STILL
NEEDS
WORK

STILL NEEDS WORK

A NOVEL

ELLEN BARKER

SHE WRITES PRESS

Published 2024
Printed in the United States of America

Print ISBN: 978-1-64742-680-4
E-ISBN: 978-1-64742-681-1
Library of Congress Control Number: 2023921599

For information, address:
She Writes Press
1569 Solano Ave #546
Berkeley, CA 94707

Interior design and typeset by Katherine Lloyd, The DESK

She Writes Press is a division of SparkPoint Studio, LLC.

For all the women I ever worked with,
especially my virtual boss in perpetuity.

CHAPTER 1

My cell phone is ringing, and I can see that it's my boss. It's 7:55 p.m. in San Francisco, where I am attending a conference, which means it's going on eleven o'clock in Baltimore, where she is. This can't be good.

"Hello, Sharon," I say into the phone.

"Marianne. I know it's late." It's not as late for me as it is for her, but she knows that, so I don't say anything. Her tone does not imply good news, like the budget increase I'm hoping for, and it doesn't imply some minor crisis that is going to keep me up all night crunching numbers, either. It implies death or disaster.

"Listen, there's no good way to say this. Your department is being shut down. You're going to be laid off."

"Oh" is the best I can come up with. This is way beyond any of the disasters swirling in my head.

"I know, and I tried everything. The assholes just don't get it." She goes on for a bit about the assholes and how they don't get it, and then gets back to me.

"I'm not supposed to be talking to you. Someone from Human Resources is going to call you tomorrow. But that's bullshit, and I wanted you to know what's coming." She gives me more details about who will call and when, and how they will inform my staff, all of whom will also get the bad news tomorrow.

"You're at that conference in San Francisco, right?"

"Yes, I'm here all week."

"You don't need to leave. Go ahead and make all the connections you can. I would love to tell those assholes that you got a job offer."

"Okay." I'm in shock and having trouble forming sentences, but eventually come up with, "I thought everyone was pretty pleased with how the last integration went?" I say that as a question.

"Yes, and now Delarosa says that since you're done with the integration, why do we need you. Now that Deanna is gone and he da man, he thinks he knows everything." And she goes on with more of who made this decision, and how she argued against it, and how she failed. I feel a little bad for her; she rarely fails.

My mind is still racing but more in the realm of how I will pay the bills than in how this happened, so I've let a silence develop.

"Marianne? Are you there? Are you okay?"

"I'm here." And I'm worried and angry, but I also feel something else—is it relief?

She pauses and then says, "You're pretty quiet. Is this like a get-out-of-jail-free card for you?"

Bingo.

"I guess it kind of is," I say slowly, because I hadn't thought of it that way. But yes, I'm in a panic but also relieved. "I've been seeing a train wreck coming with Delarosa at the throttle, and I can't stop it, so yeah, I guess this is a bit of a relief." I sigh loudly to hold onto the talking stick—I'm not finished. "But still, I can't believe this is happening."

"I'm so mad. I'm going to tell them that you're planning to sue and see if I can get you more severance."

"I'm not thinking that far ahead."

"No, but you should be. I'll support you if you do."

She lets off a little more steam about the assholes and reminds me that HR will call the next day at eleven. She says that my last day will be in two weeks and to make sure I get my expenses in for this trip as soon as I get home. I tell her not to worry, I'll be okay. I hope it's true.

I hang up and open my hotel room window, breathing in the evening fog and listening to the noise of downtown San Francisco. It occurs to me that this might be my last business trip for a long time, and that makes me wish I had found a better hotel room. This one was the best I could find without the accounting system flagging my expense report, which no longer matters. The room is tiny, but it's clean and bright and has a functioning window. The problem is that it's just outside the Chinatown gate, so the street is mobbed with tourists and conferencegoers who stay up late and drink heavily, then walk back to their hotels talking loudly. When they are all gone, the restaurant employees bang the dumpsters for an hour as they clean up. When they are finished, well after midnight, unhoused people come out and revisit the dumpsters, banging the tops over and over as one after another works the alley. I have a room and meals and no real reason to complain, but I still resent the sleepless hours.

I leave my email unanswered. I close the document I had been working on, without saving it. I take a hot bath, get in bed, and read without comprehension until I fall into a restless sleep, interrupted by dumpster diving and dreams of being a dumpster diver myself.

CHAPTER 2

The next morning, my smartphone reminds me that I am scheduled for a conference session at nine and another at eleven. I click on "will not attend" for the eleven o'clock one. I dress in jeans and sneakers and a warm sweater and walk to Union Square, where I get a coffee and croissant and sit on a bench in the October sun. I ignore all the beeps and whirs that are announcing incoming emails, messages, and calls. At eight forty-five, I head off to the nine o'clock session, because it's a topic I care a lot about. But I can't get interested. I feel like laughing at the absurdity of the earnest faces around me, people listening and asking questions. Yesterday, I was one of them; today, I feel like an adult sitting in on an eighth-grade class. But I don't want to seem churlish, so I sit it out and even submit the online evaluation, giving top marks in every category even though I absorbed exactly nothing.

I look at my phone to see if there are any alerts from my boss and realize that I'll be paying my own cell phone bill in a few weeks. And my health insurance bill. I walk outside and pick up another coffee and another croissant, chocolate. This time I pay with my corporate credit card. I walk back to my hotel, where my room has been cleaned. I make sure my corporate login works and wonder if there is anything I should email to myself in case they deactivate my account today. I can't think of anything. I've always been a little suspicious of new employees who show up with a lot of spreadsheets and documents from their old companies. I'm not going to be one of those. I don't have anything personal to delete, either; I'm careful to keep personal stuff on my own laptop. I think about leaving a few oddball files just to confuse anyone who goes looking, but I don't have the energy to figure out what it would be. I also realize that if anyone does look through my files, it will be a coworker or my local IT guy, and why make either of their lives harder? So instead, I make a list of questions to ask HR at eleven.

The call from HR is late, but I am not surprised and don't mind. The HR wonk was probably laying off someone who took more than her allotted thirty minutes to ask questions. My boss is on the phone too, and we both pretend that she didn't talk to me the night before.

"Marianne, I know this will come as a shock, but don't worry—I'm here to help."

I would think that was a bizarre way to start a layoff if I hadn't sat in on so many in the past. Eventually, she gets to the punch line. I don't respond, just to be annoying. I know she's got a script in front of her, with a list of things I might say, along with her required responses. "Silence" isn't on the list.

"Um, do you have any questions?" she finally asks.

"No, I think you covered it. I'll need to read the severance agreement; I might have questions then. You didn't mention my bonus for the year, so I want to make sure it's in there."

I know there is no bonus; one reason for doing layoffs in October and having people out before the end of the fiscal year is to make sure they are not in the bonus pool at the end of the calendar year.

"And I want to make sure that my last day is November 1, so

my health insurance is paid for November. So I'll just check all that and then get back to you if I have any questions."

My boss has been quiet, but she's IM-ing me. "You go, girl!"

I can sense that the HR wonk is gearing up to tell me that there is no bonus and no moving the date from October 31 to November 1. Those things are on her script, but I don't want to waste time with them, since she is a decision deliverer, not a decision maker.

Sharon IMs me again: "Ask for the stats on the people being laid off."

I do that, not because I care but because it will make her check the box that says there is a risk of a lawsuit for age or gender discrimination. She says she will send the report, which is standard anyway, and is curated to make sure the set of people in this particular layoff is only slightly skewed, not enough to build a case. But still, I want to make sure she has checked the box. She's uncomfortable; of course she is. She's used to hearing crying and begging and incrimination though, and at least I'm not piling that on.

I move on so that she doesn't get back to the bonus.

"You said that my department is being eliminated." I almost say "liberated" but catch myself. "Has that happened yet? Is it okay if I call them now?" I don't care if it's okay or not, but I want her to know that I'm going to be doing that.

She reads me the schedule for those calls and tells me she will email me after each is done, and then I can call them. I thank her for that. They are all going to be done today, which means she's got a team working on it.

She gets back to her script. "You don't have to work out the next two weeks before your last day. As soon as you transition your work, you can take the rest of the time off. Just code it on your time sheet as administrative time."

"Okay," I say, and then I do get a little mean. "Um, you said my department is being eliminated, correct?"

"Yes, that's correct."

"So that means that what we do isn't considered necessary, correct?"

"Well. . . ."

"I just can't think of any way to transition unnecessary work to people in other departments who don't do what my team does."

Silence.

That was unnecessary of me, of course, and unanswerable, but if she's going to do this job, she might as well know that her script has some flaws. Maybe she'll just leave out the transition-your-work point if she talks to anyone else on my team.

Sharon steps in and asks if there is anything else, in a tone that makes it clear that there isn't anything else, and we all get off the phone. Sharon is the highest-ranking female in the company, and she didn't get there by letting meetings go on past their wear date.

My phone rings again and it's Sharon, and she starts out with a string of swearing. Well-placed swearing is one of the ways she got to be the highest-ranked female in the company. That, and knowing exactly how much skin to show in any given situation, exactly how high one's heels should be each day, and exactly how much smarter she is than each of the higher-ranked men she has to deal with in every situation—all skills I try and fail to achieve. The innovative swearing cheers me up quite a bit.

"Those assholes aren't going to give you your bonus, you know. The bonus pool isn't that big this year, and all these layoffs are to make sure there's more for them."

"Of course, but you know and I know and they know that I earned the bonus on the last acquisition. All they have to do is add another ten weeks to my severance package. They can write

that off as a cost of integration. Plus another week for good measure to cover the November insurance they don't want to pay."

This amuses Sharon, and she tells me to copy her when I
return my amended severance agreement, and she will pile on
and make sure I get it. "All they really care about is reducing
head count, and your department is almost all female and therefore all expendable." She's already told me that the one male in
my group is not being let go, and neither of us wants to rehash
that right now.

We hang up, and I start working on the agreement, which is
already in my inbox. I order room service for lunch and wait for
notification that I can start calling my team.

I don't get the notifications, and the three people who are
my top level of direct reports start calling and texting. Two of
them came into the company as part of acquisitions and have
been expecting this since the day each of their acquisitions was
announced, so they are sad but not surprised. I tell them that I
will write letters of recommendation and will be a reference, even
though I know I'm not supposed to do either of those things.
Once I'm not an employee, I can't be fired for it. They are all
in other time zones, and it's getting late in the day for them, so
they don't stay on the phone long. They need to call their direct
reports, who may or may not be as philosophical about this as
they are.

I leave the hotel and walk down to the Embarcadero for
some fresh air and a bookstore. I've got two more nights here,
and I don't intend to spend my evenings responding to email and
working on spreadsheets.

At six, I change into slightly more businesslike clothes and
hairstyle, put on my game face, and go to a cocktail party hosted
by the account manager of a vendor. I'm their contact, and I see
no reason to wait to tell them. I'm also meeting a colleague there

who needs to be among the first to know, although I think there is a good chance that he knew before I did. Kyle is male and younger than me, and located at corporate headquarters. His job has been at risk since the last acquisition, and his job will be a little more secure with me out of the way. I know he wants to own the relationship with this vendor. I knew when I moved away from California that I was handing him an ace, but I couldn't afford to stay and had to take the risk.

The vendor reps act appropriately shocked and introduce me to other clients of theirs who may have need of someone like me. I talk to them quite candidly, give them my contact information, and know that nothing will happen, because I now stink of loser. My colleague doesn't show up.

I don't go to the next party—more coworkers will be there, and I no longer have the energy to talk to them right now. I walk back to my hotel and compose an email to the colleagues who will be affected by my termination. I set it to go out at various times so that everyone gets it in their nighttime and no one gets it in the next few hours. I text Kyle to meet me at Union Square for coffee the next morning and get an affirmative, then shut down all my electronics. I refuse to let myself think about what happened during the last twenty-four hours, and I read until the dumpster concert winds down and I fall asleep.

CHAPTER 3

I wake up fairly early and go outside. The idea of another room service meal has lost its appeal. I skirt the convention center area to avoid the hordes of conference attendees and stop at Old St. Mary's Cathedral. I've been wanting to see the inside. The early Mass is well attended, and the service helps me maintain the calm I've been faking for the last thirty-six hours.

I go on to Union Square and have about twenty minutes with my coffee and scone before Kyle shows up. I'm thinking about a refill when he slings his backpack into the chair next to me and sits down across from me.

"Hey, you didn't show at the party last night," I say.

"Oh, I got held up after my last session." Maybe he did, maybe not. I don't really care.

"Too bad. The food was spectacular. Want a coffee?"

He goes and orders and comes back to the table.

"So—I just wanted to let you know that my department has been shut down. My last day is in two weeks." I watch him closely. I don't pretend to be a great judge of people, but I am interested in his response, whatever it might mean.

"No! I can't believe that! How can they let you go? What's going to happen now?"

It's pretty convincing, but maybe he's been practicing.

"So really—you didn't know? Your boss had to approve it—Sharon told me that he said there would be no impact on your department if we were gone."

"No, I swear to God I did not know." I guess I believe him, but I also realize as he is talking that I don't care if he knew or not. I tell him that I'll be available for twelve more days if he needs anything, and he takes off for his next conference session.

I take a few calls but don't let anyone feel too sorry for me. I've got an underlayer of panic, but as long as I keep moving, I can revel in the knowledge that I am free of corporate politics, the end-of-year struggle over rankings and raises, the daily slog of conference calls, and the endless last-minute requests for data and analysis and crazy-ass projections that the data can't produce, no matter how important they are to someone else's bonus.

I've got my laptop with me, so I finish my response to the severance agreement and send it off, copying Sharon. I send her a separate note from my personal email with points she can use to make sure I get my bonus, even if they disguise it as extra severance. I've done the math for her.

I spend the rest of the day reading some of the responses to my announcement, which are gratifyingly outraged and supportive. My replies are along the lines of "Thanks, but don't worry. Things will be completely different but also exactly the same. It will be okay." And it will. The train wreck that is coming won't bring the company down. It will be slow and grinding and will make all their lives harder, but they will cope with each new annoyance, and some of them will leave or change roles, and new people will not know that it could be any different. The waters will close over my head, and the ripples will fade, and they will be caught up in the demands of the day. It happens every day, all over the world. It just never happened to me before.

CHAPTER 4

The next day I pack up, check out, and fly to Kansas City, where I grew up and to which I returned eighteen months ago when personal circumstances mandated a drastic life change. I'm now living in my dilapidated childhood home, in a neighborhood that has become sketchy at best. This is due to redlining and block-busting, followed by civic indifference and the crowning blow, an expressway that sliced out two streets just a block from mine. Not ideal in some ways, but very budget friendly.

On the flight, I watch movies to distract myself and make sure I maintain a cool, practical attitude toward this further reversal of fortune and don't break down and cry in my exit-row seat. I don't want to get flagged as too unstable to be trusted in the extra-legroom exit row. I'm in luck; the movie is an animated comedy, ridiculous but with no tear-jerking elements. There is a dog, but he doesn't die.

The cabdriver drops me at home without complaining about having to drive east of Troost after dark, which is a relief, because right now I'm not likely to be calm if I have to defend living there. I ring the next-door neighbor's doorbell before I go into my own house. She's got my dog, Boris, and whatever neighbor-hood news might be on offer. I'd rather have both of these before

I go into my empty house. It's a dicey neighborhood now, unlike when I grew up here.

"Dinner's ready," Josie says by way of greeting. It's not a question or an invitation. I'd rather just go home and start dealing with my new reality, but I can see that there is no point in trying that.

"Smells great," I say and shrug off my coat. Boris is trying to levitate so that he can lick my face without jumping on me, well-trained German shepherd that he is. I lean over to rub his head with both hands, which keeps all his paws on the floor. Josie's living room, like mine, is too small for dancing.

"Well, come on in and sit down," she says from the kitchen, and I step into the warm, fragrant room and do as I am told. I'm pretty sure she has something important to say and I'm about to hear it; otherwise, she would have offered dinner but not insisted. She seems as robust as ever, so I'm pretty sure it isn't anything bad about her. She's focused on serving and isn't making eye contact or giving anything away, so I don't know if it's good news or bad. Maybe it's just something interesting. I close my eyes and breathe in the smell of baked chicken. No need to rush the news. It occurs to me that whatever it is, it will occupy us to the point that I won't feel compelled to tell her that I've lost my job, which is news I will keep to myself for as long as I can. I don't want her to think I might have to move, and no one will notice anything, as I have been telecommuting for the entire eighteen months I've lived here.

Food on the table, she tells me to dig in. We talk about the food, and she asks me about the flight and if it was nice in San Francisco. I tell her the flight was uneventful and that San Francisco was lovely, October being the best—meaning warmest and sunniest—month to visit. I've never really told her what I do, because it's fairly obscure; usually I just tell people that if they've been reading the Dilbert comic strip for the last twenty years, they'll understand what my job is like. Some people probably think I'm being snooty, and others think I might work for the CIA. I'll tell anyone all about it if they insist, but they usually regret it.

Josie doesn't care, has never cared. The flight and San Francisco are just small talk so we can savor the first few bites of food before we move on.

"What's new in the neighborhood?" I ask casually, so that she can dive in if she's ready.

"Well!" she says with a huff. "Bud moved in. Bud and Jennie."

This is not a surprise; we knew they had rented the house on the other side of me.

"And Felicity, that's the little girl's name." Good to know.

And then she doesn't say anything.

I take more carrots and watch Josie pretend to be busy cutting chicken off the bone.

"They get moved in okay?" I ask.

"They did," she says, "and then. . . ." She stops again.

This isn't like Josie. As a retired kindergarten teacher, she's straightforward; she takes things as they come. She jumps with both feet, although not literally, since her hip replacement a year ago. I'm also puzzled, because she doesn't seem too upset. So why is she not forthcoming with whatever it is she's determined to tell me?

I'm a little worried, because I have history with Bud, who is a veteran with PTSD and who broke into my house shortly after I moved in. He thought it was abandoned, and, okay, I admit that it looked abandoned. He had lived there at some point with his girlfriend and was looking for some things he had left. Since then, he had been in treatment, married the girlfriend, and started a new job. The owners of the house, who also live on the block, had made sure I was okay with him living there. Which I am, or I was, until right this minute.

"And then *what*?" I finally say, loud enough to make Boris leave Josie's side and move over to me. If she's trying to build suspense and is making sure she has my attention, she has succeeded.

"And then"—she grins mischievously, finally looking me in the eye—"and then they moved out again."

"What? What happened? I was only gone six days!"

"Someone stole their big-ass TV."

I've heard Josie say "ass" only twice before, when she was describing her neighbor's truck as big-ass and her own red SUV as little-ass. I've never heard any actual swearing. So I giggle when she refers to the TV as big-ass, although it's mostly from a sudden case of nerves. The last thing I want to hear about is a break-in.

"Oh no! When? How? Were they home?" Being home during a break-in is my biggest fear.

Josie explains that they had just moved their stuff into the house, the day after I left town. They went out to pick up something for dinner, and when they got home fifteen minutes later, the back door had been kicked in and the TV was gone.

"Just like that break and entry on Chestnut last year, huh?" I say.

"Yep, same MO."

"I don't suppose they caught the perp?" I'm still curious about why her tone is light, and now I find out.

"*Yes!*" she shouts, standing up so suddenly that Boris leaps up too and barks as if agreeing with her.

"What? How?" I'm thinking CSI, DNA, maybe even FBI. I've spent too many evenings at Josie's watching cop shows and eating ice cream.

"Well!" She says that like a grand opening, a call to attention. "Liz saw it all!"

Liz Saunders and her husband and new baby recently moved out of the house Bud just rented and into the larger house across the street. They rent their old house to Bud and Jennie, and they are anxious for Bud and Jennie to qualify for a loan and buy the house. We are all anxious for that to happen. Vacant houses sometimes stay vacant for a long time and sometimes end up derelict, as mine was, or even unlivable.

"Liz saw it?"

"Yes, she was in the front room over there, nursing the baby, and she noticed this car parked on the side street with two guys in it, in black hoodies. No one ever parks there unless there's a party or something."

She's right, no one ever does park on the short side streets. When I was living there as a child, decades ago, my mother would have been suspicious too.

"Of course, everyone wears black hoodies, so that doesn't mean anything," Josie says. I picture Josie in a black hoodie and almost laugh. She gives me a look but keeps on with her story.

"Anyway," she says, narrowing her eyes as if I had interrupted her, "she saw Bud and Jennie drive away, and then she saw the two guys get out of the car. So she took a picture of the car and the license plate with her phone. She went out on the porch to do it, so she heard them smash the door." We are both wide-eyed at the idea of Liz going out on the porch with a new baby while a crime was taking place.

"She called 911—well, they made her go back inside, but she was able to tell them which direction the car went, and of course she could give them the license number."

I'm in awe of Liz. "I'm afraid I would have dithered around wondering if maybe they were friends who came over to help or something."

Josie gives me the stink eye. "You'd better not do any

dithering if you see anything going on over here!" she says emphatically.

"Yes ma'am!" I say. "Dither I will not." And I hope it's true.

"Did the cops catch them?"

"Yes they did, although not until the middle of the night. I think the perps heard the sirens and hid the car. It was a big SUV, though, so it was hard to hide. TV was still in it." She says this with so much satisfaction that it sounds as if she solved the crime herself.

"Nice," I say. Food forgotten, I'm relieved but still a little freaked out, because this break and entry happened less than forty feet from my own back door.

"Ice cream?" Josie's always got ice cream.

"Sure." No point in saying anything else.

"But they moved out anyway?" I don't blame them, but if they move away, Liz and Patrick are going to have to find a renter quickly to remain solvent. And I don't relish living next to a vacant house with a boarded-up back door.

"Yes. They left the furniture and everything, but they're staying at her mom's over on Walrond."

"So now what?" I'm still hoping the story has a good out-come, since Josie doesn't seem too upset about the whole thing.

"Well, Patrick has to put in a new back door for sure. And Jennie says she wants a dog like yours."

"But they have a dog. Wasn't it in the house?" I picture the sweet little mutt that the VA gave Bud to help him with stress. "Oh, I guess they took it with them to pick up dinner, huh?"

"Yep. So Jennie wants a real dog, like Boris."

I picture Boris in the four-room house next door with three people and another dog. It's a stretch, but they are probably pretty crowded at Jennie's mother's house, so maybe they can make it work. I just hope they keep it in the house and not in a pen outside—or worse, tied up outside.

"Or maybe a pit bull, they're smaller," Josie is saying. "But meanwhile, they're going to stay over here this weekend, since Bud won't be at work during the day. See how it goes."

"Oh! That's great." Today is Friday. Maybe they are there now, which, in spite of everything, will make me feel better about going into my dark house after six days away.

I thank Josie for the food and the dog sitting and take myself and my roller bag home. Josie watches from her porch and then goes back in the house. I see her watching from her kitchen window as I go through my house, turning on the lights as I go. I even check the basement, making Boris go with me. When I get back upstairs, I wave at Josie. She nods, and we both close our curtains and return to our own thoughts.

CHAPTER 5

Saturday morning, I complete my expense report and submit it. I spend the rest of the morning buying groceries, cooking, cleaning—anything to keep moving. More moving, less thinking. I weed the garden a little. I paint a windowsill that has needed painting since I moved in. I put the cover on the air conditioner. I bake cookies. I don't see any activity next door.

After lunch, I decide to be a good neighbor and knock on Bud and Jennie's front door. It's a little weird to welcome them to the neighborhood at this point, but I can be sympathetic or something. I debate about taking them cookies and finally decide that cookies are always appropriate.

No one answers though, and leaving the cookies seems like a bad idea. I start to take them home and then decide to knock on the Saunders's door across the street. I can give them the cookies for no particular reason, find out if there is any further news on Bud and Jennie moving back in, and then bake more cookies for Bud and Jennie tonight. Liz and Patrick don't answer either, and by now I don't want the cookies anymore, so I take them to Josie and pick up the mail that I forgot to get from her last night. She doesn't have any more news.

It's cloudy, and I'm feeling spooked by the burglary and the fact that my neighbors are gone, even though I know perfectly well that they are probably just doing their weekly shopping. I take Boris for only a short walk, not getting out of sight of my house. I can't be bothered cooking, so I have a baked potato for supper and sulk.

There are thunderstorms in the night, but it doesn't matter because I'm not sleeping anyway. When I do doze off, I dream of dumpster lids crashing like thunder.

On Sunday morning, I go to Mass and relax enough to feel like I could just lie down in the pew and fall asleep, and I think maybe I'll take a nap later. But as I'm driving home, the sun comes out, and I start feeling better. I'm even happier when I get out of the car and hear voices next door. Bud is in his backyard with Felicity.

"Hey, Bud," I say, taking the stance that the distant past is gone and we are ordinary next-door neighbors now. He looks over the fence, a little concern on his face. He doesn't say anything, so I keep going.

"I hear you had a break-in last weekend. I'm so sorry!" Then I wonder how that sounds, given that the distant past includes him breaking into my house, so I don't wait for an answer. "I hope you're still going to live here." That should sound welcoming.

He still pauses, and I remember the PTSD, but Felicity is unencumbered by past events and says, "We're playing," patting her dad on the knee and nodding vigorously. "Watch me go fast!" And she takes off running in circles.

This gives us something to smile about and something to talk about. "She's a . . . a . . . a. . . ."

I want to finish his sentence, maybe with "a wonderful little girl," but I don't. I just watch her and smile until Bud comes up with "a lot of fun!"

"Yes, I can see that she is, and she's beautiful too." I remember that I still have some cookies and say, "Hey, I made cookies for you yesterday, but I didn't catch you at home. Can I give them to you now?" I don't want to invite myself in and interrupt them; it would be easier to hand them over the fence.

At that point I hear a door open and close, and there is Jennie saying hello and that they would love cookies. She's come out on the deck. I run in to get them and hand them to her.

"Sort of a welcome to the block," I say. "I do hope you're going to stay. Josie told me what happened."

"We got a new door, a metal one," she says. "We did stay here last night. I think I can stay here when Bud's home, but I might still go to my mom's when he's at work."

"Yes, I know what it's like," I say sympathetically and then once more realize how that might sound.

"Years ago," I say, to make sure that last bit didn't sound like an accusation, "someone broke into my house while I was at work. It took a while to get over that. That's when I got my first dog. As it turned out, he wasn't much of a guard dog, not like this one." Boris is standing next to us. "But it was enough."

I think that if I were a better person I would offer to let Boris stay with her during the day, but then who would keep me safe?

"Would you like to have Boris stay with you during the day sometimes?" Did I really say that out loud?

"Oh!" she says. "That's so. . . . But I couldn't. We're thinking about getting a dog. Well, another dog. Bud's dog goes with him during the day."

"Well, if you want to just see how it feels with a dog in the house, let me know. He's kind of big, but he's good with kids." Felicity has come over to the fence and has reached through and grabbed Boris's ear. She puts her face up to his, and he licks her through the fence.

"Doggie!" she says to her mother and then zooms off again.

"Well, maybe, if I do stay here."

CHAPTER 6

On Monday I call my former supervisor, Cathy, because I have worked with her for many years and don't want to leave without talking to her. She's outraged, but as she says, nothing is surprising in the corporate world anymore. So we talk about our dogs and otherwise catch up. While we're on the phone, I get an email from HR with instructions for returning my laptop and any other corporate equipment and materials. I haven't collected any company items since moving to Kansas City. Cathy suggests sending a bag of ashes, representing the monitor and keyboard I didn't replace after the fire at my California house, and we waste more time thinking up other clever and childish ways to respond. Whatever I send will go to my old pal in IT, so we both know I won't send anything to make his job more annoying than it already is.

After we hang up, I go outside with my pruners and haphazardly trim some shrubs, pick a tomato, and check on the fall peas and lettuces coming up in my garden. I go back in and stare at my inbox but don't do anything about anything in it.

My boss, Sharon, calls later to make sure I'm okay, and I ask if she's heard anything from HR about my bonus. She says they told her no, but that was just posturing, and they'll tell her yes the next time she calls. We reiterate our agreement that there's nothing for my team to transition to anyone else, so we can all stand down during these last two weeks. My team won't, because they are supporting users who are frantic about losing them, but I encourage them to at least take time to work on their résumés and update their LinkedIn profiles and call in whatever favors they have.

HR sends another email on Tuesday, this time a personal note instead of text clipped and pasted from some official manual. I'm pretty sure I was supposed to get a call about this, but the HR wonk doesn't want to talk to me, or rather doesn't want to listen to me being snarky. The email tells me that I'm allowed to apply for other positions in the company and that the company won't dispute my unemployment claim. She makes it sound like these are special favors. I would definitely be snarky about that. The email also tells me that I can apply for health insurance through COBRA only after my company policy terminates. I think about calling her to point out that this means I will be without insurance for a month or more. But the wonk has anticipated me, and the next sentence reassures me that if I keep my receipts during that period, I'll be able to file for reimbursement after COBRA kicks in. I have some interesting thoughts about that too. She was smart not to call me.

None of this information is a surprise to me; I've had to lay off a lot of people as a result of corporate mergers and acquisitions, so I've been copied on these things and listened in on the calls. But it's different when I'm the one receiving the news. I feel bad about how cavalier I must have seemed in the past. I put that aside; today it's all about my current problems.

I wake up in the night with a sore throat and hope I've been sleeping with my mouth open, but by morning I know I've got a cold. The crowded conference rooms, the airplane, the airports, the stress. . . . It's not a surprise, and I'm just glad I got my flu shot early this year. I check my stock of cold meds and comfort foods and go out for extra tissues and groceries while I still have the energy and don't sound like a germ factory. I try not to touch anything I'm not buying, so I don't leave any germs behind.

Early the next morning, Sharon calls to tell me that I will be getting a bonus, albeit in the form of extra severance. It's not as much as I asked for, but it's as much as I expected. I thank her and tell her that I'll copy her when I get the revised agreement and return the signed copy.

My cold is coming on strong, and although I can still sound normal on the phone, I know it's going to get worse before it gets better. I take Boris out and walk for as long as I can, since he might not get much of a walk for the next few days.

Cathy calls to tell me that she can probably get approval for me to work part-time on her team doing user support and data management. She's embarrassed to offer me that and makes it clear that she knows it's beneath me, but she's trying to keep my benefits alive. I tell her I'll think about it, and I will, but I know it won't work out. Because if my email address is live, I'll be expected to do everything I do now, but with no staff.

I change the subject and tell her about the agreement I'm supposed to sign, which says that I won't post anything bad about the company on social media, or otherwise bad-mouth the company, and that I won't ever sue the company. Cathy is amused and says I should just cross those lines out when I sign it. Just a thin little line—they will never notice. She has a copy of Adobe Acrobat that allows editing of pdfs and will do it for me so I can still submit the revised pdf with an electronic signature. I hesitate about involving her in the plot, but she needs this little act of defiance, so I agree. I'm never going to post anything on social media, and I don't have the will or the money to hire a lawyer, plus I know that I can't sign away my legal right to sue. I'll do this little act of defiance just so that I know I did it. The next morning, I decide I'm not going to risk Cathy's involvement after all, so I print out the original, lightly strike out the offending text, initial the strike outs minutely, sign the last page, and then scan it all and email it. I copy Sharon without comment. She has no reason to read it, but if it ever comes up, she can retrieve her copy and say yes, look—those lines are crossed out and initialed.

I go outside and clip a few late flowers and some greenery to put in a vase. It's starting to rain, so I don't linger. I stand at the kitchen counter with the vase and the flowers and stare out the window at Bud and Jennie's house next door. The house is a couple of feet higher than mine, and the three windows are small. I seldom see any movement in any of them. A little face appears in the one that must be the back bedroom. Felicity is smiling and waving both hands. I think of my small self, doing the same thing decades ago, waving out my bedroom window on the other side of this house, at the woman in the kitchen window in what is now Josie's house. Felicity turns her head and then runs off. I finish the flowers and try to think of something to cook for dinner.

CHAPTER 7

On Friday morning, Jennie knocks on my door, and when I open it, Felicity shouts, "Boris." Jennie asks if I really meant it when I offered to lend them my dog. I assure her that I did and realize that I should have made sure they had my phone numbers. I warn Jennie that I'm sick, but she waves me off.

"This one gets every cold that comes her way. You probably got it from one of us!"

I invite them in and make small talk with Jennie while Felicity runs around with Boris. I write down my phone numbers, snap the leash on Boris, and give Jennie a few instructions. She practices "sit," "down," and "stay" until Boris does them reliably for her. I do all of this in a low voice, hoping Felicity won't try to give Boris commands, but of course she's all ears and shouts, "Sit!" Boris looks at her and wags his tail. "Stay! Down! Borrrrrrrrrisssss!" she commands. Boris keeps wagging. I look at Jennie.

"I think he knows that she's not in charge," I tell her. "Maybe we should just teach Felicity to tell him that he's a good dog."

Jennie laughs at that, and they leave for home, telling me they'll just keep Boris for an hour to see how it goes. I tell her to call if she has any questions. I close the door and spend the next hour wondering what kind of idiot I am to give my dog to the family of the guy who broke into my house, regardless of the extenuating circumstances. I worry that Boris will be the key to their staying in the house and I will let them keep him, because I can't bring myself to tell them they can't have him. I even worry that Josie will be mad, because she would love to have him but would never ever ask. I pour all the pent-up rational fear and worry about losing my job into irrational fear and worry about losing my dog. I make up scenarios in which Bud claims that Boris was his dog all along, and I cry in frustration. I cry because my house in California burned down twenty-two months ago, forcing me to live next to a crazy man who claims my dog is his. I cry because my husband died after a long and expensive illness that left me able to afford only this wretched little house in this wretched neighborhood. I get even more upset that Jennie will come back and find me crying. I wash my face and make a fresh pot of coffee and force myself to do the crossword puzzle. I want cookies with my coffee, but I've given them all away, so I start making more and am just taking the first pan out of the oven when someone knocks on the door.

Usually when the doorbell rings or someone knocks, Boris either barks like a true guard dog, or whines and wags his tail. Barking means a stranger, and whining and wagging means someone he likes is at the door. But he's not home, so I peek through the curtains. No one is there. I hear knocking again and realize it's at the back door. This unnerves me. No one has ever knocked on the back door.

"Who's there?" I use my deep serious voice. No response, just more thumping.

It must be burglars about to kick in the door. Why is this happening during the one hour when I don't have a dog? Someone has been watching and saw the dog leave. Why don't I have a peephole in my back door?

"Hello, who is it?" Deep voice again. I get out my cell phone to dial 911. Then I hear whining and a small bark. I open the door and there is Boris, tail waving back and forth, thumping against the door.

Then the doorbell rings, and Boris runs through the house barking, only to stop when he gets there and start wagging again. It's Jennie and Felicity.

"Boris!" Felicity says. I open the door and let them both in. Felicity runs into the kitchen with Boris following more slowly.

"Oh, I'm so, so sorry," Jennie says, dropping down on the sofa. "Felicity wanted to play outside, but she threw a ball over the fence, and Boris just jumped right over, and then he didn't seem to know how to get back. I'm so sorry!"

I laugh and tell her not to worry and ask her how it went up until then.

"Well, I think Felicity is on board for getting a dog, and I really did feel safer. After a while, Felicity fell asleep on the floor, and Boris stayed right there with her. I have to admit, I took a nap too. But I don't know—two dogs and a kid?"

"Maybe a slightly smaller dog would be better," I say. "And not a puppy. You want one that's already housebroken and is good with kids and will come when called." I think about it for a while, because there are a lot of dogs out there that won't come when called, including every dog I had before this one.

"I wonder if the service-dog people could help. Maybe they have dogs that don't quite make the grade to be a service dog but are still great pets. You know, like maybe they freak out when they take them on a city bus. Something that disqualifies them but that won't matter to you."

She likes that idea and says she'll call about it. She gathers up Felicity, who does not want to leave without Boris. I shamelessly bribe her with a cookie, which she will get from her mother if she says goodbye nicely to Boris and walks home holding her mother's hand.

I'm drained after that and slightly worried about the crying fit, but I'm hopeful about Bud and Jennie and their potential future pet, so I focus on that. I have a glass of wine and make a list of things I can actually do something about, like update my LinkedIn page, and then I take a hot shower and go to bed. Boris sleeps the sleep of a dog that has worked hard and done his job well.

CHAPTER 8

On Saturday, I tell myself that a week of puttering and sulking and milking my head cold by lying in bed reading is enough. I need to do some planning. I assemble all my financial records and take stock. I'm now fairly sure about how much money I'll get in the way of severance, including bonus disguised as severance, although I'm not going to count on it until I see it on my bank statement. I add in what I'll get for unused vacation and congratulate myself on not having used any in the past twelve months. I look up what I currently have in my savings account. I don't include what I've saved since I moved here; that's put away to start building up the savings lost to illness and the recession. I don't include my 401(k) or the last of my insurance payout from California, which I have socked away in case of mechanical emergencies such as car, furnace, hot-water tank, and refrigerator. Most of those are past their life expectancy. I'd like to add some of the severance pay to the mechanical fund, since the current balance won't cover all the possibilities. "And with winter coming on," I say out loud in a dramatic voice, trying for humor but not achieving it. I make a sidenote to replace the furnace filters and maybe buy an electric space heater, just in case. I don't want to have to add "replace frozen plumbing" to the list. I look up the Missouri unemployment program and calculate how much I'll get from that.

Then I work out what I've been spending each month for the last year and try to see what can be cut, other than curtailing home improvements. There isn't a lot of slack. No cable TV, no gym memberships, no Netflix or music streaming. Almost no meals out. I could drop the landline, but that won't save much if I keep Internet, and I can't look for a job without that. Plus I have two new expenses, my monthly cell phone bill and health insurance. I look up what COBRA will cost me, and after a head-ache-inducing search, I find that my unemployment payment will just about cover COBRA plus my cell phone, with a little left over if I reduce my cell phone plan. I won't be needing the unlimited plan if I'm not working. If I'm very careful and nothing unexpected occurs, I'm good for about a year. This cheers me up until I remember that something unexpected occurs regularly in my life. *Pretty much everyone's life*, I think, mentally scanning my nearest neighbors.

Well, a year is a long time and also not very long. I get up and walk around, wish my head would stop hurting, lie down for a while. I walk Boris to the other end of the block and back, trying not to have a coughing fit until I'm back in my own house.

I decide it's time to take the first steps toward looking for a job. I open my LinkedIn page and print it out. I want to rethink what it should look like, since potential employers will likely check it out early on. And I want to make all the changes at once, so people in my network only get notified one time that I've changed it. I look up a few colleagues who were laid off in the past year to see how they handled the no-job period. Not much to go on. Some haven't updated at all, so it looks like they are still employed, and some say "Experienced XYZ professional with skills in x, y, and z." That will be my page if I can't find a job quickly or think of something more clever.

Today is not a day for clever, so I look at several online job sites and make some notes about what I might post there. I wonder when I last updated my résumé and spend some time looking for it. I am not impressed when I read it; in fact, I'm pretty bored. Maybe coffee would help, but it's late in the day for caffeine. I print the résumé and put it on top of the LinkedIn printout. Great progress.

I sneeze a few times, then listen to myself breathe and think, *If I'm bored by my own résumé, how on earth am I going to find a job with it, never mind a job I'd actually enjoy?* I wonder what kind of job I would enjoy. I had liked my last job well enough, most days. But if another company offered me the same job, I suddenly realize that while I would probably take it, it would be with resignation and a dearth of enthusiasm. After all the mergers and acquisitions, all the reorgs and regime changes, all the corporate posturing and intrigue, I had no company loyalty, even before the layoff. I was only loyal to my coworkers, and only some of those. I was exhausted by my job. I'm not sure I could do it again. My game face is tattered and unconvincing.

When I'm feeling better, I try to think of what I would actually like to do. I google "career change" and find a lot of drivel about following my passion. Do I have a passion? Did I ever? I try to remember. I had passion in college about changing the world, but that was the sixties talking. By the time I was actually looking for my first job, the economy was struggling and the ten years of baby boomers ahead of me had pretty well glutted the job market. I took what I could find. The three times my husband and I moved for his job, I embraced each move with enthusiasm—a chance to find my real place in the world, discover the color of my parachute. Each time, I looked and looked, and then I took what I was offered. And it was all fine. I had good jobs, a few good bosses, some promotions, lots of business travel, kudos. But passion? I don't think so. I know a few people, mostly teachers or doctors, who are passionate about their work. But was my dad passionate about delivering furniture and appliances for Sears? Was the IT guy I appreciated so much passionate about troubleshooting the blue screen of death when my laptop crashed? Was the HR wonk passionate about sending me my forms and logging them in when I returned them?

I've thoroughly trashed the idea of following one's passion. In fact, I am pretty passionate about that. But it's only a momentary passion, and I'm bored with it before I finish thinking about it.

Okay, forget passion. What's important to me in a job? Money, of course, and benefits. I may have to take a somewhat lower salary, since any new employer will see that I'm not working and salivate over my perceived desperation. But besides money? I've grown accustomed to working at home and don't relish returning to office politics, but is remote work at all possible in a new job where I'm an unknown?

All I've done so far is determine that I want to make a living by sitting on my butt at home. I roll my eyes and tell Boris we are going for a walk. He is passionate about walks, so off we go. I try not to think about jobs or passions or the coming winter weather, and I try to stifle my coughing fits so the neighbors don't see me bent over gasping for breath and call 911. I'm actually better, but the coughing is epic.

The next time I sit down to ponder my future, I try Craigslist. The jobs are listed in a couple of dozen categories, none of which I fit neatly into. I start with nonprofits, thinking it might be a nice change from megacorporations. Yikes, most of the listings are for houseparents and laundry workers. Next I try the "etc." category, where there are listings for delivery services, egg donors, and, inexplicably, eczema sufferers. I switch to the "all" category and filter by "telecommute." This produces listings for surrogate moms, drivers, and something called "end and belly dumps." I don't even want to know.

I give up on Craigslist and open Monster again. I try filtering for "Kansas City, Missouri" and "telecommute." The results are normal jobs, just not ones I'm qualified for. The only possibility is one for a senior-care referral service, and on closer examination, it seems to be a sales job, with quotas for signing up people in care facilities. It's definitely a telecommute job, though, and they are clear that the work space has to be quiet, specifically referring to pet and child noise. I wonder if I can train Boris to stop howling along with fire truck sirens. I keep looking and find a listing for managing data and users in a fairly obscure software system. That's more up my alley. Telecommuting is an option after the first six months. That might be better than telecommuting from the start. I decide to apply for both jobs, mostly so that I can report to the unemployment office that I'm diligently looking for work.

I also check the city government job lists and some large employers. Alphapointe would be a nice five-block commute, but I remember that Bud, former burglar and current neighbor, was applying for a job there, and I don't want to crowd him. I take another break to go to the library for some new reading material. As I check out at the self-service terminal, I remember going to the library as a kid and being fascinated by librarians, with their card-stamping system and the cool little date stamp that attached to their pencils. I wanted to be a librarian then. Now I can get in and out without even making eye contact with one, which is probably best since I am likely to cough in their faces. I wonder how many germs I've left on the checkout terminal and how many new ones I picked up.

CHAPTER 9

The next day is sunny, and I'm out front planting tiny shrubs along the front of the porch, hoping they'll grow up and hide the concrete-block porch foundation. I bought them at an end-of-season sale just before I lost my job and haven't had the energy to plant them since then. It's now or never, I think. They won't survive the winter in their little plastic pots, and the ground will start freezing soon.

"Need some help there?" I hear a voice behind me—Flynn. Flynn is the only human relic of my childhood left in the neighborhood, still living a few houses up the street in the next block. He was still in grade school when I went to college, so I only knew him as a little squirt who liked to hang around when my dad was working on the car, or painting the porch, or watering the grass. His family's place was always a mess—no grass and always a wrecked car and maybe a nonworking appliance or two in the yard. The rest of the neighborhood resented them. He's cheerful and friendly and has most of his teeth, but his fashion sense and vocabulary haven't improved much since first grade. His house is one of the few that looks better than it did when I was in high school, but it still looks worse than most. I sigh softly.

"Hi, Flynn. Nice day, huh?"

"Yup. Thought I'd take a walk, get me some fresh air." He's

not walking now though. He's come up beside me and is standing, legs wide apart as if he's planning to be there a while, looking at the holes I've dug.

"Good day for that," I say. "Good for walking." Nothing happens, so I add, "Won't be many more nice days like this." I set the shovel point and take another scoop, or try to. I hear the metal hit stone and pry away at it. It's a blob of mortar left from laying up the part of the porch foundation my dad didn't build. There's quite a bit of that, and I'm worried that the shrubs won't do well if a lot of lime has leached into the soil.

"Kinda rocky there," Flynn says, taking off his Royals baseball cap and scratching his head. I can't tell if he's going to offer to help again or if the difficult digging has put him off.

"I need to get some compost to put in there," I say, picking up the shovel and turning toward the driveway, as if I'm going to get in the car and go buy compost, when in fact I'm just going to the backyard where the leaf pile is. He steps back to let me by, and I do my best to keep him in motion.

"Nice seeing you," I say, moving a little farther away.

"Well," he says, "I could. . . ."

"Seems to be clouding up," I say, although the only clouds in the sky are white and fluffy. "Better get that walk in."

I go get the compost and finish the digging and planting rather faster than necessary. I water them and hope for the best. Flynn doesn't reappear.

CHAPTER 10

The next afternoon, I get a response from the care-referral company, asking to set up a phone interview. This cheers me up quite a bit, and I work on my game voice. I take cough medicine a few minutes before the call time and make sure I have a glass of water. At the last minute, I call Jennie and ask her if Boris can visit for an hour, just to be sure he won't howl during the interview.

The phone rings. Anastacia introduces herself and tells me that she is superexcited to meet me. The company has some new products that they are superexcited about, which is puzzling until I figure out that by "products" she means various kinds of senior housing, in addition to traditional assisted living and nursing homes. She keeps referring to products, and I keep picturing mobile homes. She is also superexcited about their new incentive program for the "place team," which is what I would join. She doesn't ask me any questions at all, and I have a hard time squeezing in any comments, much less questions.

While she's talking, I hear a siren, and then I think I can hear Boris, and I'm very glad I sent him next door. I'm sure Anastacia can't hear him, given that she is talking nonstop and the howling is very faint. I put my phone on mute just to be sure.

Eventually she asks me how soon I would be available, and

I say a week from Monday, so that I don't sound too desperate and because I'm not at all interested in this job if anything else surfaces. I'm certainly not superexcited about it. I have the impression that I would be expected to be superexcited all day, every day. I ask about the salary. Basically, it pays minimum wage plus a percentage of sales. No benefits, because the place team members all work part-time. "Your husband has benefits, right?" she says.

I collect Boris and take him for a walk, ruminating on the gross injustice of health insurance in America. When a married person loses a job, switching to a spouse's benefits is easy and inexpensive. When a single person is laid off, it's a whole different problem. I fume about this as if it were something new.

When I get home, I have a message from Anastacia thanking me for taking the time to interview and saying that they don't have anything for me right now. I am super relieved but slightly disconcerted. On a positive note, I can log my attempt on the unemployment website and qualify for my week's payout.

The following Sunday, I read the comics and page through the rest of the paper, catching up on local and national news. I arrive at the want ads and remember when the Sunday job ads were pretty much the only way to find a job, when there was a whole enormous section of the paper just for jobs. For fun, I read through the single page of ads in today's paper and wonder why they are there. Some may be there to reach potential workers without computers, and others to meet legal requirements. I am surprised to find a few that are interesting, and I look up the companies and click through to their Join the Team pages. Business analyst positions look interesting; I have certainly spent a lot of time analyzing various business factors. But as I read the details, I realize that business analysts are the new admin assistants, which were once called "secretaries." I see a few chief of staff jobs that might be the new business analyst. I think, *Could I do that if I really had to—keep someone's calendar and do his expense reports and make his travel arrangements and organize off-site meetings?* Actually, no. I am spectacularly bad at doing those things even for myself, and way too cynical to do it for anyone else. More importantly, I don't have the clothes or the hair or the makeup or the manicure. I would be happier and better qualified for some of the clerk jobs that were posted, and I am not really qualified for those.

CHAPTER 11

My last day arrives, and I've got a list. I send in my final forms and turn off my company laptop one last time. I skip writing an out-of-office email response telling anyone emailing me that I've left the company to pursue other opportunities and can be reached at my personal email address. If anyone wants me, they can find me on LinkedIn. I wrap the laptop in the express-mail packaging that IT sent me and scrawl a thank-you note for the IT guy. I briefly consider walking to the post office, but it's farther away than it was when I walked there as a kid, and it's now across the expressway and slightly out of my comfort zone. I tell myself the package is too heavy to carry that far, which is silly because I hauled that laptop down endless airport concourses on countless business trips, but so what. I take Boris along, and after dropping the package, we drive to Tower Park for a long walk before I begin my new, jobless, reality.

The ringer on my cell phone is off, so I don't realize until I am back home that I've had several calls from people at work wanting this and that. It takes me a minute to realize that I don't have to respond. I text them back telling them that I don't work there anymore, and I get back the expected, "Oh, I'm so sorry—who can help me?" I cringe, because I know that I have sent that same text. It feels different from this side. But it also feels great because their problems are no longer my problems. I tell them I'm sorry, I don't know, my entire staff is gone now. I type, "Good luck, sucker!" and then delete the last word, and then delete the whole sentence and press send.

I leave the ringer off and return to job searching on my own laptop. I can't get into it and get up to find something else to do, but there is nothing else to do, unless I want to scrub the kitchen floor. I tell myself that getting a job *is* my job and sit back down. I check Monster.com, go to the bathroom, find some zydeco music on YouTube, and set it to play while I look. It's upbeat and makes me feel that finding a truly great job is possible.

I hear the mailbox open and close and get up to see what's in today's haul: credit card solicitations, real estate agents wanting to buy or sell, a grocery flier. I think about all the time I have to make a really fabulous, healthy meal. I picture myself chopping fresh vegetables and heating minced garlic. In my head, it looks and smells delicious, but I don't get the garlic out. It occurs to me that I don't even have any garlic, and I think about a trip to the grocery. That makes me think that sooner or later, the neighbors will realize that something is up, that my pattern of running errands has changed. Sooner or later, I'll probably have to tell them that I'm not working. I need a twenty-five-word speech to convey that and reassure them that I won't have to move. I'll explain that the company was not meeting financial goals and closed several departments, including mine, and that I got some severance and will be fine for a while. I realize that this speech is mostly about making me look as little like a loser as possible. I'm embarrassed that I'm unemployed. Why is that? Unemployment is pretty widespread here. Don't I want to fit in? Or do I think I'm all smart and educated and white and employed and superior? Crap. I hope not.

CHAPTER 12

I have not been to the Nelson-Atkins Museum of Art since I moved back to Kansas City, and on reflection, I'm not sure I ever went there as a child. It's free, so it fits my new financial reality, and I need to do something other than sulk and worry. Plus, going there on a workday feels like playing hooky, which the Goody Two-shoes in me never did. I take Boris next door to guard Jennie and Felicity and take myself to see some art.

Once inside, I remember that I have been here and that the gallery was and still is renowned for its Asian art. I get engrossed in the American paintings collection, however, and am feeling inspired to try watercolor painting. The classes at the gallery are reasonable, but I'm not quite ready to spend money on nonessentials, so I just think about maybe buying some basic art supplies.

I lose track of time until I realize that I'm starving. I've brought lunch, so I take it out on the lawn and wander around the huge expanse of grass, letting the giant shuttlecocks on the upper lawn amuse me. I walk all the way down the lawn to Volker Fountain and think about the war protests and rock concerts that used to materialize there on Sunday afternoons in the heady summers of the sixties and early seventies, when I was a teen. I picture myself there in my bell-bottom jeans and bandana top, hoping I was cool, feeling like I almost was cool, wondering if I could actually *be* cool when I went off to college.

Today, it's the weather that's cool. The grass is wet from the recent rain, so I take myself home and retrieve my dog, who gets five feet into the house and plops down and falls asleep. I guess he's earned his keep next door.

The trip to the art gallery makes me think that I really do need a hobby and maybe some volunteer work, or some other reason to get out of the house and talk to people. I decide to start with house projects that don't require major purchases. It's autumn again and getting chilly, so I inspect the exterior for caulking that needs to be replaced. I look very carefully for any points where mice could get in, and patch those too. I look at my windows, all of which need to be replaced, and know that isn't going to happen. But maybe insulated curtains would help. Window treatments are out of the question, but I should be able to make something that looks decent and keeps the cold at bay.

I start with my miniscule bedroom, which has a single window facing north. It has a blackout shade left from a previous tenant who used the room to grow marijuana. I never use the shade, because I have a nice batik-like curtain made from a thrift shop tablecloth. I decide that lowering the blackout shade in cold weather will insulate it quite a bit, and anyway, I like to keep this room cool for sleeping. And, for whatever reason, this room doesn't even have a heat register.

The equally small front bedroom has two windows with damaged miniblinds that I bent and tied up on the day I moved in, planning to replace them shortly after. I never touched them again. I periodically think about taking down the wall between this room and the small living room to make one not-quite-so-small living room, but I don't see that happening any time soon. So maybe I should do something with these two windows.

Inspiration strikes when I remember Mill End Fabrics, where my mother used to get bits and pieces for Girl Scout projects. I can't find that store now, but I do find some promising shops, one in Wichita and one in St. Louis. Both of those are a bit far for a day trip, but I'll keep it in mind if I'm ever headed in either direction for some other reason. What really inspires is a picture on one of the websites—they have stacks of old piecework quilts. I have my own stack of worn family quilts, not-quite heirlooms my cousins pressed upon me when I visited them last Christmas. I sleep under the best of them, and the others are taking up precious shelf space. I spread them all out on my bed and choose one of the shabbiest, which I won't mind cutting up. I can't quite picture it in the living room, but I can definitely picture quilted Roman shades for the little front bedroom.

I text the cousin who gave me the quilts, to make sure she's okay with me slicing one up. She's thrilled that it's going to be used at all and decides she might do the same thing with one of her remaining quilts. She asks how things are going and I say, "Really well," because they are, at that exact moment. Then I realize that I need to be honest with her and add, "Well, except for getting laid off at work." I quickly add that I got a nice severance package and that it's great to be catching up on projects at home. I know she's skeptical, but what can she say? She comes up with, "Well, text me pictures of the new shades," and I promise that I will.

The day passes quickly as I measure and cut and solve the problem of hardware for raising and lowering the shades. I use the cords and some of the hardware from the broken miniblinds, and by nightfall I can start to see that they might look a little better than I hoped and much better than I feared. I close the door on the naked windows and go to sleep that night, feeling a sense of accomplishment for the first time in three weeks.

The next morning is damp and chilly, and the shades-in-progress look like worn-out old quilts hacked up and strung with used miniblind hardware. I close the bedroom door on them and slog out into the morning with the dog. He is not fazed by cold and damp, so we go farther than usual, and I feel slightly better when we get back. I fill my coffee cup and sit down at my computer to do something, anything, related to finding a job.

I decide to start by thinking outside the box. I don't need a job so much as I need income. Can I get income without getting a normal job?

I have a house—can I make any money with it? Airbnb comes to mind, and I try to picture it in my head. I could put a twin bed in the front bedroom with the not-yet-finished ragged-quilt curtains. I'd need to add a small dresser and a rack to hang clothes on, easy enough. We'd have to share the bathroom, and. . . . Oh, who am I kidding? No one will stay here without a shower in the bathroom. I'm still using the unenclosed basement shower. Strike Airbnb.

Dogs don't care about showers, other than to hate them mostly, so maybe I could dog sit. I picture that and know that the fence that works for Boris would only work for smaller dogs, since I know he can get over it. That would limit things a little, but it's still doable. How would I advertise? Is there an Airbnb for dogs? I poke around and find that someone is starting one called Rover.com, but it's not in business yet, although it should be next year, in 2011. Posting on Nextdoor is possible, but I know that in my Nextdoor area, people take care of each other's dogs but not for money. Josie takes care of mine, for example, for love and cookies and the occasional chore of changing a lightbulb or getting something out of her attic for her. East-of-Troosters barter—we don't spend money on dog sitters. I'd have to advertise west of Troost or on the Kansas side, and I'd probably have to shuttle the dogs too, since the owners might not drive over here. They might not even want their dogs over here. And it's not sounding like enough money to buy groceries, so I shelve it for the moment.

Poll worker—I know I saw a Nextdoor post about that. I look it up and find that all the nearby slots are filled for the upcoming November elections. East-of-Troosters must like working the polls.

What else? I open my spam folder and scroll through some pretty disgusting stuff until I find what I'm looking for, a secret-shopper request. I move it back to my inbox. I read up and discover that while secret (or mystery) shopping jobs are a real thing, the unsolicited emails are a scam. Scratch that. I don't like to shop anyway.

I try Craigslist again, thinking that some short assignments might bring in some cash while I keep looking. I read a few that I could do, but I don't have a lot of confidence that I'd actually get paid. The ads have too many exclamation points and all-caps text.

So I'll have to put more effort into finding a real job. I check the weather forecast and see that the first frost might come tonight. I go out and pick the last of the tomatoes, peppers, and squash, none of which looks particularly appetizing. The peas and lettuces look okay, though, and a little frost won't hurt them.

I need to accomplish something, so I go back to my quilt-curtain project. I had not figured out what to use for stiffeners that will meet my requirement of costing nothing, but now I see the stiffeners staring me in the face—the miniblinds slats. I choose the ones that haven't been bent and give them a scrub. I pick apart some of the remaining bits of quilt to get enough fabric to make casings for the slats and to bind the raw edges of each shade. I'm finally ready for a test, but I need screw eyes to hang them. I don't have any and can't think of an alternative, so I decide I can spend a dollar or so after all and walk to Midtown Hardware, one of the few nearby businesses that has survived the decades since I left, and a godsend in my efforts to keep my house in working order.

CHAPTER 13

The hardware store owner greets me and asks me where I've been. "How can I stay in business if you don't buy something at least once a week?" he says, teasing. Henry has helped me through a lot of home repair in the last year and a half.

I decide to stop trying to hide my unemployed status and tell him that I've been laid off, adding as usual that I got some severance and pointing out that at least now I have time to work on the house again. I try to move right on to screw eyes, but of course he's got to sympathize. It would be cold to just let it pass.

"Oh, I'm sorry. A lot of that going on these days." I can see that he'd like to say more, but maybe there isn't much to say. Unemployment is pretty high everywhere, especially east of Troost, where we both live and where he is trying to keep an old family business afloat.

"Say, you wouldn't want to work here Tuesday mornings, would you? Matt is usually here then, but he's got a chance to work on a lab project at school." Matt is his college-student son and my yard-care guy.

"Me? I've never done anything in retail," I say while simultaneously thinking that it can't pay more than minimum wage, wondering if I would be alone, and what the chances are of a holdup on a weekday morning. But I also feel like a hardware store would be so much nicer than corporate America. I love hardware stores, small ones anyway.

"I can teach you to run the cash register, and you already know what everything is and where it goes." That's true, I've been over every inch of the store many times. "And anyway, mostly you would stock the shelves, keep things looking sharp, and watch the register if I need to go out in the yard with a customer."

I guess I'm staring blankly, because he laughs out loud. "Well, think about it. It's just minimum wage, because I can't very well pay you more than I pay my kids. But the coffee is free, and the commute is short."

"I'll do it," I say, wondering what the heck I am getting myself into. On the other hand, it's only five hours a week, so how bad can it be? Unless the store gets held up, of course. But then, Henry has survived and lets his own sons work here. And I've spent many hours in here without ever feeling any danger. Five hours a week will buy groceries—beans and rice anyway.

"Wait a minute," I say. "Is there an employee discount?"

He's ready for me. "Yes, but it's less than the contractor discount, so you pick!" He's been giving me the contractor discount, because I have bought so many tools and supplies as I try to get my neglected house into livable condition, mostly with my own two hands. I don't really deserve the discount, because he's spent so much time advising me, but I guess he often advises me to buy stuff, so it all works out.

"Now, what can I sell you?"

I am embarrassed to be making my smallest purchase ever, but he lets that slide without any teasing, and I go home feeling quite cheerful. I picture myself updating my LinkedIn page to read "quilt upcycler and part-time hardware store sweeper." I wish I were the sort of person who would do that and not mind.

CHAPTER 14

I have the shades up and working by nightfall, and they look better by lamplight, or maybe just because I'm in a better mood. As I'm raising and lowering the one in the north window to make sure it pleats properly, I see Josie closing her own curtains and give her a wave as I move the shade up and down. She puts on a "what's going on?" expression, and I raise a finger to tell her to wait, then run out the front door and across her driveway to explain.

"I got these old quilts from my cousin and decided to make them into insulated curtains. They're a little goofy, but I think I'll like them. In that room, anyway." I look at them from the outside and am glad the quilt I picked was one backed with plain white flour sacks. I know I've got one quilt that is backed with sacks that say "MFA All-Purpose Family Flour" on them, not a good look in street-facing windows.

"I guess you need to see them from the other side to get the quilt effect," I say. Now I'm not so sure about my brilliant plan.

"Okay," she says, taking that as an invitation. She picks up her keys and locks the door behind her.

"Well, I'll be darned," she says moments later as we are admiring them from the inside. "Whatever made you think of that?"

I start to repeat the line that my cousin gave me the quilts, then just tell her.

"I've been laid off and desperately needed to accomplish something. So I thought of this. My cousin gave me these old quilts last year."

I look at her to see how that is going down. She gives me a long look. I can't tell what she's thinking. My telecommuting job may not have even really registered with her, except for business trips when she took care of Boris.

"Oh, honey, I'm so sorry to hear that."

This is where I would normally toss off my, "It's okay, I got some severance, and I'll find something else" line, but I don't. I wait, and she waits. We both seem to be thinking.

One of the things I am thinking has just occurred to me now, weeks after I came home jobless from San Francisco. Joblessness for me doesn't mean what it means for my neighbors. I'm not at the edge of homelessness, not going to go hungry, not going to have to move in with relatives who don't have room for me. As soon as I have that thought, I realize that I am making assumptions about my neighbors, drawing distinctions not really based on anything. Why is that?

"How about some ice cream?" Josie says, and I realize that she is still looking at me and that I've been frowning.

"Yes!" I say, although it's dinnertime and I haven't even thought about what to eat. "Why not? I've got vanilla—will that do? There may be cookies." I know she was offering me ice cream at her house, but we're at my house already.

"Vanilla's good if you've got cookies." She prefers flavors like Moose Tracks. "Are the cookies chocolate?"

They are in fact peanut butter, but I find chocolate chips in the cupboard and a couple of bananas, and we settle in for a feast.

"This is like playing hooky—banana splits for supper!"

"You need to let loose a little sometimes," Josie says, and she's got a serious look in her eyes in spite of her grin.

"Do I seem like I'm wound a little tight?" I ask. "We could dribble some bourbon over these."

"Now that's more like it," she says and then adds, "I didn't see you as a bourbon kind of girl."

"My dad's from Kentucky. That's all they drink. Well, his generation anyway. I don't like it all that much, but I'll have a bourbon and Coke on my dad's birthday, or if my brother is visiting. Maybe on Derby Day, if I remember." I get out the bottle and a shot glass. "It's pretty good with ice cream, too."

We pass the cookies and eat in silence for a minute or two, and then Josie says, "Are you going to be all right? With no job, I mean? There's so much of that going on." She sounds concerned. "If you don't mind my asking. I feel like I know you real well, but then something like this happens, and maybe it's none of my business."

I know what she means. I still feel like an anomaly here in my childhood home, the only white woman in a Black neighborhood, and while I'm friendly with my neighbors, I still feel a bit apart. I can't figure out if I'm holding myself aloof, or if it's some lack of commonality, or what.

So now I do give her my "It's okay, I got some severance and I'll find something else" line, but I do it slowly and not with the conviction I put into it for Henry at the hardware store. I can't be sure I will find something else, and it frightens me. But I'm not ready to say that out loud.

"Actually, Henry asked me if I would work for him on Tuesday mornings at the hardware store."

She opens her eyes wide at that.

"He says I've spent so much time in there, I know where everything is and how much it costs and what you use it for." That makes her laugh. "So I said yes. It made me feel so much better, even if it's just five hours at minimum wage." I shrug. "I think I'll enjoy it."

Josie seems relieved, either because any job is good or because I seem cheerful about it.

"I'm also thinking about raising chickens and selling the eggs," I say with a face as mischievous as I can make it. I secretly want to keep chickens, and another shot of bourbon has had its effect.

She surprises me with, "Can't do that till spring," and a self-satisfied smile. "And you won't make any money, but I'll be happy to eat the extra eggs."

"What do you know from chickens?" I ask her. "I'm an expert, based on staying with my grandmother on her farm for a month one summer when I was ten years old."

"I grew up on a farm—so there! Anyway, until I was twelve, then we moved to town and my dad got a job. Way easier running a gas station instead of a farm. And I got to be a town girl—let me tell you, that's a way better deal."

"Okay then, you're the expert. When they get too old to lay anymore, will you wring their necks and dress them out?"

She ponders that. "We're just joking here, right? I mean, I think I could do that, but I'm not signing up for it."

"Yeah, me neither. I would like those fresh eggs though."

"Well, we'll talk next spring. Can't do anything with chicks in the winter."

We finish up, and Josie goes home to watch NCIS. I poke around in the refrigerator for some leftovers, because I am wound a little tight and I'm not sure I can eat only dessert for dinner.

CHAPTER 15

The first snowfall comes during the night, and I am thrilled by all the whiteness I missed all those years in California. I know I'll be sick and tired of it before spring, but this first snowfall is a joy. I open the back door, and Boris bounds into the backyard, races around the perimeter, and then sticks his nose through the fence on the Forsythe's side. Felicity shrieks and races over to give him a kiss, slips, and sits down hard on the ground, shrieks again, and offers Boris two handfuls of snow. Her mother comes over to say hello with just as much enthusiasm but no shrieking.

"She's having such a super time out here. As soon as she heard 'snow' she had to run out the door. I couldn't even get her coat on her!" I notice that Felicity is wearing footy pajamas.

"Oh well," I say. "I guess it can't hurt her for a little while. She'll get cold and want to go in soon."

"Maybe! She just gets superexcited about things. She's like me that way—hey, Bud finished his trial period at Alphapointe, and he got a raise!" Now Jennie is the one who's excited. "But realistically, I'm still going to have to keep working." Jennie works at a fast-food restaurant in the evenings when Bud is home with Felicity.

"Mommy, my feet are *coooold*!" Felicity is reaching for Jennie, who picks her up.

"Time to go in—let's get some breakfast!"

Jennie waves goodbye to me, and Felicity says goodbye to Boris, and we all go back into our warm houses—we've had enough snow for the moment. I feed Boris and think about Jennie saying "superexcited." Where have I heard that expression? I remember being annoyed by it because it was out of place—a business setting? Oh right, it was that phone interview for the senior-housing sales gig.

I think about Anastacia the interviewer and her enthusiastic voice, which is really all I know about her. I think about Jennie and her cheerful demeanor and pleasant voice. I look up the job ad at the senior-care referral company, which is still posted, probably because they have quite a few people in that position—or a lot of turnover. I know next to nothing about Jennie's qualifications, but I don't see anything in the posting that would rule her out, other than the note that children can't be in the room or under the care of the employee. I think maybe Liz, who is across the street and home with a new baby, might like to earn a few bucks babysitting to help push off the day she has to go back to work.

I feel like a matchmaker, and then I think that I'm interfering where I have no business. Maybe I am wound too tight, but I can't tell in which direction. I print out the job posting and knock on Jennie's door. When Felicity hears my voice, she comes running and yelling for Boris. When he doesn't appear, she demands to know where he is.

"He's at home, because I'm only here for a minute," I tell her. "I came to talk to your mother." At that, she shrieks and runs to the bedroom window, where we can hear her calling for Boris. Her mother and I laugh, and I wonder what Boris thinks, since it's likely that he can hear her.

I'm not quite ready with my opening pitch, still thinking that this is none of my business, but I jump in.

"I don't know if you heard, but I got laid off," I say, and then move right on to, "so I've been looking online for a new job, and I ran into this and thought of you." I thrust the printed posting at her.

"I don't even know if you're looking for a different job, but it's part-time at home, and I just thought it might suit you." I'm fumbling for words now, since I really have no idea if it suits her or not.

Jennie is busy reading. She switches to her calm voice. "I could do this," she says. Then she must have reached the part about no kids within earshot. We can still hear Felicity talking to Boris about the snow as if he were in the room with her.

"Oh. I'd still have to pay a babysitter or work in the evening—or no, evenings wouldn't work. Yeah, that could be a problem." She pauses. "You wouldn't want to watch her? I mean until you find another job? Or—you could do this job!"

I assure her that I'm not good at talking to strangers all day long, a concept she can't seem to grasp, which reinforces my impression that this job is a good fit for her. I ignore the idea of me as babysitter.

"Maybe you could work out something with another mom around here who works part-time but different hours? I don't know, maybe that would get too complicated. Maybe it was a crazy idea, but when I read it I just thought of you, so I thought I'd bring it over."

I'm repeating myself now, so it's time to go.

"Anyway, it's good to see you and always a pleasure to see Felicity." And I turn to leave.

"Wait, stay for a minute. I'm so sorry about your job. Are you going to be all right?" It's exactly what Josie had asked.

"Yes, I think so. I did get some severance pay, and I'm starting to look for a job now." I wonder what she thinks of my situation. I've learned that the mention of moving to Missouri from California makes people think I am rich, or at least richer than they are. She knows I own my house. She knows I had a job that involved trips to places like Australia and San Francisco. She knows I have a degree. She also knows a little of my recent history, which resulted in my move to this block. But I don't know what that adds up to in her mind, or Josie's. To be honest, I don't even know what it adds up to in my own mind. I don't mention my hardware store job.

"I've been looking on Craigslist and Monster.com and the state job website." I'm thinking she's the right age to know about these, but most of the people I know who are her age are college grads, and she may not be. "I'd like to find another telecommuting job, like I had before," I continue, "which is why I ran into that one." I nod at the paper, which is still in her hand.

She looks at it, reads through it again.

"Is it the kind of thing you might like to do? I don't really know what kind of experience you've got."

"Oh, I would love this!" she says. "Before Felicity, I worked in a bank, starting as a teller. I loved that too. But then. . . ." she trails off, and I think there must be some history that I don't necessarily need to know. Or more likely the subprime mortgage crisis that tanked the economy and caused a rash of bank closures.

"Well then, why don't you apply and just see what happens? Maybe it will work out and maybe it won't, but it can't hurt to ask, right?"

She's looking thoughtful, and I tell her I need to get going, although the only thing I need to get going to is lunch and another job-hunting session. She thanks me for thinking of her and tells Felicity to come and tell me goodbye, which she does very formally, with a little bow that makes her mother roll her eyes and laugh.

To prove that I'm not a liar about needing to go, I put Boris in the car and drive to a dog park where he can romp in the snow before it melts. I can't imagine that Jennie noticed or cares, but I am aware that we are all very visible to each other, which is both very nice and somewhat bothersome.

CHAPTER 16

On Sunday night, I set my alarm for five thirty, to make sure I'm not rushed on my first day at the hardware store, and then remember that I start on Tuesday. Somehow Monday is in my head—maybe from all those years of Monday through Friday at the office.

Early Tuesday morning, I take Boris for a short walk, eat breakfast, get dressed. I suddenly panic about what to wear to work at a hardware store after years of office wear. I've been in the store hundreds of times, but I can't picture what Henry is wearing. I realize that I don't have many options anyway and put on my best jeans and a long-sleeved cotton sweater. I look in the mirror and wonder if khakis would be better, then remember that I don't have any khakis, having bought very few clothes since I moved into this almost closet-less house. I feed Boris and run out the door, then go back for the car keys. I can walk, but I'll be starving by noon. If I have the car, I'll get in it and drive home. If I'm on foot, I'll very likely succumb to the smell of the fried chicken place I'll have to walk past, and I'll spend at least an hour's pay on unhealthy food.

At 6:45 a.m., I open the hardware store door, worried at the last minute that maybe I misunderstood about the rather casual job offer. Henry seems to be expecting me. Why do I have to make up things to worry about? He is wearing Dickies and a blue work shirt and leather loafers and takes no notice of my outfit, as far as I can tell. He has some paperwork for me to fill out and leaves me in his office to take care of it. This is the one part of the store I've never been in. It's clean and tidy and doubles as the staff room, with a coffee maker and cubbies labeled with each employee's name. I'm excessively pleased to see one with my name on it. I don't have anything to put in it, having worried about all the details of my first day to the point of leaving home with just my driver's license, a credit card, my keys, and my phone, all of which fit in my jeans pockets. I didn't even wear a jacket, although I did leave one in the car, just in case, although in case of what, I'm not sure. There is a new Midtown Hardware cap in my cubby, so I put it on, pull my braid through the gap in the back, and instantly feel more confident.

The store officially opens at seven, but there were trucks in the parking lot when I arrived. Henry is clearly busy, so I work through the forms as quickly as I can and hurry out to the cash register. I don't know how to use it, so I'm not sure what use I am right now, and I have another moment of panic. I should have come in during the slack afternoon and learned to use it. Well, no—Henry is the boss, and he can cope. In fact, he's talking to me right now.

"Marianne, this is Jerry," he says, nodding at one of the men standing around the counter. "He's picking up these two-by-fours and two-by-sixes." Henry hands me a slip of paper and a key. "Open up the lumber yard and check off what he takes on the tally card in each bin. You can leave the yard unlocked, but close the gate when he leaves. He's already paid." He slides his eyes over to Jerry and says, "Don't try to cheat her—she's dangerous with a crowbar."

Jerry is clearly an old customer and laughs at Henry. "Rats, I was hoping I was finally going to get a chance to pull a fast one on old Henry." I give him a smile, spin around, flip my braid over my shoulder, and lead the way outside, secure in my new cap.

I'm familiar with the grades of lumber Henry carries and have seen the tally cards, so I know that I can get through this first assignment. I even help Jerry load the lumber, which makes me realize that I need my work gloves and some sort of jacket that can take some wear and tear. The sweater wasn't a great idea.

Back inside, I'm surprised to see Henry's son, Matt, ringing up a sale at the cash register while Henry is talking to another customer about breaker boxes. Matt is wearing jeans and has a pair of work gloves sprouting from a back pocket. He calls me over and introduces me to the next customer without pausing.

"Marianne's new today," he tells the customer. "Well, new to the register. She's put in a lot of hours in the store." Matt has his father's easy way with people, and he's clearly talking to everyone in line. He finishes with the sale and then turns to me. "Just watch me for a while, and then you can take a turn." I realize that he's come in early to get me started before he leaves for his lab.

During the next few sales, while bantering with the customers, he quietly explains to me what he's doing. It's easy enough to scan anything with a barcode, but there are a lot of subtleties about lumber and small hardware that gets counted out of bins. And in spite of Henry's confidence that I know where everything is, it soon becomes clear that I don't. Lucky for me, these early-morning customers know more than I do.

"I need five of these—better make it six." A young man is showing me a tiny ball bearing. At least I know what it is, but I have no idea where they are. "Right behind you," the customer says. "Want me to get them?"

Matt nods, and the guy crowds in behind the counter with us. I pull out a small plastic ziplock bag and hold it while he counts them in. At least I know that much.

"Anything else?" I ask, pretending hard that it isn't the first time I've said that to a live customer.

"Nope, that's it."

"Here," Matt says to me. "Ring it up. Just scan the drawer label, then press the 'five' when it asks how many." I am hit with the realization that my new job is data management as much as anything else. I'm all about data management. Data management in a Midtown Hardware cap. I look up at the customer.

"That was six, right?"

"Yep, I need five, but I'm sure I'll drop one." I complete the sale and send the customer on his way.

I look at the clock over the door and see that it's 8:40 a.m. already. Henry reappears, and Matt heads out the back door. "See you next week."

"Everything going okay?" Henry asks me.

"Is it always this crazy in here at the crack of dawn?"

"Yes it is, especially Monday and Tuesday. Well, Friday too. Contractors on their way to their first jobs of the day. If they're working nearby, they'll stop in during the day. And then there's a little rush at the end—some guys would rather pick up what they need on their way home and not have to get up so early. And it depends on which way they're going and if they're taking the expressway. The expressway saved the store, really. Easy off, easy on. We give them the contractor discount and make sure they get through here as quickly as possible. The rest of the day, we're a little more relaxed. But you'll learn to recognize the ones who need to get something fast and get back to a job."

Okay, the job is a little more than data management and a cap with a logo.

By this time, there are several customers in the store, but none at the counter. Henry tells me to help myself to coffee. "I sort of hate that K-Cup thing, but Matt talked me into it. He convinced me that the packaging waste is offset by all the wasted coffee and electricity with the old pot. We'd turn it on when we got here, and then sometimes we wouldn't even have a chance to get any for a couple of hours, and by then it was all stewed and undrinkable." He chuckles. "In case you cared. I know some people really hate the whole idea of those single-cup things."

I'm guessing I look like the type who would hate them, and in fact I do hate them, but I also see his point.

"Well, I'd really like a cup of coffee right now, and I'm pretty sure I wouldn't drink the old stuff, so I say bring it on!" And I go brew myself a cup, making a mental note to bring in my own mug. I take the coffee back toward the front of the store and then wonder if that's not proper shop etiquette, so I reverse course and look over my form while Henry helps a customer. I'm appalled at how much I don't know about what to do.

The customer exits, and I leave my coffee and go ask Henry what he'd like me to do next.

"Finish your coffee. It's okay to bring it up here early in the morning—everyone expects coffee at 7:00 a.m. Just tuck it back in where it won't spill. You may not get much chance to drink it, even so. Some days are that busy. Bring an insulated mug in if you like. Just don't cling to it—you know what I mean?"

I nod. What he's saying is obvious, but I would probably have missed it.

"You can go out and lock the yard now that the morning rush is over. If anyone else wants lumber, we can just open the gate again. We've never had a problem, but I like to play it safe. Oh, and there are jackets by the back door if you ever need to grab one to go outside."

I'm glad to have a minute of fresh air and quiet. Not exactly quiet, this close to the expressway, but at least no chatter.

Henry watches me handle the next few sales, and then the store is empty for a few minutes. He shows me where the panic buttons are in case of a holdup. "Again, we've never had to use one, but you never know." I pay close attention to where they are and how they work, so that I don't push one accidentally. Henry must realize this, because he then tells me what code to enter if I do push it accidentally. "The police will come regardless," he tells me, which is both a worry and a relief.

The afternoon clerk arrives at noon. Henry tells me that his wife will go over my forms and call me if she has any questions. He tells me that the day went well and he'll see me next week, unless of course I need any hardware between now and then.

When I pull out of the parking lot, I smell the frying chicken across the street and am glad I'm in the car and headed for lunch at home. The salad that I'll probably make seems so dull and not filling, in comparison to the warm, wonderful aroma of chicken cooking in fat. I turn down my street and open the car window to clear out the chicken smell. I'll forget about it by the time I'm home, I hope.

In my own kitchen, I wash my hands and face, drink a glass of water, and sit down with my head in my hands. I'm exhausted. How does Henry work all day, every day? He must take off some afternoons. I rummage in the refrigerator for leftovers. A salad isn't going to do it today. I find broccoli and rice and pile on some cheese. While it's heating, I realize that I haven't thought about my lack of job and lack of job prospects all morning, which has let the part of my brain that worries about money take a rest. The realization is eye-opening, and I wonder if I can come up with a way to fill another chunk of another day of the week.

I read a book while I'm eating and find myself falling asleep at the kitchen table, so I give in and nap on the sofa. I dream about stuffing little bits of hardware, plumbing elbows, and screws and ball bearings into a database that keeps spilling them on the floor. The landline rings and startles me awake. Only Josie and a few coworkers ever use that number, and I've hardly heard it ring since I returned from San Francisco.

"Hello, this is Marianne." I'm businesslike out of habit.

"Oh, thank goodness. I heard a rumor that you were leaving the company." I have no clue who is speaking. I opted out of caller ID.

"Well, the rumor's correct. You've called my personal number." I remember in time not to say "home number," not wanting to sound like I'm a loser lounging at home, which is ridiculous, because I don't even know who I'm talking to.

"Oh, sorry about that! I was hoping you could help me generate a report." Clearly he's sorry on his own account, not mine. "Delarosa wants every region to email him a deck every Monday by COB showing. . . ." And he babbles on about forecasts and BLs and POS and NGD. I am amazed at how foreign it already sounds. I have to think to come up with what the initials stand for.

"Well, the system can do that," I tell him when he finally stops for breath. "But I can't help you. I'm no longer working there." I don't mention that there are dozens of people who can run reports or teach him how to do it. He has the wheedling, superior, condescending voice of a young MBA who is clueless about the business, in addition to the system.

"But could you just tell me how to—" he begins again, but I stop him midsentence.

"No, sorry. I'm working for another firm now." I giggle to myself about the thin edge of truth in that. I search the corporate archive section of my brain for a term like "fiduciary responsibility" or "managerial courage" that I can toss into the conversation, but can't find an appropriate one. Two minutes ago, I was having a dream about copper plumbing elbows, and it's a long haul from that to corpo-babble.

"I have a fiduciary responsibility to my new company," pops out of my mouth, and that shuts him up. True in some cosmic sense but bogus.

After a moment or two of silence, which bothers me not at all, he starts again, now with more wheedle and less superiority. "Could someone else help me? Can you give me another girl's name?"

At this point, I might have asked him who he was, what part of the business he was in, and helped him find someone who could do his work for him. Or told him where to post a request for help within his unit. But seriously—"another girl"?

I pause to keep from shouting, will myself not to apologize, and then I say, "Delarosa closed my department, so there isn't anyone." And then I add, "But if you want another girl's name, what about Bambi? That's a girl's name." And then I turn all cold and businesslike and tell him that I've got a meeting.

"Good luck," I say, and hang up before he can say anything.

I'm not especially proud of myself, and I'm not going to kid myself that my Bambi comment had any sort of impact at all. He's either telling the guy who sits next to him what a repressed feminist bitch I am, or he's searching Outlook for an employee named Bambi. It's a big company, and he's likely to find one. God knows how that conversation will go, but in the end he'll just think I'm mean or stupid, and he'll be at least half right.

"Boris, you and I have a meeting," I say with a sigh and get his leash.

CHAPTER 17

I have refreshment duty at church this coming Sunday. Canned pumpkin is on sale, so I decide to make pumpkin bread and bake it in cupcake pans. Cupcake pans are exactly the kind of thing I had no intention of replacing after losing everything to a fire in my last house, the last straw that ended my years in California and led me to life in Kansas City. I had been storing and moving my mother's cupcake pans for decades, after all, and I had used them maybe twice. But muffins are popular after church and at neighborhood parties, so I decide to tour my favorite resale shops.

St. Vincent de Paul is a bit of a drive, thirty blocks north on Troost. It's on the west side of the street, so technically not east of Troost, but at that latitude, it's all the same: the Troost wall has been breached. I like the store and the story behind the store, which involves the murals on the parking lot side of the building. They are larger-than-life faces of grandmothers in the neighborhood, all colors of the spectrum. I like to poke around in the store, but today I'm on a mission, so I ask the always-helpful staff for cupcake or muffin pans. They have plenty—either people have been clearing space in their cupboards, or everyone is switching to silicone. I am looking for ones that will nest together and don't have a nonstick coating to go bad or flake off.

I find some that are so like my old ones that I do a double take, momentarily wondering how they got here. I scoop them up and linger over a cast-iron muffin pan that I love but I know I will hate, because it will be a long and trying process to get it to the point where most of the muffin doesn't stick in the beautiful whorls in each well of the pan. Also, it weighs a ton. I put it back.

I'm on my way to check out when I see a rack of jackets suitable for a hardware-store employee. I detour and take a look. A store clerk materializes and holds my cupcake tins so I can use both hands. I find a fleece-lined hoodie in robin's-egg blue with a smooth finish that feels almost waxed. It's a men's size medium, so the sleeves are long enough for me, although it's a bit snug in the hips. I decide it's long enough that I can remove the too-tight ribbed band and hem the bottom edge to solve that problem. It looks new—probably because robin's-egg blue is not most guys' favorite color for jackets.

I'm hesitating, wondering if I should spend money on a jacket like this, which I don't really need for my five-hour-a-week job, although it would be good for dog walking. And it's soft enough and trim enough to wear at home like a sweater, at least when I'm just sitting around reading this winter, with the thermostat turned down because I don't have a job and am trying to save on heat. My early twenties are far in the past, but I vividly remember shivering through winter when I wasn't making much money right after college.

The clerk is hovering. "Jackets are half-price today," she says, pointing with her eyes to a sign on top of the rack. "And we have a 10 percent discount if you're over fifty-five," she adds. "Not that you look like you are, but just in case."

I laugh, and her worried look goes away. "Thank you for checking. I'll take this."

"Do you mind if I ask—is it for you?"

It is, of course, and I've been trying it on, so that should be obvious. But I guess people would try something on to gauge how it would fit on a spouse or a friend.

"I'm only asking because it's been here awhile, and I just moved it to the women's rack even though it's a men's jacket. I didn't think a man would ever buy that color."

I give her a big smile. "You are brilliant. I love this color and would never have looked on the men's rack." I tell her about my plan to alter it.

I pay and turn to leave, then turn back and tell her she has a great future in marketing. We both smile, and I can see that she's pleased, and that makes me feel good. I know perfectly well that one reason it feels good is that I hardly ever have any conversation these days, and while I like my solitude, I'm probably over the limit of how much solitude is good for me.

By the time I get home, it's snowing. A few hours later, the doorbell rings, and I find Flynn standing there with a coal shovel.

"Thought I could shovel your walk," he says, peering past me into the house. I make a show of holding Boris back, although he's just standing there waving his tail slowly.

"Oh, thanks, that's nice," I say. "But I need the exercise. Doesn't take but a minute anyway."

He stands there nodding, not making eye contact, and I suspect there is something else he wants to say, something I don't want to hear.

"Oh, that's my phone." I let go of Boris and take the phone out of my pocket. I peer at the screen. "Sorry, I've gotta get this," I say, looking up at him as if I were sorry. "I'll see you later." I pull Boris back and close the door gently, clicking the lock.

Okay, the buzz in my pocket was just an email, and it's just a newsfeed I've subscribed to. I wait until I hear Flynn's footsteps recede and then peek out. He's gone, and there's barely enough snow for him to have left footprints. I feel a little sorry for him and admire him just a little for making the attempt. And I feel just the tiniest bit guilty for pushing him off, but not nearly as sorry as I would be right now if I'd invited him in for coffee. I wonder what he would have done if I'd accepted his offer to shovel. Scraped his shovel down the almost-dry sidewalk? I cringe, imagining the sound.

CHAPTER 18

Tuesday morning, I'm up early again and excited about my second morning at the store and the distraction it will bring. I eat an extra bowl of cereal, hoping to stave off hunger pangs until I get back after noon. My coffee mug and work gloves are in the vile green tote bag that I got free when I bought the blue sweatshirt I'm wearing. I've washed the bag and the sweatshirt twice and given them extra time in the dryer, not that I'm worried about bedbugs, but still.

I walk in at 6:55 a.m. and head for my cubby as if I've been doing that for years. I put on my cap, fill my coffee cup, and stash the tote bag. The gloves are in my hip pocket, just like Matt's and Henry's. Matt is at the cash register, and I sidle up and offer to take over. Ringing up sales is so easy, until it isn't, and I want as much practice as I can get while he's there to supervise. It is excessively important to me that the customers think I'm competent.

"Sure," Matt says. "I need to run out to the yard and load up some lumber for Rolla. You met him last week. Anyone else needs lumber before I get back, send them around." He makes a point of gesturing with his head that the customers go out the front door and around. "Through the gate," he adds to make sure I get it.

"Got it," I say and smile at the next customer. His hands are full of merchandise, so I say, "Find whatcha need?" imitating what Henry has said to me dozens of times.

The next few sales go smoothly, and I'm feeling confident when a customer lays some saw blades on the counter and hands me a piece of paper. My first thought is that it's a hold-up note, and I try to remember where the alarm button is.

But he says, "Need some wood too," and I see that it's a list of lumber. I take a deep breath and put off chastising myself for later. I've got this.

I punch in the eight two-by-fours and ten two-by-sixes and then come to the "12 by 12" on his list.

"Um, I don't think we have this, uh . . . Bill," I say. I'm hoping he's Bill; that's what his jacket says.

"I'm not Bill; I work for Bill. He sent me here. Said you'd have all this stuff." His voice lacks the normal easy banter of most of our early-morning customers. "I guess he was wrong."

We both study the note again, and not-Bill is getting agitated. Then I notice that Jerry, whom I met last Tuesday, is next in line and peering over not-Bill's shoulder.

"I think that might be one two-by-twelve, not a twelve-by-twelve," he says softly. "The one is just written too close to the two."

You're an idiot, I tell myself, but shove that out of my head and say out loud, "Of course it is, and of course we carry that. Bill was right." I ring up the lumber, and just before hitting the total key, I remember the blades and add those, sparing myself another embarrassment. I hand not-Bill the receipt and tell him to go around to the yard, nodding at the front door. "Matt's out there—he'll help you."

"At least there's still one man around here," he says. I barely register the insult and see him look toward the back of the store and hope he doesn't try to go through, instead of back out the front door. I see Jerry shift his body just slightly to his right, leaving not-Bill a little less space to take the through-the-store route and more space to turn left and leave through the front. On my side of the counter, I shift slightly left, toward Jerry. My eyes are on Jerry, but my attention is on not-Bill, who has not turned to go. I expected a fast exit after his insult, so now I'm just a little spooked. I turn back to him.

"Thanks for coming in," I say, turning to smile at him. He looks like he's going to reply, but he turns and leaves instead. I watch until I see him walk toward the gate to the yard, then turn to Jerry again. Jerry drops several boxes of nails and electrical parts on the counter and says, "I just need to check with Henry about something. Go ahead and take the next guy."

I'm not sure what's going on, but I assume the best thing to do is the obvious one, so I turn to the next customer and say, "Find whatcha need?"

Jerry is back in a minute or two, and I check him out without comment beyond, "Anything else?" which he can take any way he wants.

"All good," he says, which I take to mean that all is well outside, so I thank him and tell him I'll see him soon. I got tired of "Have a nice day" in my first five minutes, so I'm working on alternatives.

After Matt leaves for school and the morning rush calms down, Henry appears and tells me I can lock the gate now. I relish my moment in the fresh air but don't waste any time getting back inside. I'm wondering if anything really happened this morning with not-Bill, but I don't want Henry to think I'm concerned. On the other hand, I don't want him to think I'm oblivious.

"Busy morning," I say when I am back inside. I wait for a response, but Henry is looking through the morning's receipts and doesn't say anything right away, so I tell him I'm going to get coffee and start in that direction. I wash my face and hands while the coffee is dripping and reappear at the counter. Henry is helping a customer, so I tidy up the racks of key chains and flashlights and other impulse items near the counter. I know Henry will walk back with the customer and ring him up.

No one else is in the store at the moment, so when the customer leaves, I ask Henry what he would like me to do next, adding that I can stock or sweep or clean the bathroom—it's all the same to me.

"Oh, is it a mess already?"

"No! Well, I don't know—I haven't looked." Why is everything so awkward all of a sudden? Why isn't he just telling me to check the stock of paintbrushes or something? Why don't I act like an adult and ask?

"Is everything okay?" I go for a light tone that assumes everything is okay but allows for something to be askew.

Finally he looks me in the face and smiles. "Yes, I'm just trying to figure out what to tell you about Mr. Friedman," he says with a hint of a laugh.

I'm relieved that he ended that sentence with "Mr. Friedman" and not anything about me, such as a cash register screwup, and I just respond with raised eyebrows and an encouraging sort of murmur.

He clarifies who Mr. Friedman is. "The guy with the twelve-by-twelve."

"Oh him," I say. "He seemed a little flustered or something." *Show no fear. Let Henry tell me what happened or didn't.*

Henry is the one who is flustered now, but he finally tells me that Mr. Friedman complained about "women who don't know anything."

"Jerry followed him out to the yard, so I thought he might have said something out of line to you."

"Oh, please," I say, relieved that there is nothing else going on. "That was nothing, nothing compared to what I put up with in the corporate world."

"Well, you got paid a lot more to put up with it there."

"I did, but still. This was nothing. Don't worry about it. I can take a lot of sexist crap and still smile and thank them for their business."

Henry is visibly relieved, so I add, "From the customers. Don't you be trying it," and laugh to let him know that I'm sure he won't.

"So really, what do you want me to do next?"

"Oh!" he says. "Matt got you a headset for the wireless intercom. It's something he put together for us to talk to each other when one of us is inside and someone is outside or in the back room. So when people need something from the yard, you can let us know before they get back there. You just clip this on your belt." He looks at me and sees no belt. "Or wherever," he says without missing a beat.

"Leave it turned on when you're working, and you can hear anything anyone says. If you get an order or have a question or anything, you just hold the green button and talk."

I put on the headset, clip the button unit to my jeans pocket, and walk out the front door to test it.

"I like it," I tell him when we're both satisfied that I've mastered it. "Do you have any code words?"

"Code words?"

"You know, code for 'someone get up here, the line is out the door,' or 'lunatic headed for the yard,' or something."

"Or armed robber in my face?" Henry is serious.

"Well, I was thinking 'paint spill,' but sure, a code for armed robbery couldn't hurt. As long as we never need to use it."

"We don't have any codes, but maybe we should. Matt's

mostly interested in the electronics. Once he gets something working, he's not so interested anymore."

I wait on a few more customers and spend some time tidying the electrical parts. I find them supremely uninteresting, so I'm trying to understand what they are called and what they are used for. That way, I can answer questions if anyone ever asks. I don't want to use the intercom to say, "Drawing a blank in electrical."

CHAPTER 19

When I get home, the front door sticks a little, meaning a little more than usual. I've been in denial that it needs attention. Door and lock maintenance scares me a little, probably because doors represent security. Also they aren't easily replaced, at least not by me, and the locks are a mystery. To my father and my husband, everything about doors was simple to the point of boring, plus they had the physical strength to lift them off their hinges and get them back on. So I never thought much about doors and locks. Until I moved here, where they are more important than ever.

But the door opens and closes well enough for the moment, and the back door, which is new, is fine, so I think about lunch instead of locks. I'm starving after my morning at work.

After lunch, though, I decide to at least figure out what is sticking, and then maybe I can figure out why. It opens just fine, but it doesn't latch when I close it. Rats, it's a lock problem. Oh wait, it's not quite flush. I give it a smart push, and it latches easily. So it's the door sticking somewhere. I think about planing the top or bottom and groan. I don't have a plane and would probably hurt myself using one if I did. Well, at least I can figure out if it's the top or bottom. I could conceivably plane the top without taking it off the hinges, although Henry would terminate my contractor discount if he ever heard about me doing something that stupid.

I remember my husband replacing hinges, so I look at the gap on the hinge edge of the door, and the gap seems even from top to bottom, so a worn hinge isn't letting the door sag. I get out my step stool and check the top. No sticking there, either. Finally, I lie down on the floor and close the door slowly. "Ah, Boris, there's the rub," I say. The weather-stripping sweep has failed and is flapping around and binding up. I open and close the door right at the sticking point and realize that I could have figured it out a lot faster if I had just noticed that the drag was at the bottom, not the top. I can feel it now. I measure the door and make a note to buy a new sweep the next time I'm at Henry's. It can probably wait a week. On the other hand, my schedule is not exactly full. I can go tomorrow.

While I'm cooking dinner, I think about the intercom at the hardware store. Matt may not be interested now that it's working, but I am. Why shouldn't he sell it? I try to think of mass-market uses and realize that there are probably dozens of similar items available online. I don't bother to google it. Surely he can make a few and sell them locally to make a little extra cash. Who east of Troost would use it though? Houses are way too small to need it, and everyone can text anyway. And then it comes to me. All those contractors passing through the hardware store every day and heading out to work sites where people need to keep in touch across a large and noisy space. Genius.

Or not. Different subcontractors every day, a different set of workers every day, headsets probably need to be sanitized, headsets get separated from the button unit, whatever that is called. Dumb idea.

Or the third possibility, which is that I'm overthinking it. I'm good at overthinking.

CHAPTER 20

On my third Tuesday at the store (or at "the office," as I call it to myself because it amuses me), I use the intercom several times to let whoever is in the yard know that someone is on the way to pick up plywood or downspouts or whatever. I love that I don't have to know who is out there; I just speak, and everyone hears. I'm startled only once by an incoming message, when Henry tells me to ring up one more sheet of quarter-inch finish plywood for Jerry, who will return to the counter to pay. "And make sure he doesn't sneak off without paying," Henry adds, and I hear them laughing and joking. I like that too. It makes me feel like all is well outside, and they know that all is well inside. I realize that I was just a little spooked last week, when Mr. Friedman was being weird and Jerry followed him out.

The store is still full of people, but no one is waiting to pay, when I hear Matt chatting about school as he is picking up his backpack to leave. When he stops talking, I say into the headset, "I wonder if any of these contractors would like one of these headset things to use on their jobsites."

Silence. I wonder if I've broken some protocol about use of the devices.

Still silence, so I add, "Oh well, just a random idea."

I've got a customer now and reach out for the caulking he is holding. I see he's got five each of two different kinds, so I separate them and verify that he wants five white and five clear. He takes five back and returns with the right ones.

"Thanks," he mumbles, barely audible.

"No problem, I've done that myself," I say, and then I look up at the face hiding under his cap. "Good to see you again, Mr. Friedman."

He almost smiles, mutters something I don't catch, and leaves.

I look up at the next customer, and Matt is next in line. He's grinning.

"Maybe," he says. "Why don't you ask around?"

I grin back at him. "Why don't you? I'm only here five hours a week."

"I got school, and it's your idea. I'll cut you in for a percentage."

We both laugh, and Matt leaves. Henry materializes. He's obviously heard the exchange.

"You should have seen Matt's face when he heard you say that over the intercom. It was like the first time he saw a Christmas tree all lit up, like he had seen something that was previously unimaginable."

"Um, it's just selling a thing he already built, to a bunch of guys he already knows."

"Yeah, but like I said, once the technical problems are solved, he loses interest. Even way back, in his Tinkertoy years. Once he was able to build the thing he saw in his head, he'd just leave it, let his brother wreck it, even if he'd spent days on it. He'd tell us all about how he made the bridge stay up, or whatever, but he didn't need to show it to us or admire it himself afterward."

"And now?"

"And now he's taking one business class, and he's supposed to come up with a business plan for some sort of business, and that doesn't interest him in the least. So I'm guessing he just saw a business that he could write a plan for."

"Well, I already thought of all the reasons it won't work, so I'm going to keep my mouth shut." I say that, but I know I won't. "Meanwhile, I need a new sweep for my front door, so I'll be checking the stock in the door-hardware department."

A few minutes later, Henry joins me. I'm stalled out deciding between loop and finned.

"This is why I can't shop at Home Depot or Lowe's. It's hard enough with just the choices you have."

Henry hands me the thirty-inch loop one. "Take this one home and try it. Leave it in the plastic, and tape it to the door with blue tape. Then lie down on the floor, and make sure it makes contact all the way across. If your threshold is original, it's probably wood, and it may be worn down in the middle."

"Got it." I know it's wood, and how can it not be worn?

"If it's worn too much, we can solve that with a different sweep or else a new threshold. That's a bit of work though." Meaning too complicated for me and my small collection of tools. "Jimmy can do it if it comes to that, but you've got some options."

I thank him and ring up the door sweep.

"You can pay for that after you're sure it will work," he tells me.

"Nope. This way I'll get some practice entering returns if it doesn't work."

CHAPTER 21

I'm tired after lunch and just lounging, trying to get up the energy to resume my job search or test my door sweep, when Boris stands up and looks at the door. His tail is wagging, so I know that someone familiar is on the other side. I wait for the doorbell to ring, though. I know it's disconcerting to be reaching for the bell and have the door open like magic. It also gives me a moment to stand up, shake off my lethargy, and put on my company face.

Jennie is at my door with Felicity, so we have the usual flurry of greetings, which involve girl and dog running all over the house, squealing (girl) and barking (dog and girl). Jennie apologizes automatically, and I tell her I like it. Felicity is just old enough to be past the stage where she has to touch every-thing and put most of it in her mouth, so I don't worry too much about where she goes. If she's quiet for more than thirty seconds, her mother will call to her without even breaking stride in our conversation.

Boris finds the superlight dog toy he got from my cousins last Christmas, and he and Felicity settle into a game of fetch. Even the most determined preschooler can't throw the toy more than about eight feet, so it's totally safe, and we can leave them to it.

"We're getting a dog," Jennie says, almost bouncing on the sofa. I interpret that to mean they've found a dog like Boris to make Jennie feel safe at home when Bud is at work with his service dog.

"Fantastic," I say, knowing that a word or two is all she needs to keep going. No need to pry it out of her. Conversation with Jennie is easy if you don't need to talk much yourself.

I've been afraid that they would be quick to adopt something loud and boisterous, with too much junkyard dog in its genes and too little training in its past. But I often underestimate Jennie, and she tells me about her search for the right age and personality and size (big enough to warn off burglars but small enough to "fit"). Her name is Wiggles. Jennie rolls her eyes.

"'Wiggles' doesn't sound like much of a guard dog, does it?" She sighs. "But she barked when we left her, so we know she sounds like a real dog. And she's thirty-five pounds, not too big but big enough to play with this one." She nods toward Felicity. The little girl walks over and leans against her mother.

"Waggo," she tells me, very seriously.

"Your new friend," I say, nodding. "When does Wiggles arrive?"

"Saddery," she says carefully, still solemn. And then she shouts, "New friend for Boris!" and Boris obligingly walks over and drops the wet toy on her toes, and they go back to their game.

"We thought Saturday morning would give us the whole weekend to get used to each other." Then she gets a little shy. "Would you like to meet her on Saturday?" she asks.

"Of course. We can let the dogs out in their own yards, and they can meet through the fence at first. Just give me a call. I think I'll be home all day, or at least all morning." I only wish I had something more on my calendar.

Jennie and Felicity leave with only a few complaints from Felicity. Jennie tells her they have to start getting ready for Wiggles, and that seems to do the trick. Boris sees them out, watching from the porch as they walk down the driveway and up onto their own porch. Once they are inside, he comes back in, flings himself on the living room rug, sighs loudly, and goes to sleep. I hope for Jennie's sake that Felicity does her own version of that. Their visit has cheered me up, and I decide to go through my fabric scraps and see if I can make a fetch toy for Wiggles.

CHAPTER 22

Two days later, Jennie and Felicity are at the door again, and again Jennie is brimming with excitement. She doesn't even wait for Boris and Felicity to finish running laps. "I got that job!"

"That job" must refer to the one I had suggested that she apply for. In the few months they've lived next door, I've learned to keep up with Jennie's enthusiastic conversation, which generally presumes that you've been thinking about whatever is foremost in her life at the moment. I suddenly worry about that trait not working so well as a senior-care referral phone employee. Or maybe it will be fine; she has a strong sense of empathy.

She tells me about the phone interview, which sounds exactly like the one I had, except that it ended with a job offer. I register one iota of hurt feelings, immediately replaced with a sort of admiration for Anastacia the interviewer, who could see—or hear—that Jennie was an obvious fit, while I was absolutely not. I follow that up with a fear that the job is a bit of a scam and that it might not actually pay off for Jennie, who will have given up her evening fast-food job. Or that she'll run into problems with the dog or Felicity making noise in the background. I tell myself to focus on Jennie, who is still talking.

"So I start Monday at ten, and I'll go into the office every day for two weeks. The first week is training, and the second week I work there in a cubicle, and it will be exactly like working at home except they'll be there with me, and they'll listen in and also record everything, so I don't have to worry if I get something wrong—they'll just bail me out."

I'm impressed with her willingness to make mistakes and trust that they will bail her out and then also be so sure that she'll be totally competent to work on her own.

"But I need a favor, and I wondered if I could ask you. . . ." She's hopeful, and I'm touched that she'd ask me for a favor but also is not counting on me to say yes. Then I panic that she's going to ask me to babysit during the training period and scramble to get an excuse ready.

She sighs and then says, "We have to have a landline—I can't use my cell phone. I think they want to make sure we are focused on work and not driving around or shopping or something." I think they are more concerned about voice quality and calls not dropping, but Jennie is young enough that she might not even realize how much better landlines still are. And then I wonder how much of her salary is going to be spent on the landline.

"The company will pay for it," she goes on. Okay, I can stop worrying about that. "But the phone guy can't come until Monday between ten and two, so I was wondering if you could let him in."

"Oh, of course!" I whip out my phone and check the calendar, as if something would have appeared there on its own. "Yep, I'm home then."

"Thanks," she says, exhaling loudly. "Liz is going to watch Felicity, and I worked out the bus schedule, and I even know what I'm going to wear, and then this came up. Liz said she'd do it if you can't, but they'll probably come when both kids are asleep."

"No problem at all," I tell her and ask if she wants me to wait at her house or leave them a note to check with me.

"They can put it in the work order to have you let them in, but . . . well, I was hoping. If it's all the same to you . . . well, it will be the first day for Wiggles to be alone all day, so it might be. . . ."

I see what she's getting at, so I tell her that I can just take my computer to her house at ten, so Wiggles will only have a half hour or so alone in the morning, and after I leave I can check back every hour or so until she or Bud gets home.

"We want to make sure Wiggles has a good first day on the job too," I tell her, and I can see that she's relieved.

"Maybe the timing isn't so good for getting the dog, but on the other hand, I'll feel better knowing she's in the house while we're all away." She sighs again but wryly this time. "I kind of wish we weren't on the corner." And that makes me worry a little about whether they really will buy the house they are only renting.

"Yeah," I say, not very helpfully. I know what she means. I feel safer tucked in between her and Josie. "On the other hand, you do have that nice big window facing south. Makes your house a lot lighter than this one, and you can see what's going on outside." I don't know if the big window is good or bad. Both maybe. But I do know that it makes the house more elegant, if anything in this neighborhood can be considered elegant. And I wish she didn't have to make this particular wish.

Saturday morning, I take Boris for a walk and then keep him inside. If Wiggles is skittish, she'll be better off exploring her new backyard without worrying about the beast on my side of the fence. She's already got Jennie, Bud, Felicity, and Bud's PTSD service dog to contend with.

All is quiet next door, and I spend my time looking for appropriate jobs and applying for inappropriate ones, since that's all I find. The only really interesting one is in Ohio, and I'm not ready to think about moving. Not yet. Maybe not ever.

Sometime after noon, Boris whimpers at the back door. I can hear Felicity and Jennie in their backyard. Boris barks softly and looks at me, but I call him to me, away from the window that looks out into the yard next door. Then I hear a tentative bark from outside, and Boris barks again, a little louder this time, wagging his tail and looking at me intently. From outside, another bark and a bit of a canine yodel, followed by Felicity shouting for Boris. I peek out and see the whole family, including the service dog, which is glued to Bud's ankle. They are all looking my way, so I wave, and Jennie gives me a two-handed "come on out" wave. So much for introducing the dogs gradually and keeping it calm for Wiggles.

I open the back door, and Boris, who was dancing with impatience a moment ago, saunters out like it's just another day and sticks his nose through the chain-link. I banish the mental image of him sailing over the fence and landing in the middle of the crowd, followed by chaos and squealing and who knows what after that. Wiggles gives him a sniff, jumps back on stiff legs, jumps forward to touch noses, and drops into a play bow. All set, then.

Felicity looks up at me and opens her eyes as wide as she can. "Waggo likes Boris," she announces carefully, eyes glued to mine. Then she shouts, "Waggo loves Boris," and runs around her yard. Wiggles leaves Boris and follows Felicity slowly, circles around her, lets her hug her. I look at the dog's glossy coat. Some Border collie there, maybe, which would explain why she's rounding up the little girl. And maybe some Lab, to account for the goofy grin. Not sure where the yodel comes from. Yorkie?

"So far so good?" I ask the parents. "Are we going to stick with 'Waggo' instead of 'Wiggles'? I actually sort of like 'Waggo.'"

"Yeah, she's a little too serious to be 'Wiggles,' huh?" This from Bud, who usually lets Jennie do the talking.

I smile at him and agree. "And who knows, it may morph into something else. I call Boris 'Boo' about half the time."

The dogs and kid talk through the fence a little longer, and then I suggest that they bring Waggo over the next day to explore our yard and have an official playdate with Boris, if it doesn't rain. Felicity pats Boris and kisses him on the nose through the fence but doesn't complain when I take him inside. Another bonus, at least for one day.

CHAPTER 23

Holidays are coming, and I'm determined not to dread them this year and not to worry about them, either. It's understood that I'll spend Christmas with my cousins in Joplin. I did that last year, and many other times over previous years, so I know that it will be low-key and comfortable and I'll come back calm and refreshed. I'm not sure about Thanksgiving, which is coming up fast. I decide to be bold and invite myself to dinner with the distant relatives in a distant suburb who invited me last year, but I come to my senses and realize that they may have other plans this year. I should keep in touch with them a little more, not leave it till the holidays.

Maybe my grade school best friend, Angie, will invite me to her large Irish German family feed. But maybe I don't want to spend a day with that many people, most of whom I haven't seen since high school (her siblings) or ever (their spouses and kids). Oh well, something will turn up, and anyway, I won't feel bad about spending Thanksgiving alone.

On Sunday, the Thanksgiving question resolves itself when I hear about the Thanks for Everything dinner being held in the church basement for anyone and everyone. Apparently it's a big deal, with two sittings. After Mass, I check the sign-up sheet, wondering how this small parish can produce enough food for the number of people who show up hungry. As I'm pondering, a voice next to me says, "You ever been to one of these?"

"No, I didn't come last year, and before that, I didn't live in Kansas City. Well, not for a long time, anyway."

Evelyn, a woman I've worked with on hospitality duty, appears and says, "Well, you'd better come this year. We need every pair of hands we can get. And we know you can cook—at least cupcakes." She puts an arm around my shoulders and introduces me to the first woman, whose name is Anna Bennet.

"Anna Bennet? You wouldn't be related to Libby Bennet, would you?"

Anna turns out to be the mother of a girl I sang in guitar choir with in the late 1960s. Her husband was my brother's scoutmaster. We start talking about Libby and her brother.

"Y'all go ahead and reminisce," Evelyn says, rolling her eyes but grinning while she does. Then she looks at me with mock fierceness. "But you better show up with a lot of cupcakes on Thanksgiving. Or something else just as good. Actually, you better show up on Wednesday too. We need tall people to get stuff off the high shelves." She laughs and goes off to talk to someone else.

I turn to Anna and ask how many people they serve and how they manage to serve them all.

"Oh, it all works out. We get unsold turkeys and sweet potatoes on Wednesday night from some of the groceries. We soak the turkeys in warm salt water overnight to thaw them—course that's called 'brining' now, so we're all in style. We bake the sweets first thing in the morning, and a bunch of ladies make them up into casseroles. That's sit-down work for folks like me who don't stand up so well anymore. After that, it's a loaves-and-fishes thing. People bring whatever they've got. Even if it's just a bag of potato chips from 7-Eleven, everyone brings something.

Kid comes in with a can of tuna, we'll put it on a plate on a lettuce leaf with some celery sticks or something. Kid will just beam. Of course, we all"—she swings her head around to include everyone in the parish—"buy canned green beans and corn and stuff all year and then make it up on the day. Oh, and B&R already gave us their leftover Halloween cakes. They're back there in one of the freezers. We just scrape off the witches and ghosts and top them up with a squirt of whipped cream. Day after Thanksgiving, we'll get the turkey cakes to fix up for Christmas."

"You do this again at Christmas? I mean, *we* do it again?"

"We do, although this is bigger for some reason."

I'm impressed and excited and sign up for Wednesday and Thursday shifts. I'm thankful just to have a place to be thankful. I ate lunch every school day for eight years in this church basement, so I've already eaten more meals here than in any place, other than my own kitchen. As I'm leaving, Anna smiles at me: "Good to have you back."

CHAPTER 24

Monday morning at ten, I take my laptop next door to wait for the phone company to install Jennie's new landline. At eleven, I have a phone interview and realize I'll have to take it on my cell phone. I hope I don't have to go outside to keep the call from dropping. Just in case, I sit on the floor next to the big south window. This makes Waggo happy, and she snuggles up beside me. No face licking, I'm glad to note.

At noon, I wish I had remembered to bring something to eat and run home for a banana. Boris sniffs my leg and wags his tail hopefully, but I tell him he's on duty at home.

Just before one o'clock, I hear Boris bark twice at my house, his usual greeting to the letter carrier. Waggo's ears perk up, and she stands and looks at me.

"Speak," I tell her. "Speak!" And I bark in her face. I grab a toy and squeak it. "Speak!" She barks tentatively, and we hear footsteps on the porch. "Speak!" I tell her, and she barks again.

"Good girl!" The mailbox lid clinks shut. "Speak!" Waggo yodels, and I pet her all over and tell her she's a good dog. I don't know if she's learned anything or not, but it feels like progress.

The phone company hasn't arrived at two, but I don't want to miss them if they are running late, so I stay on. I hear a car door slam at three thirty. I look at Waggo, but she's at the door, dancing. A few minutes later, Jennie and Felicity burst in, full of energy and excitement about their days. Felicity and Waggo dance out of the room.

"Is the phone here?" Jennie asks. "I know why I need a landline now!"

I tell her that they didn't show, and she shifts gears and gets out her cell phone to call them.

"I'll let all of you get squared away and check back in an hour or two. Oh, and I can wait for them on Wednesday, but not tomorrow. Or anyway, not before about two o'clock."

She's already talking on the phone and just nods at me with a face that says she understands, and she's grateful, and she's going to give the phone company a piece of her mind.

At five thirty, I'm thinking it's time to find out where things stand, but Jennie beats me to it. She's at the door. I briefly wonder why we don't phone or text in this neighborhood.

"I just wanted to thank you in person, especially since it was a big waste."

"No problem at all; you can't help it. What did they say? Do you need me on Wednesday?"

"No way—I told them to be here tomorrow morning at eight o'clock sharp. That gives them an hour and a half before I have to leave, and they'd better be here! I know it will make them late for someone else tomorrow, but I'm not going to feel bad about that. They need to feel bad about that, not me!"

I have to admire her attitude, and I wonder if I can get some of that to rub off on me.

"So you're sold on landlines now?" I ask, feeling a little smug and expecting to hear about dropped calls.

"I love that thing," she almost shouts. "It sits there on the desk and doesn't move! You can't lose it or forget to take it out of your pocket, and drop it in the toilet. You don't have to charge it. And all those buttons! You can see if you have someone on mute or not—you're not wondering if you said something you shouldn't have."

I realize that like most of her age group, she's never seen a desk phone before, and I smile, amused at her enthusiasm and her youth.

"I better go. Bud's starting dinner, and Little Miss is talking nonstop about her day. I think it's going to work out with Liz. Well, at least from Felicity's side. I guess I'd better make sure she isn't too much for Liz." She gets thoughtful. "And I'd better ask when I get a paycheck, so I can pay Liz."

CHAPTER 25

Tuesday morning is very cold, with flurries in the forecast. I put on a warm jacket and walk to the hardware store. It's even busier than usual.

"Everyone's got a project they want finished before Thanksgiving," Henry says by way of explanation when the early rush lasts until after nine-thirty. "Plus snow in the forecast always brings people out. When you get a minute, bring another carton of snow shovels out front. The contractors bought the first batch, and the moms will be in after school. Bring out more Ice Melt too. They see it, they buy it."

"What about windshield scrapers and snow brushes?" I ask him. "And insulated work gloves."

"Sure, bring them all out. Move the rakes and leaf bags back to the garden section to make space. We'll let the garden stock shrink until March. I'm going to look for the SNOW SHOVELS sign." Henry always has a large sign outside, visible from the freeway. The current FALL CLEANUP one replaced the BEDBUG SUPPLIES one that haunted me last summer.

As I am leaving the store for home, I check my phone and see that Jennie sent me a text as she left for work, saying that the phone installer is at her house but working outside. When he needs to get back inside, he'll knock on my door or text me.

"And there he is," I say as I pull into my driveway and see him on my porch. I get the key and open the door and decide to stay while he works. Five minutes later, he tells me he needs to run to the hardware store for a minute; he's misplaced his wire cutters.

"Midtown? On Prospect?"

"Yeah. Well, no—on Troost."

"They have wire cutters at the one on Prospect. Only four blocks." My face dares him to go to Troost.

"Oh. Okay then, back in a flash."

I'm pretty sure he goes to Henry's, because he is back in a few minutes. I hear the van door slam and hear Boris bark once next door. Waggo looks at me. "Speak!" I tell her. We hear footsteps on the porch, and I tell her again. She barks, the doorbell rings, and she barks again. "Good dog," I whisper.

That night, I wait until I think dinner is over next door and check in. I don't text neighbors, either, I guess. I ring the doorbell and hear barking inside. Bud opens the door holding a sleepy Felicity. She's sucking her thumb and only waves at me. I think she's had another busy day across the street.

I hear Jennie's voice and see that she has brought home a desk phone. She is talking to someone, her mother I think. She waves at me and then hangs up.

"I love this thing," she says. "I can hear my mom perfectly. I always thought her phone was just bad."

I smile at her and tell her I wanted to make sure everything worked out. I return the front door key, but she insists that I keep it. "Just in case of . . . well, I don't know, but just in case."

I decide it's best to agree and hope they don't expect me to give them a key in return. They are turning out to be good neighbors, but it's impossible to forget that Bud broke into my house less than two years ago. So I change the subject and ask if Waggo always barks when someone comes to the door.

"I don't know—did she bark when you got here?"

"She did," I say. "She's a great dog." I lean down to pet her. "If she forgets, just remind her. I think she knows the 'speak' command." I blow Felicity a goodbye kiss, then turn back to Jennie. "On the other hand, maybe you don't want certain little people to learn that particular command."

CHAPTER 26

At the last minute, Angie does call and invite me for Thanksgiving, apologizing for the late call. But by now I'm fully committed to the St. Louis Church feast. I've made pumpkin cupcakes and have the piecrusts ready for pies. I've had a couple of calls from parishioners asking if I happen to have any of this or that—apparently some of them have apple trees, or grow butternut squash, or otherwise garden specifically for this day. I offer what flowers I have left, although it's not much. I'll plan my gardening differently next year.

Wednesday and Thanksgiving Day both pass in a whirlwind. The food is fabulous, a mix of my childhood memories and all the cuisines that live in my parish. Even though we send leftovers home with people we think are underfed, there is still plenty for the last of the workers to take home for Friday. We are all glad that we will not have to cook the next day. I've completely forgotten all my problems for two days, or really for most of the week, while my mind was taken up with food and decorations and more food. But best of all, I feel like I really belong in this parish again, in a way that I haven't since I first crept in the door nineteen months ago. I know many more people now, and they know me. We've worked together and made casual conversation. We know a little about each other.

— — —

The Tuesday after Thanksgiving, I'm still in a holiday mood, and as I walk into the store, I look around wonderingly and ask Henry why he doesn't have his store decorated for Christmas. "You're already a month late," I tell him with as much seriousness as I can muster. He snorts and tells me to get a move on, that I'm late, although I'm not, and he's just not coming up with a better rejoinder. The store is very busy, so I don't bother with coffee. I just put on my cap and headset and take over at the cash register.

Not-Bill is my first customer, and I wish I knew his real first name but decide to stick with the joke and see how it is wearing.

"Not-Bill, how's it going? What can I help you with?" He needs Sheetrock, and I press the button on the intercom and relay his order. I ring up the Sheetrock and the drywall tape he's holding and ask if he's got all the mud he needs.

"You're out," he says. He sounds like it's my fault.

"Oh, let me check," I say.

He seems to take that as an insult to his ability to find a large white bucket in the drywall section and says that there isn't any, and now he's going to have to make another stop.

"Matt, Henry—do we have any extra drywall mud stashed somewhere? To go with that Sheetrock for Not-Bill?" I say into the intercom. "We seem to be out up here."

Not-Bill's head comes up. Apparently I wasn't insulting him after all.

I hear Henry tell Matt to check the loading dock—which is what we call the shed attached to the back of the store.

"He's checking in the back," I say, mostly to fill the conversational gap; it's hard to make light conversation with Not-Bill.

ELLEN BARKER

"Thanks, Matt," I say into the intercom and then give Not-Bill a half smile, keeping "I told you so" out of my voice. "Matt's taking it out to the yard. I guess it just got delivered." And then I add, "Sorry about that," for good measure, then wish I hadn't, remembering that men don't say sorry, and it makes women seem like we're taking the blame.

That seems to be the case here. Not-Bill smirks a little as he hands me his credit card. I'm not going to let my very first customer of the day ruin my mood or goad me into smirking back, so I look at the name on the credit card, thinking that maybe he would be friendlier if I use his actual name. Duncan Friedman. As I hand him the receipt to sign, I say, "Here you go—" and then I stop myself as he realizes I'm about to call him by his first name. So I say, "Thanks, Duncan Friedman. Now I don't have to call you Not-Bill."

"Just Duncan is fine," he says. "Thank you." And then he does smile and duck out the door.

The next customer is Sam, short for "Samantha," who is always cheerful and talkative. She's a project manager on a series of municipal jobs, so she's not usually hauling lumber. She mostly stops in to replace a worker's lost safety equipment or pick up a specialty tool. Today she's got a bit of a crisis and wants all the spray-foam insulation we've got. She's brought all she can find to the counter. I use the intercom to see if there is any more.

"Is that Bluetooth?" she asks, and it takes me a second to realize she's talking about the intercom and not the spray-foam.

"I don't know," I say and then press the button and add, "Matt, is this thing Bluetooth?"

Matt replies, but I don't catch what he says, because Sam is asking more questions, the last of which is, "Would that work on my jobsite?"

"Matt, if you've got a minute, Samantha has more questions

101

about the intercom. Or I could give her a card and have her call you."

Samantha remembers her emergency and says, "Have him call me tonight. I've got to get this stuff back to the site." She hands me her credit card and fishes out a business card while I'm completing the sale. Matt comes out with another case of spray-foam, and he talks to Sam while I ring up the second charge. He helps her carry it all out, and as they exit, I hear her tell him, "Damn, I need that right now!"

I move on to the next customer, which is Jerry.

"You know," he says, "she's got a point. That kind of thing could really be useful. Course I mostly work alone . . . but even if it's just one other guy. . . ."

"I'll have him call you too."

"Nah, I'll talk to him the next time I'm in the store."

When things calm down enough to catch up with Henry, I tell him about Sam and Jerry. "If his business plan includes a focus group, I think I know where he can find one."

CHAPTER 27

I've let the job search slip, putting it off day by day. I take long walks "for Boris." I build shelves in the basement from old pallets, even though I don't really have much to put on them. I go to weekday Mass some days and help out with whatever projects are going on there. I draw up plans for home improvements. I read books. I visit museums. I think about what I want to do with my life that involves making enough money to live that life. And occasionally, just enough to keep the unemployment coming in, I brave the demeaning and demoralizing work of looking for a job.

I know there are jobs. I could probably get hired for fast-food shifts that are during school hours or later than teen work curfews. Maybe I could sign on with a cleaning crew, although age is against me there. Cashier in a megastore is possible. But so far, I have not been able to bring myself to seek out these jobs. I wonder why that is—I am, after all, working in a retail job for minimum wage. I can only assume that I see Henry and Matt as professionals. Or maybe since it's only five hours a week, I don't feel trapped. I don't feel like a minimum wage retail job in a dilapidated neighborhood east of Troost is all I am good enough to get. I am sure there is a better job for me somewhere, if only I can find it.

I feel guilty about this, because in my chosen neighborhood, these are normal jobs, not to be devalued. People are glad to have them. And these are people who, I can tell, are often as intelligent as I am, but not as educated and not credentialed and not as confident in their ability to work in the corporate world, behind a desk, as I am used to doing. They are, for the most part, not as white, and the value of whiteness in the corporate job search is more obvious to me than ever before, because whiteness is erroneously equated with education and skill and work ethic and reliability. No one would ever say that out loud, and most people won't even think it. But as I review my LinkedIn page, and look through my LinkedIn connections, and scroll down through the pages of faces that LinkedIn has recommended for me to connect to, almost all I see are white faces. Back when I was traveling for business, if I had a coach seat, I counted the number of women in business class as I passed through and noted that the ratio was usually about one in ten. No need to count Black or Hispanic people in business class. There were seldom any to count, and back then, I was only interested in evidence of discrimination against my own group—white women.

This thinking isn't getting me anywhere. I go back to my current LinkedIn contacts and the recommended ones, this time ignoring skin color and evaluating only whether I actually know them and whether they have any potential for helping me find a job. Many of them have moved on since I last had contact with them, and I wonder if they will even remember me. I understand why LinkedIn is always pestering me to congratulate these people on their work anniversaries and their new jobs or titles. It's so they will remember me when the time comes, as it has, for me to ask for help.

I click on Notifications, to find all of my connections with recent anniversaries and new jobs, and I choose a few to congratulate. I add a note that I'm looking for something new and ask them to let me know if they have any leads. I'm going for light and breezy—lots of opportunities for me, no panic here! Then I scroll through the recommended connections and choose a few of those. I accept invitations to connect from people I don't really know, and I ask them for ideas too. I get curious about some former colleagues and look them up, and find more than a few who appear to be unemployed, either looking for work or available for consulting. I look at my own profile, which is sadly out of date. I add the end date for my last job, rewrite my "About" section, and become yet another of those many people interested in new opportunities.

It all leaves me a little depressed, but at least I've done something, and it's always possible that I'll hear something from one of my connections, even if it's just an encouraging note.

CHAPTER 28

It's December now, with more cold days than not, and of course the daylight hours are few. I spend as much time as possible outside in the sun, trying to fend off the winter blues. I refuse to diagnose myself as having seasonal affective disorder, but I know I'm a little anxious when the streetlights come on so early. I'm also anxious because the property taxes are due at the end of the month, and the bill sits on the kitchen table mocking me every day. But it's not going away, so I sit down and open the envelope. It's $340, less than it was last year. In California, we were paying something over $10,000 a year. Somehow I forgot that I live in a different universe now. I write the check and stop worrying about it.

I'm outside on Saturday afternoon, throwing a ball for Boris, when Jennie and Felicity come out with Waggo. Jennie tells me about her job, which is going well so far, although sometimes Liz can't keep Felicity, so Jennie has to work when Felicity is home. She's teaching her about "quiet time," when Mommy works at her desk and Felicity colors or plays with Lego, "which don't tumble down as loudly as her wooden blocks." We talk about the nearby options for free nursery school.

The dogs come over for petting, and we talk about putting a gate in the fence so the dogs can play together. I ask her if Waggo is barking at the right times and making her feel safe.

"Sometimes I forget that's why we have her. It's like she's just here to be Felicity's best friend. Although that's good too. Mostly, I do feel safer. Maybe I'm just too busy to be scared during the daytime. I do get a little nervous when it's dark out and Bud isn't home from work yet."

"Does she ever bark when she hears noise outside?"

"She barks if someone comes to the front door, but I don't know if she barks at anything else."

"Should we find out? I could go around and tap on your side window, and we can see what she does."

We decide to try this, and I tell her I'll put on a hood or a hat or something so she won't recognize me and I'll tap on the window in ten minutes. As I'm walking down my driveway, I wonder if anyone is going to see me and call the cops, so I push back the hood of my sweatshirt and wave in the general direction of Liz and Patrick's house across the street. Then I put the hood back up, cinch it down so that most of my face is covered, and creep up to the big south window.

I reach up and tap, and nothing happens, so I knock harder and hear a tentative woof through the window. I knock again and raise my head up, keeping my face low. Another woof, and then a little high-pitched voice: "It's the Boris lady!"

Who knows if that means anything to Waggo, but she probably realizes that no one inside is scared, so I'm not sure we've accomplished anything. I duck down, push the hood back, and head home. Bud is pulling into the driveway, so I give him a short version of the experiment and tell him we can try again another day.

CHAPTER 29

The next Tuesday, I remind Henry that Christmas is coming and he should cash in like every other store in America. We argue about Christmas at a hardware store, and he insists that "The guys don't want to see all that junk that the chain stores pile up around the checkout." I tell him that "the guys" don't want to have to shop at the mall, either, and I'm not talking about impulse gifts that are yuppie or girlie or whatever. We just need to give them the idea that they can make it easy on themselves by buying stuff we already carry. Do we have any sleds? We certainly have warm hats and gloves. Christmas is all about warm hats and gloves, even if ours are utilitarian rather than fashionable. And flashlights. Every kid wants a flashlight. Every *person* wants a cool flashlight.

In the midmorning lull, Samantha the project manager stops by asking for Matt. She's been talking to him about the headset intercom. Matt has already left for school, so she asks me a few questions about the technology, which I can't answer, and about the user interface, which I can help her with. Henry is in the store, so I ask him if we can let her try mine for sound quality, and he obligingly talks to her as he moves to the back of the store, then outside, then to the far edge of the back lot. She seems satisfied and asks Henry over the intercom when

Matt will be in. He tells her to give him another ten days to get through finals.

"Anything else while you're here?" I ask. "Avoid the crowds at the mall, do your Christmas shopping right here. Free parking!" I leer at Henry behind her back.

She blinks a few times. "Why not?" she says and disappears down the plumbing aisle. Not where I would have started, but she must know what she's doing.

Henry comes back in as she is piling things on the counter. She's talking to herself.

"Insulated gloves for my crew. And my dad. Oh, I should get him a new hand trowel too. I left his out in the rain and it got rusty, so now it's mine. What about my mom? A broom?"

"Are you nuts? She'll use it on you!"

"You're right. You have any Wellies? I know she'd like some shiny red boots for mucking in the garden. Oh, and hey, look what I got for my nephew: plastic plumbing parts. I'll cut the pipe into short lengths, and he can put them together with all these Ts and elbows and things. Way cooler than Lego—he can make something sturdy enough to sit on."

Henry is watching.

"Did Marianne put you up to this?"

Sam says, "What, plumbing parts? No. Do you think ABS or PVC?" She goes back down the plumbing aisle with Henry and comes back with more parts and several rolls of colored duct tape.

"Great idea, giving the kid tape to put the parts together. Everyone likes tape, especially colors. I got some for my mom, too."

Henry helps her carry it all to her car, and when he gets back, he puts his hands in the air.

"Okay, okay, you win. But no tinsel and no music. Just a hint or two."

"We don't have to decorate at all; just tell whoever is on the register to ask people if they need to pick up any Christmas gifts while they're here."

The afternoon clerk comes in the front door, waves, and goes to the back to leave his coat and get his cap. Henry looks at him and sighs.

"Okay, no one but you is going to do that. So think up something simple."

"I'm on it," I say, and get ready to leave. "Gift wrapping is probably out, huh?"

At home, I try to come up with subtle ways to get contractors to do their Christmas shopping at Henry's without going boutiquey. "Subtle" and "the Christmas shopping experience" are hard to work into a single script. Add in guys who don't want to shop and are not thinking about Christmas gifts and would rather not ever think about Christmas shopping at all, and it's looking like mission impossible. I want them to walk past stuff on the way in, and see stuff while they are waiting to pay, and pick it up and buy it. But they won't associate it with Christmas without a little tinsel and Santa faces, will they? And if they do, will they be embarrassed to pick up a couple of shiny red flashlights, knowing we've conned them into Christmas shopping? I can't see it. Sam would do it, but she's a woman, and that might make the guys in the room roll their eyes, if they even notice—at least for the moment. But maybe not entirely.

I've been picturing a grouping of those five-gallon buckets with canvas pockets on the outside, stocked with shiny hand tools tied with red bows. Another with digital levels and measuring devices, and more with other things I'll find on the racks. That may be too subtle to have any effect, and not subtle enough for

Henry. I give up on that, mentally put it all back on the shelves. I picture myself as not-Bill, making a beeline for the things he needs. That's what he looks at. So that's where I have to get into his field of vision.

I've still got buckets on the brain, so I picture them, stacked on the floor at the end of an aisle. I can put a sign on them: "Buckets, the original gift bags." These guys know about gift bags, right? But "original"—does that grab them? Nope. Doesn't even grab me. What about, "Skip the wrapping paper, use a bucket." Okay, maybe.

I need to get them to buy something to not-wrap in a bucket. I mentally wander up and down the aisles, stare up at things hanging on the walls. Sam raved about the colored tape. "Kids Love Tape" on a little card with a Santa sticker? "Everyone Wants a Flashlight for Christmas" with a little clip art of a kid with a flashlight looking for Santa? I spend the rest of the afternoon coming up with more ideas and laying out four-by-five-inch cards with subtle hints and Christmassy art. I print them out, cut them apart, and hang them around the house to see if I really think Henry will go for it.

In the morning, I decide it's worth a shot. Almost everyone will run into at least one little sign, and they can pick up things as if they needed them anyway, pretend they aren't Christmas shopping at all. Contractors are a creative bunch, I've come to realize. If we can just get them to think of Midtown Hardware as an easy place to do their Christmas shopping, they'll see potential gifts everywhere. I'll try to rearrange the buckets just a little, so they see them on their way back to the counter, and I'll make sure the bucket lids are obvious. I make another sign to hang near the tool belts: "Stockings Are for Wusses" and cobble together some clip art showing Santa putting toys in a tool belt hung on a fireplace. I delete the text and print the artwork a little larger. It speaks for itself.

When I walk into the store with my plans and my signs, I'm actually nervous. Henry looks up, a little surprised to see me on a Wednesday morning. I've timed my trip for the late-morning lull and waited outside until there was only one truck in the parking lot.

"So, about Christmas." I hold up a large brown envelope. "No tinsel, no lights, no elves."

Henry rolls his eyes, but he's smiling, and he's curious.

"Okay then, let's take a look."

I may be good at selling hardware as presents, but I'm not good at selling myself or my ideas. Decades of corporate life have taught me that if you want it done, you get a woman to do it, but if you want it said, get a man to say it. Maybe it's not that way everywhere, but it's been that way everywhere that I have worked.

Today, though, I'm the one who did it and the one who has to say it, and convincingly too. I lay them all out on the counter and look up at Henry, arms akimbo, face as full of confidence as I can make it. He looks them over carefully, then looks up at me and raises his eyebrows. I still haven't quite worked out my pitch, so I just pick up the nearest one and march down an aisle with it. Henry tags along. Things get dicey for a moment when I can't find a good place to secure it, but I grab a clamp and solve that problem.

"Well?" I finally speak.

Henry shrugs, rolls his eyes, and concedes. "I think the red two-inch clamp would be better."

"I'll leave you to it then," I say. "It's my day off. Let me know if you think it's working. I'm sure I can cook up a few more. Don't want to overdo it though!"

And I saunter off, proud of my little victory and savoring it while I can. I know that if anyone teases Henry about the promo signs, he'll take them down. I'm also proud of my speech, which involved no speech at all. Would that have worked in the boardroom in Silicon Valley?

CHAPTER 30

I've told myself that job hunting is useless until after the holidays, but I need to record something every week to get my unemployment money, and I'm also afraid of missing that one job that is out there for me. So while I'm still feeling good about pushing Christmas at Midtown, I make myself sit down and go through potential jobs at Monster and LinkedIn. I visit the websites of companies like the one I used to work for, clicking on the Join our Team! links. Nothing. I try to think out of the box and remember the civil service exam. I discover that it is no longer used, although there is talk of reviving it. I go back to LinkedIn and check for messages from people I contacted last week—two greetings, no hint of a job lead. I wander down some rabbit holes, reading about the wonderful opportunities of the new post-recession gig economy, rife with side hustles and short-term projects. I go down a rabbit hole far enough to bid on one before I take a breath, open a new window, do a little reality checking, and decide that a lot more research is needed to make sure I don't end up making less than minimum wage.

I think back to college when I worked at temp jobs and look up Kelly Services. At least it's not called Kelly Girl any more. Substitute teachers, call centers, dishwasher, machine operators, weeders. I'm intrigued by "weeder"—it can't mean what it sounds like. It doesn't mean weeding lawns, but I'm not sure what it does mean. I understand the lines about "flexible hours" and "must have résumé," but I don't understand "signs that go on the doors of trucks." It insists that applicants must have at least one year of weeding/signage experience, so I move on. I finally apply for a data entry job, just because I have to apply for something, and I could enter data. Anyone could enter data. I could also wash dishes, but I can enter data sitting down, so that's what I apply for. "Data entry" does not appear on my résumé, and I can't come up with any way to make my management jobs look like data entry jobs, so I don't attach my résumé. I just list my employers and dates of employment. I click the submit button and call it a day.

The next morning, I'm at a loss. I walk the dog and poke around the yard looking for chores and find nothing. I clip some evergreen branches and make a wreath for the front door, which gets me to eleven o'clock. I have a leisurely lunch. I stare at the calendar and think, *Oh no—Christmas cards.*

I didn't send any two years ago, because my husband was dying, and I didn't send them last year, because I was barely able to make it through the holidays. This year I've lost my job, but that seems pale in comparison. I need to keep in touch with those old friends and distant relatives. I go back to my computer.

I stare at the blank Word document for quite a while. I obviously can't write the sort of holiday newsletter my husband and I used to compose. And I can't send everyone a litany of all I've been through since the last time they heard from me. I also can't pretend none of it happened.

So I open the Word file with the address labels from three years ago and work on updating that, while I stew about what to write. I go outside and take a tight photo of my front door with its homemade wreath. I sit back down and open PowerPoint and make a card with the photo on the front, my address in a Copperplate font across the middle. On the inside, just a holly border from free clip art. I print the page, take out a pen, and write a letter to the first person on my list. I get teary at the beginning but work on through it. When I get to the bottom of the white space, I read it through, sign my name, and fold it. I am mentally exhausted and a little stiff from sitting. I get up and put Boris in the car, and we go out to buy envelopes and stamps.

Writing notes takes up a lot of the day. I stop at three o'clock and take the day's work to the mailbox. I laugh at myself because I don't know where a mailbox is, other than at the new post office, and I'm not willing to walk there. When I was six, there were at least three within a couple of blocks, and my mother knew the pickup schedule for each one and sent me to the one with the next pickup time if she wanted a letter to get to someone quickly. Now I have to find a website and look it up. The closest is a little over a mile, near my old high school. It's a nice brisk walk and clears my head.

I finish up the next day, having saved for last the people I don't know very well, mostly my husband's college friends and work colleagues. I've written exactly the same thing to each of them, but made myself finish them all by hand. I try to channel my aunt Katy and her beautiful penmanship, and I apologize in my head to Sister Mary Augustina for the poor showing I make. Decades at the keyboard have degraded my cursive, but at least it's legible. I mail the last of the cards and feel like I've turned a corner. I wonder if I should have done this last year, then decide it's a waste to even think about that.

Then it's Sunday again, and we're into Advent. I spend the afternoon making an Advent wreath. Advent wreaths have three purple candles and one pink one, but the only candles I have are the plumber's candles I've stockpiled in case of power outage. They are white and about as ugly as a candle can be. I rummage through my kitchen drawer, which after twenty months is almost as full of junk as a kitchen drawer should be, but it yields nothing to dress up the plumber's candles. Ditto my sewing stash, which is nowhere near what it should be at my age. I try the basement and think about sawing up some wood blocks to use as candle holders, but they will still be ugly candles and still white. I open my kitchen cupboards and stare. They are not as bare as they once were, but there is nothing to even spark an idea.

"Well, Boris, we can afford a small splurge at the dollar store," I tell him. "Let's see what we can find."

Boris waits in the car, and I return with tea lights and small canning jars and two bottles of translucent fingernail polish, one purple and one pink.

I set up the wreath on the kitchen table, turn off the lights, and touch a match to one candle in a purple-rimmed jar. The daily rituals are in the church bulletin, so I don't have to google them and read from my phone. I haven't done this homey little practice for decades. I like it.

CHAPTER 31

The next Tuesday, I see Sam at the store, and she tells me that the pipe idea was a success and a failure.

"My sister stopped by my house with my nephew when I wasn't expecting them. He made a beeline for the bag. We couldn't separate him from the plumbing parts, so he got his present early. Now I don't have a present for him for Christmas. My sister says not to worry about it, but he's so adorable. I love giving him stuff."

"Well, I say you're in luck! We have the expansion pack to add onto the starter kit!" I'm thinking fast, making it up. "And I think we can solve the shopping bag problem too."

I point her to the buckets for a new gift bag, and then I send her to the clamps and bungie shelves.

I go back to the register, but I can hear her rummaging in the bins.

"I love this stuff," she calls out. "I wish my aunts had given me toys like this."

"Never too late," I call back in her direction. I turn back to my customer. "Christmas shopping," I say by way of explanation, swinging my head in Sam's direction. "Who knew that kids prefer hardware to toys?"

The customer looks thoughtful and then picks up the weather

stripping I was about to ring up. "I'll be right back," he says and disappears in Sam's direction.

I picture the two of them on a treasure hunt through the store, with flashlights. Or rather, with headlamps so they can shop with both hands. The next time I have a pause between customers, I draw a cartoon of kids with headlamps and the caption "Light Up Christmas." I try again, making the kids older, more like teens. I find a red Sharpie and draw a border, then clip it to the rack with the headlamps. As I hurry back to the counter, my eye catches an unfamiliar card attached to a little metal box of screwdrivers. It says, "Don't Screw Up. We'll Help You Finish Your Christmas Shopping." I think it's Henry's printing, but it might be Matt's.

Just before I leave, Henry asks if I can work a few extra mornings before Christmas.

"Matt finished his finals, but Sam wants him to build a prototype of the intercom for her jobsite. If it's a success, her boss wants to equip all the sites." He pauses. "I know we only agreed that you would work through this semester, but if Matt gets involved in this thing, he'll need to spend more time on that, so we might be able to keep you around, maybe give you another shift or two. Maybe. Depending. And only if you're interested, of course."

I've been worrying that my time here is almost up, and even though it's not much money, it's something. And I really like, and probably desperately need, this bit of scheduled social interaction.

"Yes, I'd love that!" I tell him. And then I stop and put my nose in the air. "I mean, I'll take it under consideration, sir, and let you know. My people will contact your people." And I swirl around and leave. Then I stick my head back in. "Okay if I take off on Christmas Eve and Boxing Day? I want to go see my cousins in Joplin. It's okay if you need me though."

He waves me off. "Go, we'll be fine. Matt wants to go hiking over New Year's anyway, so he won't squawk about working around Christmas."

The two wreaths and the Christmas cards and the extra hours at the store have put me in a holiday mood—the good kind, not the desperate sort I learned all about during the last two seasons. I see Christmas lights in other people's houses and want a tree of my own. I don't have room for a tree, I tell myself, which is ridiculous, because we always had a tree when I was a kid and four people managed to live in this space. I look through my scanned photos and find an early color photo of my toddler self, reaching out to touch a two-foot-tall tree on a lamp table in the front window. I can do that again. The lamp can take a vacation in the basement for a few weeks.

I go out looking, but there are very few tiny trees available, and they are no cheaper than large trees. So I stop at a resale shop and pay fifty cents for the largest florist's vase they have, then search my yard and Josie's for more greenery. I'm trimming pine branches from the huge tree that overhangs her yard from the next lot down the hill when I notice very small pine seedlings sprouting in the shade of the big tree. I get a trowel and scoop up six of them and take them home. I plant a little grove in my backyard and picture it in a few years, dusted with snow. As long as I'm still here, I will be able to cut my own trees. I hope I can make myself do that. Otherwise, they'll take over, shade the garden, drip sap on the clotheslines, and provide cover for the bogeyman. For now, they are only six inches tall, and I just hope they take root.

I go back inside and string popcorn to hang on the pretend tree in the florist's vase. It's harder than I thought, but Boris and I both enjoy eating the ones that shatter when I try to shove the needle through. I sculpt a star out of crumpled aluminum foil and tell myself it will do for now; now I just need something to put under it. Or near it, given that it's just a vase.

I decide to make something I've wanted for years—a swing. Not a porch swing, although I'd like one of those too. No, I just want a wide, flat wooden-seat swing. The difficulty is that I want it to swing in a wide arc, which means it has to be hung a lot higher than a standard kids' swing set. I don't know where I'm going to hang it yet, but I can start with the swing itself.

I've become very particular about the pallets I scavenge, only choosing solid wood ones. Last summer, I found one with two one-by-six boards, which I've hoarded ever since. I get them out, lay them side by side across two kitchen chairs, and sit on them. I decide I want twenty-four inches to sit on, plus about three inches on each end to accommodate the rope attachment. I cut two lengths and carefully round the edges a little. I line them up side by side with a bit of gap and cut short lengths to join them on the bottom. I pat myself of the back for buying tools and jars of hardware junk at garage sales back when I still had a job. The screws don't all match, but I come up with sixteen that are the right length. I'm careful about placement so the screws are out of the way of the holes for the rope.

I think about drilling the holes but decide to wait until I have the rope. I'm picturing the thick rope on old-fashioned swings, but I know that may not be possible. I'll take it to Henry's and see what he's got.

That's all I can do for now, so I go outside and consider where I can hang it. The trees around my backyard are all volunteers that have sprouted since my family moved away, and none have sturdy horizontal branches. And most of them are the weak non-native elms that proliferated after Dutch elm disease decimated the native elms in this part of America. There is one hard maple, at the edge of my property, but its only sturdy branch points north, over Josie's backyard. I go through the gate and knock on her back door.

"Not good enough for the front door today?" she asks.

"Just testing your back doorbell. And I have a backyard question for you."

"You knocked; you didn't ring the bell. But go ahead and ask your question." She's pulled on a sweater and come outside and is petting Boris.

"Your backyard needs a swing," I say firmly.

"That's not a question."

"Do you realize your backyard needs a swing?" I bat my eyes at her. She sighs.

"Apparently it does. But why are you talking about swings in December?"

I tell her about my Christmas present to myself and point out the perfect place to hang it. She laughs, and I tell her that actually it will be her swing, and she will always have first dibs, which makes her laugh even more.

Then we get sidetracked and talk about other things, but I know where the swing is going now.

The next Tuesday, I leave the swing seat in the office, where Matt finds it. On his way out the door, he puts it on the counter and asks if it's mine. I explain about the swing, although I don't say that I'm making it for myself.

"I need to decide what kind of rope to use, and I may need to buy a hole saw."

He tells me to pick out the rope and mark where the holes go, and he or Henry will drill or cut them before my next shift. I thank him and turn to the next customer in line, who has been listening to us, of course, since we're right in front of him and his hands are too full for him to be fiddling with his cell phone.

"That a Christmas present?" he asks.

"It is. I'm thinking about painting it red." I hadn't been thinking about paint at all, but now I am.

"Nice," he says thoughtfully, taking his change and receipt.

A few minutes later, I get a chance to run back and look at the rope selection. For a small store, the choice of material and diameter is amazing. I grab a spool that might work and hurry back to the counter, where a customer is waiting. I put the rope on the swing seat and smile at him.

"That a swing?"

"It is. I'm thinking about painting it red." I smile broadly and suppress a giggle. No room for giggles in a hardware store.

"Green would be nice."

Before I leave, Henry comes up to the counter.

"Swing, huh?"

"It is. I'm thinking about painting it red." I want to see what happens the third time I say it.

"I'd use porch paint. Won't need much. This the rope? Just get the sisal, it's plenty strong. You might need a hole saw, unless you've got a really big bit. Want me to cut the holes? No point buying a hole saw just for one swing."

This is what makes Henry so good at his business, but today it strikes me as hilarious, and I laugh, and he starts laughing too.

"What are we laughing at?"

"Who knows. I guess it's a Christmas thing."

Midway through my Friday shift, Matt drops the seat and two lengths of rope on the counter.

"When you get a minute, take a look and make sure it's what you wanted."

This is my first time working on Friday, and the clientele is slightly different, so I don't know everyone. A couple of minutes later, a customer I don't know points to the swing parts, which are still on the counter.

"That a swing?"

"It will be soon." I'm busy scanning codes on his drill bits, so I don't add my line about red paint.

"Is it a kit?"

I pause and look up at him.

"It could be." *Well, why not?* "Sure, you want one?"

"Yeah. Two of them would be better. Well, hold on—how much is it?"

I look on the bottom, where of course there is no price.

"Let me check." I press the button on my intercom. "Matt, Henry? I need a price on the swing kit up here. You know, the one on the counter?" I'm trying to give them time to figure out what I'm talking about. "Got a customer who wants two of them."

No response on the intercom, and then I hear laughter in the back of the store. Henry comes in and takes over, and I move on to the next customer. I can hear him making small talk while he calculates in his head what the rope and lumber and screws cost, plus something for time.

"There's an unfinished version and a painted one," I say while I'm ringing up a big lumber order for the next customer. And then I think that if I get stuck making the swing kits, I don't want to deal with oil-based paint in December. "The painted one just means that the kit includes a little can of enamel—red or green." Henry looks at me. I wonder if we even carry red and green enamel in the small cans. "And an optional paintbrush, if you're going to give it as a kit. Kids like to paint stuff."

In the end, we sell him my swing, along with paint and a bit of sandpaper and a promise to have a second kit ready by the end of the day. Henry tells me I have to stay late and make up the second kit. But when I go out to the yard at noon, I find he's already cut the lumber and planed the edges and done a much nicer job than I did. He has, in fact, cut enough for five swings and has screwed on the bottom pieces and cut the rope holes. I'm glad the guy didn't take mine with him, because now he'll have two of the nicer ones. I get busy and cut the rope and assemble paint and brushes and sandpaper. I have to think for a while to come up with a way to assemble the parts into kits, and finally Henry suggests wrapping it all in the heavy plastic wrap we keep on a roll on the loading dock. I tell Henry they really need some kind of label and that I'll do that at home and bring them back in an hour or two.

"What about instructions? Do we need assembly instructions?" I have a vague idea about how I'm going to fasten the rope, but I know I'll probably try a few things before I'm happy with it.

"These guys build stuff all day long. They can figure this out," he says. "In fact, don't bother with the label even. I think the charm is that there is no charm. It's just stuff we have in the store. Isn't that what you said we should sell these guys?"

"Yes, it is. And I'm outta here!" This means I can go home and eat lunch.

"Not quite. You need to wrap up these other three and figure out where to put them in the store. Let's see if we can sell a few more, now that we're in the swing business."

I wrap the extras and stack them on the counter. They take up far too much space, so I get the beat-up red coaster wagon that we occasionally use to move small things around in the yard. I put the swings in it and park it by the front door. I smile a private Cheshire cat smile. Someone's going to want a wagon too.

CHAPTER 32

Working more hours surprisingly gives me more energy on the other days of the week. I know this is probably psychological, but I push that thought aside. If I go back to fewer hours or no hours in January, I will deal with it then. Meanwhile, I push on with the job search, hoping I'll find a "real" job and not have to worry about it at all.

And bingo! There it is, on the website of Sarmes, a firm that competes with my old employer. I know people there. I message one of them, and he is encouraging. I spend an hour sharpening up my résumé and honing my cover letter. I've got this! I click the Submit button and get back the automated "We have received your submission" email. I go through my wardrobe, deciding on interview attire. I take Boris for a celebratory stroll and let him sniff all he wants. A real job for Christmas! I'm fully aware that I don't have the job yet, but I let myself be happy about it anyway. I'm used to disappointment. I can deal with that if it comes, but meanwhile I'll enjoy an afternoon of hope and happiness.

While Boris is sniffing at a particularly interesting bush, I'm gazing at the overgrown lot behind it, picturing the lush family garden that was in this spot many years ago. I picture myself contacting the current owner, getting permission to plant my own garden here—maybe a few fruit trees too. It would be a lot of work in the hot, humid months—maybe not a good idea after all. Or maybe some of the neighbors would like to share the space and the work. I'm not so sure about that though. I don't see all that many tomato patches around. Still, a few fruit trees would be good, if I could teach myself how to prune them and avoid all the pests without resorting to chemicals. Two apple trees would produce plenty for Thanksgiving pies and more to share with the neighbors.

When I get home, I look up "community gardens in Kansas City" and discover KCCG. I assume it is either in the distant suburbs, where space is plentiful, or else in the densely populated low-income areas closer to downtown. I look at the address and recognize my own zip code. The office is in Swope Park, less than a mile away. I read about its history and discover that it's been "supporting home and community gardens for thirty years." Thirty years! How did I not know about this? *Well*, I tell myself, *thirty years ago you had already left town*. Head smack. After less than two years back here, there are moments when I can almost believe I never left.

I click the Employment Opportunities link on the KCCG site, just in case. There is an opening as a family gardens assistant. Sounds like a low-wage job, but I could do that, if I somehow don't get the job at Sarmes. I read on and see that it's an Ameri-Corps position, and I'm not eligible for those. Still, there are lots of volunteer positions and lots of resources for home and community gardening. I dream about the plot down the street again and wonder if a border of raspberry bushes would keep critters out. More likely it will just provide cover for them.

Now my days begin and end with checking my email for a response to my job application at Sarmes. I make sure my cell phone ringer is on day and night, except for when I'm at work or in church. I conduct imaginary interviews in which I am confident and professional, enthusiastic but not too enthusiastic. I make sure my laptop camera is working and try several angles and backgrounds and lighting options, until I'm satisfied that I've found the best one possible in case they want a video interview. I think about using a little makeup, but I have never been very good at it and wonder if I should practice.

We have a few warm days, and I stay outside as much as possible, soaking up the weak rays of sun. I rake the last of the leaves and dig them into the garden, and extend the garden a few more feet. I find the bag of tulip bulbs I bought at an end-of-autumn sale and plant them along the path from my back door to the garden shed, where I can see them from my desk. I drive in a few stakes to mark the spots so I don't forget I did it. Then I think it would be nice to brighten up the front yard too, but I can't find any more bulbs on sale, so I give it up until spring, when a few marigold seeds will go a long way.

I check my phone so often, I start to feel like a teenager. I remember when I got my first-generation BlackBerry. The first thing we oh-so-cool business types did when our flights hit the runway was to whip them out and turn them on. Other people had their cell phones and were listening to voice mails and returning calls. But we, the coolest, the elite ones blessed with BlackBerry éclat, were reading email, sometimes laughing, mostly faking concerned and important faces. We were it. And that wasn't very long ago. But now, every tween has a much cooler device, and I'm acting like one of them.

Christmas is creeping closer. I light the second purple candle on my Advent wreath and then the pink one. Only one more Sunday to go. I make final plans with my cousins in Joplin, and I make another swing for their first grandchild, who is not even due until spring.

On my last day at the store before Christmas, the swings are all gone and so is the red coaster wagon.

"The swings, sure, but the wagon? You sold that rusty old wagon?"

"You know how kids are—every kid loves a wagon. It was safe in the back, but no—you had to bring it up front." Henry is teasing me. "The first kid in here sat in it and put on her adorable face, and her grandpa just had to have it for her. He rolled her right out to the parking lot with it and the last swing kit."

I see that he's hung a swing from the rafters over the spot where the wagon used to be.

"Oh, and by the way, you have a job in the back. We've got five more swing orders to wrap up. You can stack them on that swing"—he motions toward the hanging one—"until the wagon shipment comes in this afternoon." He's shaking his head in mock horror.

When the afternoon clerk comes in, I go to the back to wrap the last kits. Henry hands me an envelope.

"Merry Christmas," he says.

It doesn't look like a Christmas card; it looks like a paycheck envelope, and it will be bigger than usual, which will make for a merry Christmas indeed.

"Thanks," I say and stick it in my pocket.

I'm wondering how to ask him if I still have a job, since our agreement was only through the end of Matt's semester. And maybe the week between Christmas and New Year's is slow and he can manage without me, so for all I know, this is my last day. I need to ask him, and I don't want to sound surly or desperate. I don't notice that he's still standing there, arms crossed, looking at me.

"Aren't you going to open it?" he asks.

"Oh. Um, sure." I get it out and open my eyes wide at the

amount. I know exactly what it should be, and this is more than that, plus a certificate for store credit.

"What's this all about?" I'm thinking that it can't be severance pay, which would in the corporate world be about fifty cents, based on salary and length of service. And a temporary minimum-wage clerk doesn't get a Christmas bonus after eight weeks, which in my case is less than a hundred hours—a lot less.

"Well, Matt did tell you he'd cut you in for a percentage if he sold his intercom thing, and Sam has bought one and ordered another one. Matt's at home working on it right now. Our markup on those is pretty high."

"Cool. I've got more ideas about that thing, by the way," I start, but Henry cuts me off.

"And then there was your little Christmas nonsense, which netted us quite an uptick over December."

"You can't tell whether those cards did anything or not!"

"You really aren't very good at selling yourself, are you? You're supposed to be the one convincing me that you've sent profits through the roof." He's pretending to be exasperated with me and with good reason, as I'm wrecking his very nice little speech.

"Okay, it was fun for me, and I'm just glad no one complained about it."

Henry raises his eyebrows. "No one complained, Marianne. Now if you'll just listen. Matt decided to make a list of everything near one of your little Christmas sign things."

"And yours too? Or were the rogue ones Matt's?"

"Not telling." But he's grinning in a way that makes me think they were his.

"Anyway." He goes back to being serious, or trying to be. "Matt is a numbers guy. He figured out how much more we sold of those things this month than we did last month and also compared with last December. We decided to give you a percentage of that increase too." He sees me open my mouth and rushes on. "And then there were the swings—you get a percentage of the profit on those too. And we used all scrap lumber and some from a pallet or two, and we even used up some ends of rope, so the profit was pretty good. And don't say, 'But what about labor?' because I counted that too. Paid myself more than I pay you, I'll have you know." He's finished with his speech and smiling. "Plus, as you can see, you didn't get it all in cash—it's mostly in store credit." He stops smiling. "Look, I know how it is. You're working, and you don't have time to do things to your house. Then you get laid off, and you have the time, but you don't want to spend the money. You get another job, and you don't have time again. So things don't get done. That's why we gave you store credit instead of cash, so you'll get some things done while you have time. And I'll move some inventory."

I'm 90 percent convinced that it's all true and he's not just being generous, so I thank him profusely and quickly move on before we get embarrassed.

"Do you need me at all after Christmas?" I figure he can take that to mean the week after or going forward after that. I want to let him know that I understand that our deal was only until Matt had his Tuesday mornings available again.

"Yes, if you're back from Joplin."

That sounds like he's talking about the week after Christmas.

"Sure! I thought that might be a slow week here."

"Oh, you'll be surprised then. Lots of guys are ready to get out of the house after Christmas. They'll get back to the jobsite or get things to work on their own places. Plus, it always seems to snow that week, and we'll go through a lot of snow shovels. And there's a chance that everyone who sees one of those swings is going to want one."

"More red ones for Valentine's Day! Easter egg colors—swing into spring! Or bungee swings—bounce into spring."

"Get out of here!" he laughs and then gets serious again.

"Oh, one more thing. In January, can you still work Tuesdays and Fridays? Matt's going to take another semester of that lab on Tuesday, and he wants Fridays to work on his intercom. I'm afraid he's going to want to spin out on his own. He's taking two more business classes in the spring, Entrepreneurial something and Business Finance, or maybe it's something in marketing."

"Good for him—he can make the big bucks and pay off his loans faster."

"Oh, he doesn't have much in the way of loans." He doesn't elaborate. "But he's talking about a double major now, so it will mean another year."

"Or maybe he should go ahead and graduate and then get a master's in business. Doesn't have to be a three-year MBA; he could do a two-year program in business."

"Well, maybe. Anyway, you have a good Christmas, and we'll see you back here after."

CHAPTER 33

I do have a good Christmas and get home refreshed and hopeful about my job prospects, even though my constant checking has not produced any response about the Sarmes job. *People are away over holidays*, I tell myself. *They'll get back to me after New Year's.*

A few weeks later, I take Boris and go to my childhood pal Angie's for dinner. We get home after dark. As I pull into the driveway, I see that the gate is open. Boris jumps out and runs along the driveway, whining and sniffing. Inside, the landline is ringing.

"Marianne, are you home?" It's Jennie, and she's upset. I don't point out that of course I'm home, I answered the phone, plus she can see that my car is in the driveway and my lights are on.

"Yes, I'm here. What's going on? Boris seems to be all wound up."

"Waggo started barking like crazy, and I looked out and thought I saw someone with a flashlight in your backyard."

I immediately jump to the conclusion that the guy who broke into my house the week I moved in has returned, then shake myself. That "guy" is Jennie's husband, and the break-in wasn't quite what it seemed.

"Oh no! Did you call the police?" I don't know how much

confidence Jennie has in the police, but they did recover a TV stolen from her house, so maybe.

"I did, and you'll never guess what?" I hear a little pride in her voice.

"They caught the guy?"

"Well, no, he was gone when they got here. But Felicity heard all the barking, and she woke up and was looking out her window when the guy left. She saw him run down your driveway, and she told the police all about it."

I can actually picture that, three-year-old Felicity enjoying being the center of attention and talking their ears off. I don't think she'd make things up, but she *is* only three and she does love an audience. So even though I'm a bit freaked out by the whole thing, I focus on Felicity.

"She is an amazing little girl," I say to Little Miss Amazing's mother. "What did the police think?"

"They were really nice to her and treated her like an adult. Well, nicer than an adult, but you know—very serious. They wrote it all down. She loved that. They said they would be back in the daylight to dust for fingerprints. I don't think they would do that for a shed normally." She sounds like Felicity's interview brought on the additional attention. Maybe it did.

"Yes," I say. "They had an eyewitness and got a description, so maybe that's why." I hope it's that and not because I'm the white person on the block. Depending on who responded, they might or might not know that. I'm also thinking this conversation would be better in person, but I can see that Felicity's bedroom light is out, so I don't want to go over there and risk waking her up.

"Did the guy get in? Do you know? I'm a little scared to go out there now."

"They didn't say. Bud was going over, but he decided to wait for you. He'll go now if you want."

I do want to see, and I also don't want to go out there. But better to know, and surely with Boris and Bud along . . . and anyway, no one would have stuck around after the police showed up. My brain says all that, but I'm still scared.

"Oh, that's so nice of him. I guess I would like to see if they got in. If he really doesn't mind." And then I add as an afterthought, "And if you don't mind. Are you worried?"

"Me? Oh—no, I want to know too. And I can see you from the back window. Turn on your backyard light."

Of course. I turn on the yard light and meet Bud at my back door, and together we walk toward the garden shed, careful to stay on the path.

The garden shed is not the original. I had this one built the previous year, and it was built to be secure, exactly because I was afraid it would be the target it was today. Even when I lived here as a kid, the shed was occasionally "visited" when we were away, although the house was never touched. The new shed is concrete block with windows too small for entry and a plug-ugly metal door that I got for almost nothing at the FreeStore shop, because it's scratched and dented.

We shine flashlights on the door but don't touch anything. There might be a few new marks, but it's pretty clear that no one got the door open. I'm ready to retreat, but Bud is braver than I am and walks all the way around the little building. Boris goes with him, leaving me alone, although for less than thirty seconds. It's a long time.

"It all looks fine," Bud says. It's a short sentence but firmly stated—no hesitating, no waiting for a word to emerge. I think it's a sign that Bud is coping well with his PTSD. This must be at least a little stressful for him.

"I really appreciate your coming over to check," I tell him. He makes a dismissive little sound and I add, "I mean it. I would worry about it all night." He starts to stammer, so I move on to something less stressful for him. "And that Felicity—she's something else!"

That pleases him, as it's meant to do, and he heads on home.

The trip to the shed really does help me take the incident in stride, and I sleep better than I thought I would. At 10:15 the next morning, the doorbell rings and Boris does a happy dance. I look out and see Officer Carl Benning, who got me through the day Bud broke into my house plus all the aftermath of that. I'm glad to see him but surprised he didn't send someone far more junior. It's only fingerprinting, and no real crime seems to have occurred, other than trespass, maybe. Carl pets Boris, and we all troop out back. I hear Waggo barking next door—not frantic, just making a statement.

"You do something bad and get busted down to fingerprinting now?" I ask as he gets his kit out.

"Just staying in practice." He looks up and smiles, and I think I see a little mischief in the look. "Not likely he left any prints, though. The marks look like he just tried to pry it open, so he wouldn't have touched anything." Carl looks around on the ground. "Probably brought his own crowbar." Boris is snuffling along the back fence. "But we might as well take a look around, see if he panicked about all the barking going on."

Carl goes over to Boris to see what he's sniffing, but it's nothing as far as humans can tell. Carl squints, keeps looking, walks back toward the gate. "He left this way, right?"

"As far as I know. That's what the little girl next door says. Her window is right there, so that's the only way she could have seen him leave." I pause. "You think a three-year-old is a valid witness?"

"She is if there's no reason for her to make things up, and no inconsistencies." Carl smiles at me again. "They were still talking about her this morning. Played the recording and everything. I think they want to catch the perp just so they can use her testimony. She's something."

"They wouldn't do that, would they? I mean, wouldn't that expose her to revenge or something?"

"They probably wouldn't. Depends. Also, they can use a filter in court so the voice sounds like an adult or something. Depends on the parents too." His voice trails off. We're outside the gate now. "Would you look at that?" He's pointing at a crowbar in the hedge. "Is it yours? Has anyone been doing any work for you?"

"No way I would leave something like that out here. But you know, it does look a lot like mine." We look at each other. "Should we go in the basement and see if mine is there?" It didn't occur to me to check to see if someone broke in through one of my basement windows.

We walk around the house together, then go inside and down the basement stairs. I let Carl go first.

"Mine is here," I say with relief, when we get to the bottom of the steps and I can see into the workshop. "I think I'll put it in a less-obvious spot though." I put it on the floor and shove it under the workbench with my toe. I wonder if I'll remember what I did with it the next time I need it.

"Good, so that means he stayed outside, and it also means I can take the one outside into evidence."

I watch as he takes pictures and bags the crowbar. It really does look like mine, but I guess crowbars are pretty much all the same.

"This is pretty minor though, right?" I ask. "Is it really worth your time and trouble?"

"Oh, you never know where something might lead," he says. "We'll let you know if anything pops." He heads for his car.

"And, of course, you have great neighbors. Not everyone looks out for other folks like that."

"They are pretty terrific," I say, and I mean it, no matter what Bud did in the past.

We're both quiet for a moment, thinking about the whole Bud incident, or at least I am.

"You're not going to let this worry you too much, are you?" He's looking at me more intently than I'm really comfortable with, and for a second, I wonder again why he is dusting for prints for an extremely petty crime. A thought passes through my head and moves on.

"Nah, I'm fine. Nothing happened, really."

The intense look softens just a little and changes to a smile. We thank each other, and he leaves, and I go back inside feeling better about my neighborhood, instead of worse.

I'm feeling especially good about the shed, that it was worth the planning and expense of making it burglarproof. I call Sean to let him know that we were successful. Sean is the concrete guy I hired to pave my driveway and who ended up helping me build the shed too. To be honest, I helped him, not the other way around. And it probably took him only a little longer than if I had stayed out of his way. But I did like helping with the masonry work, and he was nice about making sure my work was as good as his.

Sean does not respond with the enthusiasm I expect. He lives way out in the country, where nothing ever happens, and is worried when I say that someone tried to pry their way in. I reassure him that it's okay, that the dog next door scared him away and that the neighbors saw the guy and called the police. I don't tell him that a three-year-old was the star of the show. He asks if I checked to make sure the lock wasn't damaged, that it still works. I am forced to admit that I have not checked, and as we are talking, I get the key and go outside. Now I'm worried that he did get in, that maybe I left it unlocked. I convince myself against all odds that someone is in there now. But Boris is along and unconcerned, and of course the lock is secure and works just fine. I peek inside and lock it up again.

"Well, good talking to you," Sean says. "And maybe you should get some sensors, you know—the ones that turn the lights on if someone walks by."

He's right, and I tell him so, and we end the call.

I let a few days go by, but nothing "pops" and I'm more relieved than not. Of course I'd like the perp to be apprehended, but all in all it was nothing, and I don't want to relive it with police statements and so on. I don't let myself think about the crowbar, and I tell myself it was a small one anyway and that I'm not thinking about it.

I take my store credit to Henry's and look through the outdoor motion sensors and don't say why I'm looking.

"I'm taking your advice and getting some projects done," I tell Henry, which is perfectly true. "I'm putting one of these up by my back door." I look at the specs on the box. "Might as well get one that can see the whole area between the houses. I should have measured, but I know it's less than fifteen feet, house to house, so any of them will do. I'll let Jennie and Bud know and then get Jimmy to install it, if I decide I can't do it myself. For that matter, I should get another one for the north side, as long as Josie is okay with it."

Henry gives me a long look, but he doesn't say anything as he checks me out. I make sure he deducts the full amount from my store credit, minus the contractor's discount. He sees me looking.

"Yeah, yeah," Henry says. "I heard you slip that in about Jimmy. You're the contractor, he's the sub. I get it."

So there is no awkwardness about the gift, and we are on normal footing.

Before I call Jimmy, I knock on Bud and Jennie's door. I show them the sensor and explain my plan. I just want them to know that it might come on at odd times and it won't always mean anything.

"It might come on if a squirrel runs down the driveway," I say, "or a cat. I don't know how sensitive it is yet."

A little voice pipes up. "Boris would knows that." Maybe she's saying, "Boris would nose that," but I'm not going to ask and risk the disdain of a three-year-old. I didn't realize she was listening, although of course she was—it's a tiny house, and she loves to listen to grown-ups when she's not running full tilt.

"Yes, he would," I agree solemnly, then turn to the adults. "So if you guys are good with this, I'll see about installing it. Or I'll get someone."

Bud lights up. "I could do it. I'm pretty good with electrical." His voice is confident.

I start to object, tell him he's busy, he doesn't have to, and then I realize how that would sound.

"Oh," I say instead. "That would be great. I mean, I would really appreciate that."

He's beaming, and Jennie's beaming at him, and I'm beaming all around, and Felicity says, "Why didn't you bring Boris? Because Waggo just wants Boris to be here."

There's really no answer to that, so I tell her that it's Boris's dinnertime, and I need to go home and feed him and that we'll see each other soon. I leave the sensor for Bud to study and tell him to let me know when he's ready, no rush.

Walking back home in the dark, although it's only a few feet, I think that yes, there is a rush—that I wish it had somehow installed itself already, today, before the sun went down.

CHAPTER 34

The next morning, I forget all about the shed and the lights and the would-be burglar, because when I check my email, I have a response from Sarmes. *Finally,* I think. *Interview!*

But no. It's an automated email thanking me for applying. They had many excellent candidates, they tell me, and regret to say that I was not selected. They go on to assure me that they will keep my information on file. They will, of course, because it's all in an electronic data system. But it will never be looked at again. I know all about keeping information; it's what I do. Or did. And may never do again if I can't even get an interview for a job that is perfect for my qualifications. I steam a little, and then I droop. How did this happen? What is it about me? What in my application or résumé or cover note screamed "loser" to them?

I tell myself that I'm not the only person on earth who can do that job, and maybe they just wanted someone who was . . . what?

The end of the "no thanks" email tells me that I'm welcome to apply for other positions, so after I roll my eyes, I click on the link to the company website and scroll through the open positions, but of course there isn't anything else that's even close. I click on News and Press Releases, and there it is, the announcement that Phil Marx has been appointed to the job I was expecting to get—as a VP, no less.

I am dumbstruck. I know Phil Marx. I have worked with Phil Marx. Phil has no background for this job. I check the title in the press release and cross-check it with the position title in the email they just sent me. They are identical. I read the press release, which basically repeats the position description, which of course I copied and saved in my job-search folder. I get up and walk around the room. I read the end of the press release, which is a bit of bio on Phil, telling one and all what Phil "brings to the company." It is, almost word for word, the bio at the top of my own résumé.

I'm a little angry, but mostly I'm puzzled. Did wires cross? Did someone at Sarmes sneak him my résumé and tell him, "Make yours look like this"? HR data systems don't move data around on their own. Some person did this deliberately. But I can't prove it, and if I could, who would I prove it to?

I do have one place to look, and that's LinkedIn. I look up the Phil Marx I know and see he has already updated his profile with his new job and title, liked Sarmes, and posted links to the Sarmes website. No surprise; that's what LinkedIn is for.

I read his About section—and it's an exact copy of mine. He didn't even bother to change a word or two.

I check his job history. It's a copy of mine also, although he did mistype some dates. He barely disguised the company names. Everything else is a copy and paste from my own profile. I feel like I've been smacked in the head. I feel like my identity has been stolen. I feel like. . . . I don't know what. I've never felt like this before.

I print out his profile and save a screenshot while I'm at it. And then I think that while contacting Sarmes will be futile, maybe I can report him to LinkedIn. It's not much, but it's something. So I google "LinkedIn profile report" and find that LinkedIn has a process, an online form, for reporting inaccurate information on another member's profile. I look through the form, make some notes, and decide to take a breather.

The only useful breather is a walk outside, so even though it's spitting snow, Boris and I go out and skid around on the sidewalks for an hour. I'm a little calmer when we get back, and I methodically lay out my complaint. I let it sit while I cook, eat, and wash dishes, and then I read through it again and submit it.

I instantly get back a message that my form has been logged and will be processed in the order it was received. I feel like that's where this whole mess started.

I think about connecting with Phil, and I think about messaging him, but I don't. It can't do any good.

Instead, I click on my LinkedIn messages and find one from a former colleague saying that the board of directors has fired Delarosa, the CEO who closed my department last year, eliminating my job. I discover that his bonus last year was more than my entire departmental budget—just the bonus, not including the eight-digit salary. After that, I have no more interest. It's just too absurd. I also have a LinkedIn notification asking me to congratulate my former colleague Kyle on his new title, so I know that his position was solidified with my leaving, but I don't care about that, either. The Delarosa train wreck is coming, and he'll have to deal with it. I'm free of that.

On Thursday, I'm washing dishes and putting them in the drainer and wondering why I don't miss having a dishwasher. I hated washing dishes by hand as a kid. Hated it. Now, it's almost relaxing. I don't look forward to it, and I admit there are times when I'd like to shove everything out of sight in a dishwasher, but mostly I'm perfectly happy gazing out the window, washing and drying and putting away. It's not only the years that make the difference. I'm only washing for one person now, and I cook a little differently, not much in the way of skillets and the dreaded broiler to scrub. And I don't ever make a meal with four or five or six dishes, so there are fewer pans and no serving dishes. Less civilized, and yet more civilized. Anyway, there's not much room for a dishwasher in this kitchen or in my current budget.

CHAPTER 35

It's late January, and snow is falling, and I'm sick of it. I'm also grateful that I have so little to shovel, exactly forty feet of public sidewalk and about fifteen feet up to the house. I'm fanatical about keeping that clear for Esther, the letter carrier. Might as well make her job easier. Since the house faces west and the driveway slopes just a little in that direction, I let the solar shovel clear the driveway unless it gets really deep. Some days I get outside in time to clear Josie's sidewalk too, but some days another neighbor beats me to it, or she does it herself. I love the self-satisfied "hah!" she gives me when she's the first one out.

But right now, I'm sick of it, and I'm thinking about gardening. I know I can't grow enough to actually feed myself, and I know that some years I've spent more money on gardening than I would have on buying the vegetables I did manage to produce. But that wasn't in Missouri, where the tropical summers practically guarantee success. My own backyard is too shady to add much more garden area, and I'm wondering about tomatoes in the front yard. I peer out the front window and realize that the tree the city program planted last fall will soon shade the front yard too. That was the point, of course, but it pretty well nixes front-yard tomatoes.

I wander around the house, looking out my windows at snow on my car, on the roof next door, on my backyard garden shed, on Josie's yard. The side yards are miniscule here, no space there. The backyard is all I've got. I stare at the snow, trying to picture the lush green of July. It's a stretch. But the leafless, snowy Zen look is nice too, and I squint at the backyard and wonder if I should try a pen-and-ink drawing.

Something crosses my field of view, far in the distance. Well, not very far, but across the back fence in the next yard, at the house where I have never seen anyone, never managed to meet the neighbor who lives there. The other neighbors are vague about them. They are a bit of a mystery. To myself, I call them the Logans, because that's who lived there during the entirety of my childhood. Mrs. Logan, older than my parents, was still there when they moved away in the mid-1970s. Now I don't even know how many people live there.

Without giving it much thought, I put on my coat and boots and open the back door. Boris leaps out—he loves the snow as much now as he did in November. He runs a lap and proceeds to sniff the fence lines for recent squirrel visitors, paying no attention to the figure in the yard behind us. Well, maybe that's because the figure has disappeared. I trudge to the back fence, pretending to look at my snow-covered garden plot, and I picture extending it all the way across the back. I wish I had planted leeks and kale last spring, the two things I would be able to harvest all winter, if I had planted them and if I had buried them deeply in mulch in the fall.

Whoever was in the yard behind doesn't reappear. I gaze across the fence into the space where the Logans' peach trees once grew and on into the lot next to them where the Logans had tended a huge vegetable garden in a sunny, well-fenced space patrolled by their beagle-ish dog, Cookie. I picture myself picking green beans there. I picture myself walking around to the front door, stamping the snow off my boots, and asking if I can plant beans there in the spring. I know people who could do that, but I'm not one of them.

Boris and I go for a walk anyway, and we do walk past the house behind me, which looks as deserted as ever. There are no public sidewalks on this street, and the walk from the curb to the house isn't shoveled and shows no footprints. I sigh and wonder if I'm hallucinating neighbors now.

The snow stops, and the temperature drops that night and keeps dropping the next day. I look up my gas bill and worry about how much I'm using and how much the gas bills are going to reduce my savings account before the summer heat arrives and the electric bills make further inroads. Surely I'll have a job by summer.

I turn down the thermostat and put on another sweater. I close the furnace vent in the front bedroom and close the door. By nightfall, the outside temperature is well below zero, and the furnace is running pretty much full-time. I hang a quilt in the doorway between the kitchen and the back room and shut off those vents. I wonder if it really does any good. My bedroom doesn't have a furnace vent, and the bed feels icy. I pull all the covers off, shut the door, and curl up on the living room sofa. I warm up pretty quickly, pressed against the sofa back, with sofa pillows toppled over on top of me. I snuggle in and fall asleep.

The next morning, it's still below zero. I can't face the cold basement shower, but I can't go to work without washing my hair. It's just a hardware store, but still. I should have washed it yesterday or even the day before. It's gross. The kitchen sink will have to do. We all washed our hair in the kitchen sink, until I rebelled and insisted on using the showerhead suspended over the basement floor drain and open to the entire basement. Surely I can manage one shampoo in the sink.

I forgot that we used a shampoo attachment, a rubbery hose that fit over the spigot on one end and had a soft diffuser on the other end. I get the water temperature just right, stick my head under the spigot, and immediately raise my head just enough to cover the spigot and spray water in all directions, starting with down the back of my neck. Crap.

I get on with it, regretting every second, until I can finish and wrap myself in towels. Shivering, I change into dry clothes, spin my wet hair up in a bun, and drive to work with the heat on full blast.

"Nice look," Henry says when I walk in a few minutes late.

"What?" I look down at myself. My sweatshirt is wrong side out, and I can feel loose wet hair sliding down my neck. I race to the office, unpin my hair, and yank it through the back of my Midtown cap.

"I'm taking today's pay in a space heater," I tell Matt, shoving him away from the counter so he can leave for school. "A giant industrial one."

"No can do," he says. "Sold out yesterday."

When I'm sweeping the store later in the morning, I run across the dryer-vent kits, which makes me think about disconnecting my dryer vent and diverting the hot outflow to the basement. When I get home, I comb out my hair again and realize it's still got conditioner in it, or maybe shampoo. I go downstairs and put a load of laundry in. Thirty minutes later, when it's in the drier, I reroute the drier vent hose so that it blows directly at the shower. I undress, get in the shower, slather on conditioner, rinse it all out, and pull a hot towel out of the drier, slamming it shut and turning it back on.

When I get back upstairs, warm for once, I take a long look

at my bathroom and wonder again how I can install a shower. The next time I go out, I stop at the dollar store and get a shampoo hose. I test it out in the bathtub, but it splits the first time I use it. I fix it with duct tape, which doesn't really work, and feel like a complete loser.

CHAPTER 36

In March, I get a message from LinkedIn saying that my complaint about Phil has been resolved. They thank me for my interest and encourage me to complete a survey on my experience. Before I do that, I look at Phil's profile and see that Phil has changed it up a little. His degrees don't mirror mine now; in fact, they are probably the correct ones. His jobs have been modified a little also, and as far as I can tell, they now have the right dates and employers, although his responsibilities are still remarkably like mine. I make a copy of the new version and decide to think about it for a while.

While I'm thinking about LinkedIn, I log in, and LinkedIn informs me that Kyle from my old job has changed companies. I wish him well in my head but don't even click the Congratulate Kyle button. I don't look up my old company to see what's going on there. I'm not interested.

A few days later, I look up Phil again, thinking I might protest the job descriptions, at least the ones I'm absolutely certain are wrong. But his profile has disappeared completely. I check the Sarmes website and see that the press release about him is gone too. So I email my friend at Sarmes and ask about the position, without mentioning my rejection or anything at all about Phil. A few days go by, and he gets back to me saying that he was told that the department "is going in a new direction." So maybe I got Phil fired, but I didn't do myself any favors. I wonder if Phil is the vengeful type. I wonder if reporting him was wise. I decide it was worth it. He needs to be held accountable. There is a lot of gray area in the world, but there was nothing foggy about what he did. I go back to my own LinkedIn profile, though, and make sure there is no clue about my current city of residence.

The weather is warming up, and the days are longer, and I start thinking about planting peas and lettuce. At the store, Henry reminds me that I've still got store credit and spring is a good time to do house projects. I promise that I will come up with something. When I get home, I open the kitchen window to let in some fresh air and then go in the bathroom and open that window too. The bathroom never smells as clean as I would like. I hear Henry in my head and take a serious look around the room. I turn the light on and stare at the floor. I know where the problem is. I know what that cracked and curled linoleum tile means. It means that water, and who knows what, has been collecting for decades. I bend down and pry up the edge of the worst tile, at the corner of the tub. It cracks and comes away in my hand. It's black underneath.

"Ick," I say out loud, and I go back to the kitchen and eat lunch and make a list.

I spend the rest of the day chipping up the nasty linoleum tile. It's a small room, and I get all the tile up before dark, but there is a mangled layer of paper and adhesive under it. Over dinner, I read up and learn that heat or alcohol will help. Early the next morning, I try my hair dryer, but it is the wall-mounted kind, so it's not much use. I try the iron, which is tricky, but I make some headway. That night, I read that there may be asbestos in the paper and that I need a certified contractor to test and remove it. Rats. I keep reading and finally decide to soak it all down with soapy water to prevent asbestos dust, and then pour boiling water in small areas and scrape it. That works well enough, and I finally get down to the wood subfloor. I put a fan in the window, sponge bleach water all over the floor, close the door, and leave the house for a few hours. When I get back, the smell is gone. The temperature is dropping, so I leave the window up about an inch and close the bathroom door.

Friday morning, it's twenty-nine degrees when I get up, and the bathroom is freezing. I close the window, brush my teeth, and head to the store for my Friday shift.

"Well?" says Henry when the morning rush calms down. "Did you start a project?"

I tell him what I've done, and he nods thoughtfully. "Now what?"

"Oh, I can't decide. I'd like to put down ceramic tile, but I'd have to put down backer board, right? And that would raise the floor some. Plus I would probably need to stiffen the floor. It's a small room, but still. I might have to sister some of the floor joists." I barely know what sistering means, but I saw a lot of YouTube advice about that. I'm not excited about nailing sections of two-by-sixes to the floor joists, although I am sure I can manage it. "Sure," as in I watched a couple of videos and understood what was going on.

"I also thought about a concrete floor, but same issues, of course. I suppose I can just get new linoleum tiles. They still make it, right? I don't want vinyl. Wood seems too fussy; I'd worry all the time about water leaks. I guess there's Pergo, but I just don't like it." I've covered the whole gamut, so I shut up.

"Well, there's always carpet. Easy in, easy out."

"Yuck."

"Okay then, back to tile. Are you going to replace the tub?"

"Oh, the tub's okay. I just need to put in a shower, which is a problem because the window is over the tub, and there's no way to rearrange the fixtures. But I think I figured it out—a long U-shaped shower rod fasted to the wall where the plumbing is. I could tile that wall, or else put up melamine. Which I like about as well as vinyl flooring, but I'm getting to the point where I don't care."

Henry laughs and tells me that if I want tile, I should do it. "Just take your time, go slow. Matt can cut the sisters and help you hold them in place. He can help you shift the toilet too."

I guess he sees my face fall. I do not want to move the toilet and had visions of tiling up to it.

"If you were thinking of tiling around the toilet, you can just forget about that," he says. "I'd have to fire you if I found out. Because sooner or later, you're going to have to replace that toilet, and let me tell you, you will be sorry then." He lets that sink in, and I know he's right. "Also, it would require a lot of fussy tile cutting that you don't want to do."

After lunch, I take careful measurements and make some drawings. Henry has pointed out that tiling will be far, far easier if I buy tiles that will fit the space, allowing for grout lines, without having to cut the last row of tiles. So if the space is forty-eight inches, and I buy four-inch tiles and allow one-eighth-inch grout lines, it won't work—I'd have a three-inch gap at the end and have to cut a whole row of tiles. Even if I rent a tile cutter and miraculously do a perfect job, it's still going to be a row of cut tiles. I keep calculating, wishing we used metric in America so I could work in decimals, and finally feel ready to go to Habitat for Humanity's ReStore resale shop and see if they even have any tile. At this point, I'm ready to install Pergo, until I realize that I'll have the same problem. Maybe Henry was right about the carpet. If it gets icky, I can easily toss it and get more.

ReStore has a dearth of floor tile, but I learn a lot from a woman who is there looking for tile to make mosaics. She thinks I should mix it up, use different colors and sizes.

"But make sure they're all the same thickness, you know?" she says. "For me, different thicknesses are good. My stuff is kind of 3D. But you want a smooth floor, see." She puts a lot of *o*'s in "smooth" and moves her hands back and forth, as if making a surface perfectly flat.

I nod enthusiastically, then less enthusiastically as I realize that my project just got more complicated. She watches my face and laughs. "Here's what you do—you go find a piece of low-pile carpet over there"—she waves an arm—"and get a bunch of tile too. Then you go home, and cut that carpet to fit. Just lay it down loose. You can pick it up and keep working on your tile till you get it where you want it. Maybe it takes two trips up here, maybe it takes five trips. You'll get it sooner or later. Then you can cut up the carpet to make door mats. Or put it on the floor in front of your washing machine."

It's nuts, but I do what she says, mostly because I can't think of anything else to do. I'm so sick of the nasty subfloor that I'm ready to spray-paint it black.

CHAPTER 37

The next week, I'm telling Henry how easy it was to install the sister joists when I get a text from Sharon, my old boss: "You working?"

I start typing *yes* when her next message arrives: "Or still looking?"

It takes me a few seconds to realize that she wouldn't consider my hardware store job "working," so I delete the "yes" and type, "Still looking" instead.

"Call me," she replies.

I check the time. "In about an hour?"

"Sure."

I float home, excited—this must mean that they have realized their mistake at last and are ready to rehire me. I'll demand more salary and a bigger budget. I picture myself picking up the threads and saving the day. Then I have a sort of flashback to my old life—eight hours or more of conference calls every day, late nights catching up on reports and emails, middle-of-the-night calls with staff on the other side of the globe. Airports, hotel rooms. Same meetings, same topics, same arguments. Same train wreck looming. On the other hand, the money will be nice, as will the health insurance. I can get someone else to figure out the tile, install the shower, sister any future joists.

Or I can move to a normal house with a normal bathroom that already has a shower and tile. But then Josie won't live next door to that house. By the time I get home, I've deflated and have to drag myself up the steps to the front door. They probably only want me back for a week to explain things to someone they've hired, at a VP level of course, to do my old job, which they now call something completely different so they don't have to actually rehire me.

I eat a banana and tell myself to get over myself. I sign into LinkedIn and make sure that Sharon is still at the same job. Then I call her.

"Sharon, what's up?" I try to sound cool and casual and busy all at once.

"Hey, listen, I've got a call in fifteen minutes. You remember Deanna, right? Deanna Bailey?"

"Of course." How could I not? She was CEO before our last acquisition.

"I talked to her this morning. She's got a new gig. She's CEO of a startup; they just got funding."

"Cool—what is it, where is it?"

"Chicago. I told her I didn't know if you'd want to move but you'd probably be willing to telecommute. I just put that out there so she could think about it. You could move if you want."

"But what is it?"

"The company is called Magetech or something like that. I'm not sure. It involves a lot of data, so she was looking for you."

"What kind of data? Did she say?"

"Hell, I don't know. Data. Everyone wants data these days. Look, I gotta go. Just call her."

I want to ask a lot of questions, but I don't think Sharon has the answers. And she sounds rushed and uninterested in small talk. So I thank her and tell her I'll call Deanna right away.

"Good to talk to you," Sharon says. I look at my phone. *Call ended.*

The phone buzzes—incoming text. "Forgot to give you the number," it says, followed by the number. It's not a Chicago area code, but the last I heard, Deanna was in Pittsburgh, so who knows.

I google Magetech, with various spellings, and get nothing. I google Deanna's name and get zillions of hits, mostly having to do with her previous jobs, her philanthropy, and her pet causes. Nothing about a new startup. I'll have to call blind, which every book, article, and job counselor tells you not to do. On the other hand, they all tell you to use your network, and that's what just happened. I make a few notes and practice a few opening lines on Boris, who yawns and rolls onto his other side. I put the number in my contacts and call it.

"Hello, this is. . . ." I don't catch the name.

"This is Marianne. I'm calling for Deanna Bailey," I say, but the voice on the other end is still talking. I realize it's a recording, just as the voice stops. It must be waiting for my message. "I'm calling for Deanna," I try again, but the voice interrupts.

"I'm sorry, I didn't quite get that. To transfer to one of our associates, press. . . ."

The phone buzzes, and a text appears. "I gave you the wrong number. Try this one."

I disconnect the call, swap out the number in my contacts, and try again. This time it is a Chicago area code.

"Hi, Marianne." Deanna picks up immediately. I'm startled and forget the opening lines I'd just practiced.

"Oh, hi, Deanna. How are you?" Brilliant. She doesn't say anything, so I go on. "I just heard from Sharon. She says you're in a new startup." Still silence. "Deanna?"

"I'm back. Someone asking questions. You've talked to Sharon?" She didn't say sorry—I have to remember that.

"Yes, she was telling me about your new startup."

"Great, what did she say?"

"Well. . . ." I stall. Sharon told me exactly nothing. That's all I've got, so I go with it. "Just that it's a startup, and it's in Chicago. That was about it. I think she thought you would be better at explaining it."

"Ah, still the diplomatic one, I see. She knows more than that, but she signed a nondisclosure agreement, and you haven't. I'll fax you one. Can you come to Chicago next week?"

It sounds more like a directive than a question, but she's a CEO, so directives are what she does.

"I do have some commitments next week," I hedge. "I could fly out Tuesday afternoon, and I'll need to fly back Thursday evening. Would that work?"

"Great. We'll have dinner when you get in. I'll have someone call you about travel." The line goes dead, and I stare at my phone. While I'm staring, it rings—a Chicago area code.

"Hello, this is Marianne."

"Hi, Marianne, it's Cassie. Remember me?"

I don't remember anyone named Cassie. There was a Cassandra in my grade school, but this can't be her.

"Uhhh," I say. "Cassie." I wish I had used the landline so I could use my iPhone to text someone and ask if we ever worked with a Cassie.

"Cassie!" I say. "Can you call me back on my landline? I'm out of battery on my mobile." I'm not out of battery, but I'm out of memory cells, and isn't that sort of close? I give Cassie the number, hang up, and message Cathy from my old job. The landline rings before I can even click Send.

"Isn't it great to be working together again?" Cassie says by way of hello. I have an immediate suspicion that she's confused me with someone else, and it's going to be awkward in Chicago next week if I pretend to know her now. Cathy hasn't responded; she's probably on a conference call with a screen share and has wisely shut off everything else.

"It will be good to see you," I tell Cassie. That's pretty non-committal. "I can fly anytime after three on Tuesday, and I'll need a return flight on Thursday, maybe late afternoon?" I make it a question, hoping she'll be forced to switch gears from old times to travel. That seems to work, and she becomes quite busi-nesslike and competent, even asking which airline I prefer. She tells me she'll forward airline and hotel reservations shortly and that she'll reimburse cab fare when I arrive and meals after the trip. I'm impressed and relieved that Deanna hasn't hired a ditz, and also relieved that I'll have a last name once I get the email. Unless, of course, it's the kind of startup where everyone is first-name@startup.com, which is surely not a mistake Deanna would make.

The reservations arrive by email within an hour, all in order, along with the NDA, which I print out, sign, scan, and email back. Cassie's last name is Mettlin, which is vaguely familiar. I haven't heard from Cathy, so I send Sharon an email thanking her for the lead and telling her that I've talked to both Deanna and Cassie and that I will be going to Chicago next week to interview. "By the way," my note ends, "who is Cassie? She seems to know me, but I can't place her."

CHAPTER 38

When I get to Chicago, I text Deanna, letting her know that I've checked in.

"Great!" she replies. "See you in the morning." So obviously, dinner is off, and I go out and walk up Michigan Avenue until I'm freezing. I go into a store to warm up and think about how nice it will be to feel free to buy something here if I want to. When I get the job. If I get the job. I wander back toward the Club Quarters where I'm staying, looking for a little Italian restaurant whose name and location I can't quite remember. I finally stumble on it and have dinner without feeling too weird about eating alone. Room service seemed too pathetic.

The next morning, I present myself at the office, and Cassie is friendly and businesslike and doesn't mention anything about working together in the past, so I leave that alone and fill out more forms. Deanna isn't available until afternoon, but I'm spending the morning with the technical leads, which is just as well. I'm anxious to find out what the company does.

The two men I meet with are circumspect. They tell me they are developing a system to monitor urban infrastructure, but don't specify what. They keep talking about monitors, and backup, and benefits of knowing what's happening in real time. "Oh," I say, "like water, sewer, electric? Or more like roads and bridges?" Finally I get them to admit that it could be any of those. They are the idea men, they say. They don't ask me anything. I try to talk about data access and volume and security, but they don't seem interested.

Everyone disappears at lunchtime, so I text Cassie about next appointments. She tells me engineers at one o'clock, so I go out and eat a salad at the Corner Bakery, wondering just how big and how far along this startup is. At 12:55 p.m., I'm back in the lobby. Cassie appears and takes me to a conference room and tells me the engineers will be in shortly. She seems distracted, not at all like she was on the phone a few days ago. When the engineers show up, I recognize them immediately from many years and many acquisitions ago. They are much more open about what they are doing, which is installing monitors and cameras in stormwater systems. They have a small contract to do proof of concept for an industrial section of the city. They are storing data in a spreadsheet and need someone with better Excel skills to handle the volume and complexity, which is increasing daily. I tell them they need a database, and they are skeptical for a while but finally come around. They get nervous again when I say they need to store it in the cloud. I step back and ask them about their IT support, which they admit is minimal, and we get back around to the idea of not trying to manage our own server farm and uptime and security. Their eyes get wide, and I tell them we'll figure it out when we know more.

Deanna appears as we are wrapping up and invites the three of us to go out for a drink. The guys decline—they've spent the entire afternoon with me and need to catch up on their real jobs. But they shake my hand enthusiastically and tell Deanna that they're relieved to have someone on board to worry about data.

Over drinks, which turns into dinner, Deanna fills me in a little. I've met the entire staff, I discover, although she's interviewing for a lot more people and has outsourced HR and payroll and legal for the time being. Gradually we move on to other topics and people we know, who is now working where. We don't linger over dinner, and as we are leaving, she tells me she has an all-day meeting the next day, something that came up at the last minute.

I realize that I don't know if I'm interviewing or if I can assume I have a job, so I tell her I'm really excited about the business and ask about next steps. "I'll call you in a few days," she says and then adds that I should check in with Cassie in the morning to make sure she has everything she needs, and then I'm free to leave.

On Thursday morning, Cassie is again all business as we go over my file and expenses. By ten o'clock, I'm back on the street. I've got hours and hours before my flight leaves, so I go to the Field Museum and puzzle over what just happened. But I cling to the idea that I'll know more in a few days, and I catch a cab to Midway with a lot of time to spare.

When I pick up Boris from Josie's house, she asks about the interview, and I tell her I think it went well, but I can't say for sure. It's a startup, I tell her, and I'm used to big companies. Maybe that's all it is—just a different sort of business.

"Startups," she says. "Seems like they either go wild and everyone gets rich, or they fizzle out and disappear." I'm afraid she's right, and the odds are on fizzle.

CHAPTER 39

Friday morning, I'm back at the hardware store. It's busy, and the interview and the excitement of Chicago and a potential job fade to nothing, almost like I never went to Chicago at all. It comes back to me on the walk home, and I check to make sure my phone is on with the ringer turned up, just in case. I remind myself that it's too early—Deanna said "a few days," so she must mean Monday or Tuesday.

Monday and Tuesday come and go, and so do Wednesday and Thursday. On Friday morning, I send Deanna a short text: "Great to see you last week. Look forward to hearing from you." I realize I should have sent it in a more formal email, and I should have sent it a week ago, but at the time, it just seemed so casual and certain.

Over the weekend, I log into the unemployment website to record my interview and look for more jobs to apply for, to keep the unemployment coming. The weather turns gloomy, threatening snow but only delivering clouds and drizzle. Not unusual for late March, but I'd like some wind or sun or something other than the pall of November when it's almost April. Taxes are due soon, so I decide a gloomy day is a good day for a gloomy job, so I install TurboTax and get started. I'm gloomier still when I finish. I've had my fingers crossed for months that enough taxes were taken out of the severance pay and vacation payout. But no—my income was inflated, and I owe money, both to the feds and in Missouri. At least it's not at California rates. I set up the money transfers and sit around feeling sick to my stomach. I remind myself that at least I have the money to transfer.

Every trip past the bathroom reminds me about the tiling project, and every chilly trip to the basement shower reminds me that a bathroom shower is only a few days of hard work away. I drive to a different ReStore with my bathroom floor drawing, which shows two big ceramic tiles in the middle, the decorative tiles I got along with the carpet scrap on my last trip to ReStore. I picture the perfect edging and background tiles to fill in around them. What I find instead is a box of ten gray twenty-inch linoleum tiles. They are on a bottom shelf, and I sit on the floor, open the box, and slide them out. There are only seven, and four of them are dark turquoise. Leftovers from someone's checkerboard-patterned floor project, no doubt. I stare at them. The colors are nothing like the apple-blossom pink and green of the ceramic tiles, which I already have and have been picturing with matching towels and paint and shower curtain. But I love the feel of the linoleum tiles, and I know they will go down on the existing subfloor and be even with the hall floor. I can cut them to fit and not worry about grout lines. And not spend months looking for the right ceramic tile to finish the project I've been imagining. And the lino is only eight bucks. I can barely lift the box, but I get it into my cart, pay for it, and go home, stopping at Henry's for a linoleum knife and a long metal ruler. Henry's not there to advise me on adhesives, so I don't buy that. I'm also reluctant to use my store credit with a cashier I don't know and who may or may not have gotten his own bonus. I pay cash and keep the receipt. When I get home, I find my store credit sitting on the kitchen table, so it's just as well I didn't try to use it. I can honestly tell Henry I forgot to take it.

When I spread out the tiles on the bathroom floor, I realize the twenty-inch tiles will make a bizarre statement covering a space that is about forty by sixty, with another twenty-by-ten recess where the toilet tank tucks in between the tub and a stack of cupboards. I could cut them all in quarters and do a checkerboard pattern, or cut them in half and make stripes. Or put two big turquoise ones in the middle with gray around the sides, cut to fit around the tub and the cupboards. Or, or . . . . Why aren't they all the same color, so I don't have to stew about it? I heat up some soup and think about it while I eat.

After lunch, I tape newspaper together to make an exact pattern of the bathroom floor, which involves careful measurements of the dodgy area behind the toilet that I'm most anxious to rehab. I bleach it all again, open the window, shut the door, and make a note to look at bathroom exhaust fans at Henry's. Moving the toilet to install the floor tile is a nagging worry that I keep at bay.

The newspaper sheets have perfectly square corners that send me back to the bathroom, holding my breath. The corners that will show are close enough to square that the baseboard will resolve any discrepancy. Thanks, Dad. He replaced the lath and plaster in here back in the 1950s—he must have squared it up then.

By nightfall, I'm ready to cut but decide to wait until morning. I watch a few more YouTube videos on linoleum and convince myself that I can use the linoleum knife without disemboweling myself.

On Monday morning, I arrive at Henry's at ten, when I know the morning rush will have calmed down. Henry does a double take and then realizes I'm there to buy, not to work. I tell him about my projects, and we choose an adhesive and look at exhaust fans. He points out that I can easily replace the existing ceiling light with a combination light and fan, or light-fan-heater combination. I like the glass ceiling light I have, but I see his point about cutting a new hole in the ceiling and wiring it separately for the fan, so I cave and choose the combo. We both make sure it's the type for remodeling, not new construction. Something about insulation, I think. He cautions me about tracing out the wire and replacing it with Romex if it's anything other than perfect.

"Get professional help if you're the least bit concerned," he says. We both laugh at that, and I assure him that I'll call an electrician or the suicide hotline, whichever is appropriate. It feels good to laugh, and I tell myself I need to go to the library and get a comedy or two on DVD that I can play on my computer—or else just spend more time with other people. That seems harder.

Henry also sells me a wax ring for resetting the toilet and makes sure I have wrenches to take the toilet out and put it back in.

"Do not reuse the old seal," he says. "It will leak. Maybe not the first hour or the first day, but soon enough. That won't burn your house down like the bad wiring, but still."

"Enough already," I say, plugging my ears. "I'll even get Matt over to help me seat it. I think I can do it, but I've watched the videos. Crucial to get it right on the mark in one shot."

He rings up the sale, and I don't bother with the receipts from Saturday. I'll easily use up the bonus soon enough.

"Watch a few more YouTubes on cutting that linoleum," he calls after me. "You need all your fingers to work here."

"I'll report you to the ADA people," I call back and head home, wondering if I can cut lino with a jigsaw. That hooked linoleum knife scares me. I watch a few more videos of people cutting linoleum with saws and resist the urge to click on drywall and baseboard videos. All in good time.

On Tuesday, I get home from work at the store, ready to start. It's cool but dry outside, so I set up the jigsaw in the driveway, using a short stack of pallets as a work surface. Sawing takes longer than I thought it would, because I clamp a guide for every single cut, and possibly because I'm using the wrong sort of blade. I get tired of it and try cutting a scrap with the lino knife and metal ruler, which goes much faster. Then I get out one of the large ceramic tiles and use it as a straightedge, which keeps my left hand a lot farther from the finger-threatening knife blade. I put the saw away and move operations to the bathroom floor, which is cramped but has the advantage of being near enough to test fit immediately.

By dark, my hands are cramping, so I stack everything in the bathtub and take Boris for a very short walk. It's not that late, and people are out and about, but I am still nervous about being outside alone when it's dark enough for the streetlights to be on. After supper I watch the trailers of the comedy DVDs I got from the library and settle down with a book instead.

Wednesday morning, I zip through the rest of the cutting without losing any fingers, and I lay out all the tiles on the floor. I'm pleased with the look and with myself. I admire it for a few minutes and then turn my attention to the toilet. I don't want to take it out until I have to, since it's the only one I've got. I'd like to be the sort of person who wouldn't mind running next door to pee once or twice, but I'm not that sort of person. It's the toilet or the basement floor drain. I start installing at the other end and work my way toward the toilet, stopping short of the point of no return. The rest can wait until tomorrow, I decide. My knees, back, and hands are aching. I shower and lie on my back until I can bring myself to find something to eat for supper.

Thursday morning, it registers that it's April Fool's Day and maybe not a good idea to tempt fate by removing the toilet. Plus

I remember that you're supposed to treat newly installed tiles gently for a few days, not squirm around on them and set heavy porcelain fixtures on them. I take the day off and catch up on email. I log in to look for jobs I can apply for—it's almost time to record another week's efforts. I realize that it's now been two weeks since I returned from Chicago. What the heck? I scroll carefully through my emails, texts, and calls. Not a peep. I google Deanna and Magetech again; still nothing. I waste forty-five minutes thinking of an excuse to call. All those job-seeking discourses about networking and following up replay in my head. I try a few notes, trying to catch the right balance of professionalism, friendliness, interest, and lack of desperation. Finally, I email Cassie: "Just checking back to see if there is anything else you need from me." I'm pretty sure she's smart enough to see through that. I'd be disappointed if she didn't. But I don't know exactly what her role is. And while I'll want to bond with her if I do get hired, I also want to make sure my role is in tech, not admin. If I were male, this would be understood, but even in a woman-led company, I know that any female role is automatically admin unless forcefully positioned elsewhere. I delete the unsent message and text Deanna instead: "Still excited about joining your team. Keep me posted."

And then, even though it's the middle of the afternoon, I make myself watch one of the comedy DVDs until I can get the futility of job hunting back in the cage where it belongs. I have a now-rare glass of wine with dinner and then watch another DVD. It's not particularly comfortable, sitting at the kitchen table watching on my laptop, but lounging on the sofa with it propped up on my stomach isn't so great, either. Maybe I'll think about getting a TV eventually. Or maybe just a monitor, if I'm only going to watch DVDs.

On Friday, the afternoon clerk calls in sick, so Henry asks

me to stay for the afternoon shift. I take the opportunity to treat myself to the mouthwatering chicken that calls to me every time I leave the store. I offer to get some for Henry, but he's got a sandwich from home and besides, he says, years of smelling that chicken have pretty much inured him to its seductive power. I'm back in fifteen minutes with enough extra for Saturday's lunch, which pleases me more than it should. I'm not that poor, I tell myself. I can have a fast-food chicken meal once in a while.

I'm far too tired to deal with the floor when I get home, so I eat salad for supper and read until I fall asleep. Saturday is the day. I layer cardboard on the bathroom floor, wish myself luck, turn off the water supply to the toilet, and flush it one last time. I immediately wish I had peed one more time, but I roll my eyes and start bailing the last of the water out of the bowl and tank. YouTube is open on my laptop in the kitchen, where I can refer to it if I somehow forget something I've seen a dozen times now.

It takes a little prying to separate the base from the floor, and I'm glad I've assembled more rags than necessary. I really should have taken it out before laying the tile as close as I did, but I get away with it, and the old wax seal gets scraped into a plastic bag and dumped into the trash. I check the clock. Henry will be open for hours yet, if anything goes south. I'm wishing I had bought two wax seals, just in case I mess it up the first time. I roll my eyes again and get going on the tile. Even with the toilet out of the way, it's awkward, and I don't do as good a job as I did in the rest of the room, but it's good enough. No gaps, anyway. A little filler piece in the dark corner will be seen by no one but me.

At three o'clock, I take a break and go to the library to return the DVDs and use the bathroom. I get a few more DVDs while I'm there and check out at the desk instead of the self-checkout, just to talk to someone for a few minutes. I go back to the home section and check out two books on bathroom remodeling. One is from *This Old House,* and one is from *Popular Mechanics.* I try to picture Bob Villa taking on my house. I'm pretty sure no one but me would watch that series. Maybe not even me.

It's after four when I get home, and I realize that if I'm going to get the toilet back in today, now is the time. Matt is not likely to be free on a Saturday evening. I text him, and he says he can be there in thirty minutes. That gives me time to read the instructions on the wax seal box three more times and watch two more YouTube videos. Kant-Leak is the brand, spelling that would normally annoy me, but I'm too nervous to worry about it. I put the seal in place and let Matt in. He picks up the toilet, sets it down perfectly straight on the bolts, and presses it into place like he's done this a hundred times.

"Looks like this isn't your first time at this," I say admiringly. I had been expecting to crouch on the floor checking the alignment and helping ease the toilet onto the seal.

"Just once before, but Dad made me watch a YouTube video before I came over." He's busy with the washers and screws. He pulls out a cutter and snips off the excess bolt and drops the caps on.

"All set." He gets up and washes his hands. I hand him some cash, and he makes a show of leaping back as if it were poison. "No way. I still owe you," he says, and darts out the door. I stand in the door and wave. He never even took off his jacket. He was here for ten minutes, tops. Why was I so stressed about this?

"Uh-oh," I say out loud. Just because it's all back together doesn't mean it doesn't leak. I wonder if I should let it all sit for a day before I use it, so the adhesive can cure a little more if anything does leak. Or do I need the weight of the water in the toilet, pressing down on the wax seal to make sure it doesn't leak?

I get out the rags, reconnect the water supply, slowly turn on the water. The tank fills. No leaks. I flush. So far, so good. It might seep, of course, but I'll just have to watch for that. I tuck a few paper towels around the base so it will be obvious if it does leak, and then I force myself to admire the floor and leave any trouble for later. I take a picture and text it to my brother, who returns a smiley face and something that looks like a toilet plunger.

On Sunday morning, the paper towel–leak indicators are dry, and I go to Mass feeling grateful but spend the entire hour certain that it's leaking directly into the basement and kicking myself for not checking there.

When I get home, I run downstairs. It's not leaking into the basement, of course. It's dry and perfect, and I am inordinately proud of myself. I smile every time I think about it.

The afternoon is warm and not too windy, and I take my library books out onto the front porch. I sit on the steps in the sun and leaf through the pages. I want to start on the shower project, but I tell myself to get the exhaust fan in first. The sun is warm, and I go in for a glass of cold water. When I get back, a group of teenagers is headed up the hill, walking on the sidewalk and sometimes spilling into the street. I wave and say, "Hi, kids," in a way that says I see them but don't need to engage. Boris is looking out the storm door. He shuffles his feet and whimpers softly, wanting in on the conversation.

"We not kids," one of the girls says, shoving the boy's shoulder. She seems to be trying to impress him. "Yeah, we grown-*up*," says another girl, shoving her chest forward and upward, bumping into the boy. The third girl has the boy by the arm and is being proprietary; she ignores me. The boy is trying to be über-cool, but it's pretty clear that being the center of a three-girl fan group is new to him, and his cool-kid face keeps breaking into happy-kid grins. They're passing the house now, and he looks sideways and sees Boris.

"Oh, cool dog!" he says, shaking off the girls and heading toward me. I let Boris out, and they have a little lovefest in the front yard. The kids switch from acting like twelve-going-on-twenty-year-olds to seven-going-on-eight. Boris finds a pine cone and coaxes them to toss it for him. Finally, they continue on their way, and I murmur, "See you later, grown-up kids," as they saunter off.

The next time I look up, Flynn is standing in the driveway.

"Hi, Flynn. Nice day, huh?" I suspect that's what I always say to him.

"Yep, just taking a walk. Nice to see tulips up."

Flynn's walks, as far as I can tell, take him a little past my house and then he turns around and goes back up the hill. Better than no exercise, I guess, but I'm starting to think he's trying to be more than just a friendly neighbor. I hope it's just because he remembers my dad.

We talk about the weather while I try to come up with a way to gracefully push him on down the street.

"Them bushes you put in, they're nice," he says.

I turn to look. They are just starting to leaf out, and at least one of them seems to be dead, but I nod a thank-you and look out across the yard. I don't say anything.

"Okay, well, I need to get going," he says and waves as he heads back up the hill.

I sigh, pick up my library books, and go inside. Enough interaction with the general public for today.

CHAPTER 40

Throughout April, the weather does what it always does in mid-spring: threatens but doesn't produce snow, heats up to almost too warm, delivers lashings of rain and hail and at least one tornado warning, and, in between, sets out new green leaves, flowering shrubs, and tulips under skies that make me sigh. I watch a dozen YouTube videos on installing my bathroom fan and exchange my bathroom books for *Electricity for Dummies*. It is not that hard. My husband, my dad, and my brother could all do it without thinking. I've replaced outlets and light fixtures myself. But still I dawdle.

I dawdle until the day I get a call about a market research job I've applied for, a job in a new field but one that sounds interesting. I go to the interview and impress them by understanding better than they do how their new software works. It's only five or six miles away, by the expressway, and I think there is some possibility of telecommuting at some point. My unemployment benefits end on April 30, so I ignore the fact that the salary is quite a bit less than I was making previously and that the job is going to be pretty routine, with no travel, no decision-making, and very little problem-solving. It's full-time, with health insurance, after all.

The call offering me the job comes on a Friday afternoon,

and I am upbeat and positive and ask if I can let them know on Monday. I want to check in one last time with Deanna, although I don't say that.

"Of course, of course," the hiring manager gushes. "Monday is fine. We want you to be sure."

I text Deanna: "I've got a job offer locally and wanted to see where we stand with the Magetech job. You are probably my first choice."

I don't hear back right away and obsess about the wording of my text. I don't hear on Saturday or Sunday either, and on Monday morning, I decide that I'll give her until noon and then accept the marketing research job. Noon comes, one o'clock, two o'clock. I stare at my phone, check the Junk folder one last time, and make the call.

"Oh, we offered the job to someone else, and she accepted," the hiring manager says.

"But we agreed on today, didn't we?" I keep my tone professional but friendly, although it's dawned on me that it doesn't matter.

"If you were the right one for the job, you would have accepted right away," she says, and then she ends the call. I get up and stomp around the house, which isn't big enough to stomp effectively. So I put Boris in the car and drive to the park, where I can scowl and mutter to myself without alarming the neighbors.

I get home feeling a little less stompy and ready to tackle something that requires concentration. I get the step stool, the toolbox, the fan, and the new switch. It takes a little fishing to get the new wires to the switch box, until I realize I can attach all the new wires to the old ceiling light wire and use it to pull in the new ones. Voilà: wires in place, including a new wire replacing the old. Chipping out plaster to make a hole for the fan vent is annoying, because I should have done it before I put in the new floor. But after all that, it only takes two hours, if I don't count the time I wasted taking the ladder and the tools and everything else out of the bathroom and laying down the carpet scrap to protect the new floor. I test the light, fan, and heater, one at a time. It all works, no sparks. "Well done," I say to Boris. "No electricity leaks." I snap the escutcheon in place and take the tools and the carpet back to the basement.

Henry is pleased when I report my success and tells me to push on and get the shower done while I can. "You don't have forever," he says. "That job is out there; it's on its way." It's a little odd to hear him say this. We never talk about the eventuality of me getting a "real" job and leaving the hardware store. I don't talk about my job search, and he doesn't ask. I didn't even tell him when I went to Chicago to interview. It's out there, but it's not tethered to anything here, so it never comes up. I, for one, don't like to think about the time when I don't work here, even though my current situation can't go on forever. One more unemployment payment, and that's it. I've looked into the extension program that was in place a few years ago but can't find anything on the state website. I finally find an article in the *Kansas City Star* from six months ago, saying it was discontinued due to improvements in the job outlook.

I respond to Henry by telling him I'm looking at shower-conversion kits, where I can replace the tub faucet with one that has a riser outside the wall. I won't have to dig into the drywall. I won't have to do any plumbing really, just replace the existing faucets and attach the wall bracket that anchors the showerhead. I've even located the stud I can hang that on.

Henry doesn't respond. He believes in doing things the right way, so they will last. But I show him pictures on my phone and point out that I can use a shower rod that rings the whole tub, eliminating the need to tile, which eliminates the need to take out the drywall and replace it with waterproof backer board, a job I don't really want to get into. We talk through the one-piece tub-and-shower option again but can't resolve the window problem in a way that suits either of us, so we give that up for good. He looks at the plumbing fixtures on my phone and at my sketches. A customer comes in and then another, and I go back to stocking electrical parts. I go home and read the reviews for the shower-conversion kits, but they all seem to be written about fifteen seconds after the installation is complete, when euphoria is high and no leaks could possibly have occurred. No one has yet slipped and grabbed the riser and ripped it out of the wall. I go back and read the anchoring procedures.

Wednesday morning, I drive to ReStore, mostly so I can feel like I'm doing something related to finishing my bathroom remodel. They have lots of one-piece tub-and-shower combos, none of which I can use, and I've lost interest in them anyway. The tubs, I've read, are plastic and have to be set in a bed of sand to support the bottom. Mine is steel, and I'm happy to keep it. I find lots of showerheads and other bathroom plumbing but nothing like what I want. I also find shower rods, lots of those, mostly in good condition. I don't buy any. They'll be here when I'm ready.

I move on to the shower doors, just in case there is something there that will magically work. There are quite a few that would fit my tub, and I imagine how sleek they would look and how they wouldn't block the light and would be so much nicer than a plastic shower curtain that will billow and also get mildew in humid weather, which is most of the weather we have. I picture the sleek doors, and then I picture myself in the room with them and realize that while a curtain can be pushed entirely out of the way, a shower door can't, and it will essentially put a wall down the middle of the already tiny bathroom. I'll wave my arms around and whack the door. My six-foot-five brother will feel like Gulliver.

And then I see something that makes me forget about shower doors. At the end of the display, I come across two separate tub-enclosure panels that fit together to make a corner with a set of shelves where they meet. I get out my tape measure and my sketch. They will fit the faucet end of the tub and the outside wall next to it almost as far as the window. That will protect the most vulnerable part of the walls, and the shower curtains will do the rest. I measure again to make sure they won't run into the ceiling—they are not made to be cut to fit. I pay for the panels and slide them into the back of my station wagon and go home feeling ready to work.

When I get them into the bathroom, I take down the towel rods and prop up the panels. I go back to reading to make sure I don't need to replace the drywall with backer board, although I'm now convinced that I can manage it. When the Home Depot website assures me that the panels can go up on regular drywall, I'm relieved anyway. I don't get started, though, other than to clean the walls, patch the holes where the towel bars came down, and draw lines to mark the top edges. Now that I've talked about it with Henry so many times, I decide to wait two more days, until I can talk to him again.

I spend most of Thursday applying for jobs, none of which interest me, although I'm now mostly concerned about income and health insurance. I even check the other hardware stores and am relieved when I don't find anything. I submit my last unemployment qualification and resolutely think of something else.

Friday, I get to the store excited, sketches and photos ready to show Henry. He's in the yard, and Matt is clerking. He's glad to see me arrive early and charges out the door. The semester is almost over, and he's got projects due.

The morning rush gradually subsides, but Henry doesn't come inside. I press the button on my intercom and say, "Henry, everything okay out there? Need any help?"

"Be inside in a second. You okay? No code words?"

We now have actual code words in case of emergency, but "code word" has become a shorthand way for all the rest of the employees to tease me about them, since I'm the one who dreamed them up.

"No code words." I sort through the bits of this and that that have collected on the counter, returning some rolls of tape to their hangers and sorting a few dozen screws back into their bins. I wait on a couple of customers, and then Henry walks in looking like the cat that ate the canary. He's pushing a dolly, and on the dolly is a very small bathtub, with a shower conversion kit installed. I walk over and look closely. He's made it up himself out of plumbing we have in stock. It looks just industrial enough to be cool. I walk around it.

"I can't believe you did this. Does this mean you approve?"

"Actually, Andrew did it." Andrew is his younger son, who is just graduating from high school.

"He's been itching to invent something ever since Matt started selling that intercom thing. I was talking about your conundrum at dinner Monday night, and his eyes lit up, and he's spent the last three nights here going through scrap stock. I don't know where he got the tub." Henry rolls his eyes. "Probably under an overpass somewhere. I'm not going to ask."

"So can I buy it? How much is it? It's perfect, isn't it?" It seems much sturdier than the ones I've been looking at. It has two risers, and I grab one and shake it. Solid.

"You can buy it, and I don't know how much yet. But I promised Andrew I would leave it out here on the floor for one week and see if anyone asks about it. You okay with that?"

"Of course, that's totally fine." I want to take it home right now, but I also want to see if it sells. I want it to sell, of course. I love it when the store tries something new and it works. "There are probably a lot of houses around here like mine—still no shower."

"Yeah, well, the guys who come in here are contractors—they've already converted their own."

"We'll see. The local moms come in later in the day. They're the ones who'll see the potential." Assuming I'm not the last house east of Troost with no shower. I have no idea, really. I don't even know if Josie's house has a shower, but I'm thinking it does. The family that put in central air in the 1960s surely remodeled the bath to include a shower stall.

I almost forget about the panels, and when I do remember to show him my photos, it's all an afterthought. He says sure, that's a good idea, and we go back to discussing the shower. I go home and watch YouTube one more time and then put the panels in place. I stand in the tub and pretend to take a shower. I can't wait. Well, I have to wait a week at least, but I can go ahead with the shower curtain rods now so that will be ready when the shower is in, seven days from now.

But none of that happens. At 7:00 p.m., my phone rings and I wonder who is calling me on Friday night. Most people text first, unless something bad has happened. I pull out my phone—Deanna Bailey.

"Deanna, hello."

"Marianne, can you be here Monday morning? Strategy session."

"I can, but is this an interview or a job offer?"

"You talked to Cassie, didn't you? We're putting you on contract for now."

"Okay, I'll need to see the contract. I haven't heard from Cassie since I left your office."

"We'll straighten it out on Monday when you get here," she says, in a tone that says she's not going to straighten it out right now, no matter what.

I don't want to blow this opportunity, since I've got nothing else pending, so I say, "Okay, sounds great. See you Monday." Then I decide to push back just a little. "But I've got a long-standing commitment Tuesday morning, so I'll need to fly home Monday night. Is that okay?" I try for a tone that says that while there might be the slightest bit of wiggle room, she owes me this one.

The long pause that follows unnerves me, but it turns out she's just put me on mute to talk to someone else.

"I'm back," she says, and her tone has changed. Less CEO, more best buddies. "Sure, you can leave Monday night, but make it as late as you can. Look, why don't you come in on Sunday? We can get all the HR stuff out of the way."

HR stuff sounds like a job offer, although I'm not especially happy about that contractor comment earlier. But it's worth a trip to Chicago, so I agree and arrange to text her when I get in. Then I think about travel arrangements. "Wait, one more thing," I say before she can hang up. "Are you making the travel arrangements since I'm not on board yet?"

Another silence, and then she's back and all business again. "Cassie will make the arrangements." So now I'm pretty sure Cassie is in the room. I end the call and wonder how much crap Cassie is getting right now and how much she's going to take it out on me. She won't, I decide. I'm going to be her best friend.

— — —

As it turns out, that doesn't happen. Oh, I try. I show up at the office friendly and cheerful. I breathe and stay cool when Deanna tells me that I'll be on a three-quarter-time contract "for now," reporting to Cassie. "She's my new chief of staff." It sounds like Deanna is not used to saying "chief of staff." I see a glow of victory on Cassie's face, tinged with a smirk. I breathe evenly and turn to Cassie with a smile, no idea what I'm going to say, hoping my face isn't giving me away. "Great," I say. "We'll talk about goals and deliverables when we have a few hours. I assume you've got some background in data management."

"Of course," she says promptly, too promptly. I think about asking her if she's familiar with Beezel software, which I make up on the spot, just to see what she'll say, but decide not to be that mean, especially since she might call me on it.

"Do you have a preferred format for use cases and test cases?" I ask instead. "Maybe you use Jira?"

Cassie looks quickly at Deanna and then puts her chin up and turns back to me. "Oh, that will be up to you and the . . . the guys," she says. "I'm more on the management side." She puts a lot of stress on the word "management."

"You're my direct report." That comes out pretty awkward, but I'm guessing she really wants to say "direct report" out loud. I give her a steady look and a perfectly cooperative smile.

"Got it," I say. "Who else is on our team?"

The thing about working for a man is that he would have taken this conversation at face value and said to himself: *This is working out perfectly. They are great together. I'm brilliant.* But however CEO-ish Deanna has become in her many years of management, she knows this is not off to a good start. I can only hope she's not blaming me. No need to blame Cassie, either, I suppose. Cassie's just trying to put herself out there, get ahead. She probably took a class in empowerment.

Deanna doesn't give anything away; she just picks up the reins. "I can't have everyone report to me, so Cassie is going to take over most of the staff management for the time being." She looks over her glasses at Cassie as she finishes the sentence, then turns back to me. "You're first, because you're first onboard. She'll approve time sheets, and travel and expense reports."

"And weekly reports and evals," Cassie adds quickly, and I wonder how that will work out. Deanna looks at Cassie over her glasses again, and I detect the slightest tightening of lips, a shake of the head that is more implied than real. Cassie looks down. I breathe a little easier and wonder who forced Cassie on Deanna and why Deanna, of all people, let it happen.

I want to sit quietly and see where this goes, but I decide to move us on to what I really want, which is to find out what the contract says in terms of hours, and dollars, and months, and health insurance.

"Maybe we could go over the employment offer," I say, because I want an employment offer and not a contract. "Or 'contract,' did you call it?" I ask innocently.

Deanna gives Cassie a few more seconds of stare and then turns to me. "Excellent," she says cheerfully. "Cassie can do that. I've got a few things to take care of, but interrupt me if you have any questions." She stands up and picks up her cell phone, turning slightly toward the window. Time for us to exit.

"Maybe you could give me an office tour," I say to Cassie as we walk out. She's happy to do that, and it gives us a little time to shake off the posturing and insinuations and questionable juju of the meeting. The tour doesn't take long; most of the office is still a big empty area. Walking into the chilly space, we both take deep breaths and look at each other and laugh, a little self-consciously. I don't press her about how and when the space will be filled. We go back to the furnished area, and she whisks me past the small interior cubicle with her name on it. I pretend not to notice, and we settle in a large conference area with a wide view of Navy Pier.

"This is great," I say, looking out at Lake Michigan. "I love Chicago."

"Oh good—then you'll move here? Deanna was hoping you would, although I know you talked about telecommuting." Cassie would like to give Deanna the good news, a little victory.

"Well, not while I'm just on contract," I say lightly. "Let's take a look at that."

She takes a document out of the envelope she's been carrying around and lays it on the table but doesn't sit.

"I'm just going to run to the ladies' room for a minute," she says and looks at me with a little grimace that tells me she's having a bad period.

"Of course, take all the time you want. I'll just read through this." I look at her. "Maybe coffee would help."

She grimaces again and shakes her head, pressing a hand to her stomach.

"Maybe a Coke then? A tiny bite to eat?"

She gives me a grateful look and disappears. I'm grateful too, for a chance to look this over quietly. I get out a pen and start reading.

A few minutes later, I hear the door open and look up. Deanna sticks her head in and asks if everything is okay.

"Yes, I'm just taking a look at the contract. Cassie's multitasking while I read through it. We're good."

"Multitasking is crap."

"Okay then, let's say I sent her off to see about something

while I read through this carefully." I look up at her. "Beats having to tell you I'm going to let my attorney review it."

She smiles at that and walks over, close enough to see my long list of notes. She tilts her head, raises her eyebrows. "A few problems there?"

"No problems. Cassie will give you solutions." I emphasize the "solutions," and Deanna laughs. Her mantra when we worked together in the past was, "Don't bring me problems, bring me solutions."

She looks at the list again. "I'm looking forward to seeing that," she says and walks out.

Cassie gets back a few minutes later and looks better. She sees my list and says, "I don't think we can change anything."

"Just a few things; let's take them one at a time."

I start with things I don't really care much about so we can get past them and feel like we're making progress. I tell her a one-year contract is too long, I'd like to convert to regular staff within six months. She tells me the legal team says all employment contracts are to be one year. I'm not looking at her but hear the catch at the end that tells me she's given away something she wasn't supposed to. It must be "legal team." The company is too small at this point to have a legal team. Something is up. But I don't really care about the one-year term, so I tell her that's fine and cross it off my list. She smiles brightly.

I do care about the hours, and the contract says three-quarter time, thirty hours a week. I decide to let her have this one, since I can keep working at Henry's. I tell her that thirty hours is okay for now and tell her I can work ten-hour days Monday, Wednesday, and Thursday, and that if necessary, I can schedule calls for Tuesday and Friday afternoons. She makes a note, and I check that off my list. She's happy.

Health insurance is trickier. It's not mentioned in the contract, and I'm sure it's not going to be available, but I ask her the question anyway. She knows the answer and tells me it's not possible. I tell her I'm going to be honest with her, and then I tell her how much I pay for insurance. "So the solution is easy," I say. "Just add that much to the contract. Or better, don't add it to the rate— include a monthly 'in lieu of benefits' amount. And remember, I'm not asking for the other typical employee benefits. I won't be getting any 401(k) or life insurance or anything. No vacation, and no pay for holidays."

She looks a little worried, but I can't tell if it's astonishment about not getting vacation or fear of taking this to Deanna, so I encourage her. "It's just accounting," I say, "and probably within your scope to decide." She straightens up a bit at that and makes a note without commenting.

That hurdle passed, I read through some routine contract stuff and ask her bland questions about it, just to sally along before I tackle the big issue. She doesn't know about a company credit card, so I tell her it's fine, just a question, and she can get back to me tomorrow. I give her a few more assignments like that, and she seems happy to have a managerial-type to-do list. All is going well.

"So just one last thing," I say, "and that's the hourly rate. The going rate for this sort of work is about 35 percent higher than this." I don't really have any idea, but I want to make about as much as I used to, so that's the figure I give her. She blanches, as I knew she would.

"Or more, in some geographies, but I live in Kansas City, so we'll stay with thirty-five." She opens her mouth, but I don't want her to say anything yet, because she is inexperienced enough to stick with whatever she says first, thinking that's what a hard-nosed manager would do.

"And I know it's a new position in a new company, so you

two"—I include Deanna to make her feel less at fault—"you two are still figuring it out. I can send you some statistics if you want." I'm pretty sure she doesn't want, so I press a little to make sure she doesn't want statistics: "Means, medians, corrected for geography, and with a gender spread."

"But that's more than I make," she says, and now I know the real issue. Statistics won't get us around this. But knowledge is power, and I use it.

"Oh," I say, as if this were the easiest thing in the world. "That's okay. I've had people report to me who made more than I did. It's very common, especially when you are chief of staff. You'll have all kinds of people reporting to you." I let that sink in and then deliver the carrot. "And it helps keep your salary at the top of the grade." I give her a conspiratorial smile, nodding. She smiles back, and I make the change in the contract and initial it, then flip back and add the "in lieu of" sentence and initial that, and finally turn to the end and sign and date the document.

"There you go, good work!" I tell her, and stand up. "I'm going to get coffee. Want some?"

She's savvy enough to see that I'm giving her a chance to run off and talk to Deanna if she wants to, so she says no to coffee, and I take my time going to the ladies' room myself, and then I putter in the kitchen for several minutes. I'm still there, sipping a glass of water and reading the bulletin board for the third time, when Cassie rushes in.

"There you are!" she says. "She agreed to everything! You start tomorrow—we forgot about start date. Just initial that part here."

I suppose that means I'm not getting paid for today, but that's okay. I initial, and she says she's leaving now and will see me tomorrow, and impulsively gives me a hug. "Oh, Deanna said to stop in and see her before you go back to the hotel. She has a question about the user cases."

I don't correct her, and I saunter off to find Deanna. She's on the phone, so I miss my chance to make an entrance. She's standing up while she talks and motions for me to sit down. She's planning to be in charge.

But no—when she hangs up, she reaches across the desk and shakes my hand. "Welcome aboard," she says and sits. "You were ruthless," she goes on, leafing through the contract she's already signed.

"You got off cheap," I shoot back, and we both laugh. "But what's the deal? All hurry and then nothing, and all of a sudden, I start tomorrow?"

"What do you think?"

"I think you're being acquired."

"Cassie let it out of the bag?"

"Come on, I've been to this rodeo before. I recognize the signs."

"So Cassie did let it out of the bag."

"No, seriously. She did not. Mostly it was the radio silence and then being brought in on contract. Either the buyer won't let you hire actual employees, because they don't want to have to lay them off, or you're trying to make payroll look small. I know the tricks."

"Okay, you got me. We are out of the quiet phase as of today, so I can at least tell you now, although it's still not for public knowledge."

"So who is it, the buyer?"

"Oh, it's just investment bankers buying up this and that. They are going to use our name, though, and start integrating some other acquisitions into our org."

I heave a great sigh. "Okay, so this is about system integration more than data management. You want me to do systems integration."

"Yes. Well, we do need to do data management for the Magetech system—that's a real thing. But I'll let you find someone to do the heavy lifting there, once integrations start. You good with that?"

I heave another sigh. "I am." And I really am, mostly. Investment bankers are usually in it to buy and sell quickly, which could make this a short gig, but better than a gig with Kelly Services.

We go out for a drink, and I know she can hold her liquor a lot better than I can, so I have one glass of wine and switch to fizzy water. I wait until she's near the end of her second single malt.

"So really, you can't put me on an org chart reporting to Cassie. You know how it is the minute the takeover is announced. All the jockeying. No one will take my calls if I'm reporting to Cassie. Unless you hire a bunch of guys—lawyers and your heads of state like finance and IT, and put them all under Cassie. Then I'm good with it."

She sighs this time. "I thought women were supposed to lean in now, help each other. Didn't you read Sheryl Sandberg?"

"I leaned in all afternoon. Cassie learned all kinds of things from me today."

"Yeah, I hope I don't regret that. 'It's just accounting.' Sheesh."

"I'll lean, but not so far I get trampled on. Because that would be a problem. And the solution is a C-suite boss."

"Okay, you win. I'll make it happen. Just not this week—agreed?"

She signals for the check, and we go our separate ways. I walk out to the end of the pier and go back to the hotel and read.

Monday is all business, data management for the Magetech system. We write out high-level use cases and system requirements and decide that in the interest of a fast start, we will go with the vendor we already know can meet the requirements, unless we hit a fatal flaw. I'm amazed at how much the engineers have come around about data management since we last discussed it. They are now the ones insisting on cloud storage and system flexibility. I call my vendor contact and set up a conference call for Wednesday afternoon. Late in the day, I stop by Cassie's desk and tell her we both need accounts for conference calls and ask if that's something she can approve. She says she'll get them set up, as I knew she would. It's not management, but it's something she can do and check off.

Before I get in my cab, I stop to say goodbye to Deanna.

"Leaving already? I saw you want off Tuesday and Friday mornings. What gives?"

"I'm just part-time here, remember?" I say as casually as possible. "I've got commitments I can't get out of when I've just got a part-time job. Let me know when you want me back here."

"I'm pretty sure you'll be back here when you think you need to be. Just bcc me on your weekly reports." She turns back to the call she's had on mute and waves me off. On the way to the airport, I realize the loaner laptop the IT guy gave me puts me over the carry-on limit and I'm going to have to check luggage, which I don't have time to do now. I repack in the back of the cab, stuffing everything I can into my small suitcase and then trying to cram the laptop case into my backpack. It won't work. It's a generic free case anyway. When I get to the gate at Midway, I shake out all the pockets, turn it wrong side out so it doesn't look like abandoned luggage, and leave it in a trash can. I get on the plane and start making lists for the rest of the week. Life is different now.

CHAPTER 41

Tuesday morning, I'm up early thinking about Magetech. I have to remind myself that this morning my job is hardware, as in hardware store, not computer hardware. I start off up the hill, which magically shifts my attention to the right place. By the time I walk in the door, I'm excited about seeing my shower set up near the checkout counter. But I don't—it's not there. As usual, the store is busy, and I take over the register while Matt picks up his backpack and gets ready to head off to his lab.

"By the way," he says as he leaves, "Andrew is here. He's getting a new shower thing ready for you." Jerry is next in line, and I get on the intercom and pass on his lumber order. While I'm ringing up nails and sealants, he asks about the shower.

"You adding a basement shower at home or something?"

"Got that already. I'm putting one in the bathroom now. Over the tub. I wanted one where the plumbing stays outside the wall, you know what I mean? Replaces the tub faucets, has a riser directly from the faucets?" I wave my arms, demonstrating. "Andrew made one for me last week—it was right over there. But it's gone now. Maybe someone bought it off the floor." I'm very casual, trying to gauge his reaction without staring at him.

"Hmm, I guess I saw that yesterday," he says and takes his slip outside and off to the yard.

"How's that work, the shower thing?" says the next guy in line, Duncan Friedman. I flip through my phone and show him a few pictures.

"Only the one Andrew made is better, sturdier," I say.

"You guys watching cat videos? I'm in a hurry here." The guy in line behind Duncan is waiting.

"Just plumbing stuff. See?" I hold up my phone, but he's not interested. I check him out quickly, and he leaves, still muttering about cat videos.

I shrug my shoulders and turn back to Duncan. "Sounds like Andrew is making up another one."

"Mmmp," he says and plunks down a double handful of small items. I ring them up and process his credit card. "Andrew around?" he asks.

I speak into the intercom and tell Andrew someone has a question at the front counter. As far as I know, Drew has never gotten a call to the front. He practically skids to a stop. "Huh?"

I nod toward Duncan, and the two of them start talking. I wait on the next customer, and when I'm through with him, I notice that Duncan and Andrew have both disappeared.

When Henry comes to the front of the store around ten, Andrew is with him and talking nonstop. Henry tells him to take a breath and asks me if all is well. I assure him that nothing unusual has happened and raise my eyebrows in Andrew's direction.

"So this woman, on Saturday, she comes in for, I don't know, a hose or something. She'd been down the street at Van Liew's— buying a fountain or whatever—and needed something they didn't have. She came in here all nervous like, like I don't know, like maybe we were some kind of man-zone place."

I can picture this. "Sounds like someone from the Kansas side who heard about Van Liew's but had never ventured east of Troost."

"Yeah, she was from Prairie Village. Anyway, she comes in and sees your shower thing and says, like, 'I have got to have that for my pool house.' And I was working at the counter"—working at the counter is new, since he turned eighteen—"and so I sold it to her."

"Nice!" I say to him. "How much?"

He takes a quick look at his dad. "Three hundred. I think she would have paid more though." He looks back at me, eyes blazing. "*And then*, right at closing time, this other woman roars up in a BMW and wants one just like it for her birdbath, except not really like it at all as it turns out. I guess she was a friend of the first woman. So I say"—he pauses dramatically and looks at his dad, who is smiling proudly—"I say, 'Oh, a custom job, no problem. Let's talk about some options.' And so *we did*, and now I have a commission for this awesome bird thing."

I put him on pause with a significant look and tend to a few customers. Henry drags him off to the back, and I can hear them talking about copper piping, and welding versus solder. Henry comes back alone.

"Pretty amazing," I say.

"Yeah, I just wish it had all been one week later, after his finals. But yes, it's great to see him so excited."

I check out another customer and send him on his way and then turn back to Henry.

"You know," he says, "I never expected either boy to want to take over the store. I mean, I do it because I like it but mostly to make sure they can go to college and do whatever they want. But still, it feels good when they get charged up about something related to hardware." He stops and chuckles a little. "Birdbaths, oh my. I blame you, with your Christmas schmaltz." But I know he's kidding.

"Think I'll ever get my shower made, or should I just buy

something dreary on Amazon?" I'm kidding too, and he knows it. "Or wait, I've got a vision. I want sound effects, a rumble of thunder, maybe birds chirping."

"Oh no, don't say that around Drew—he'll actually do it."

"Well, he actually should offer that, just not to me."

I rush home at noon, head full of Magetech, and am startled when I pass Flynn's house and he calls out to me. I've never seen him on my way to and from work, and I generally avoid walking past his house otherwise.

"I'm planting tomatoes. You want some plants?" he says.

"I've already got mine," I lie without pausing. "But thanks." I hurry on down the hill and turn on my laptop.

The rest of the day, and the next two days, are full of Magetech conference calls and use cases and test cases. Thursday night, I text Cassie asking when and how she wants my hours and expenses. I don't hear back, but I write up a report on the week's progress and send it off to her, bcc to Deanna. By then, it's close to midnight and I'm exhausted.

Friday morning, I wake up with a headache and leave for the store a few minutes later than usual. I think about driving, but I know I need the exercise, so I take my coffee with me and start off at a brisk pace. I make it through the door before seven, on time but later than usual, and see a wave of relief pass across Matt's face.

"Here," he says, taking off his cap and slapping it on my head. "Gotta git." I take over in midsale.

It's busier than usual for a Friday, and I don't even think to look around for my shower until after nine. I see the miniature clawfoot tub but no shower. An hour later, Henry asks over the intercom if there are any more contractors who might want something from the yard, and I say no. "Coming up front then," he says. "I'll lock the gate today."

He brings a new shower setup with him, this one a little different. It's sleek and shiny chrome, or maybe stainless steel. "This one isn't yours," he says before I can ask. "I made this one so Drew can finish up his last term paper today. Yours is in the back. I had to hide it so he wouldn't sell it. We've created a monster."

"A profit-making monster, I hope."

"Oh yeah, I told him that's the first rule."

"So is he selling garden art or actual bathroom plumbing?"

"Two garden, two bathroom—three, if you count yours."

"I'll count it when I get it . . . which is when?"

"For you, a special deal—he wants to install it himself. Tomorrow morning? I'll tell him ten if that's good for you."

I detect a smile that Henry is suppressing, but I decide not to call him on it. We move on to what's going on in the store, and I ask him about the Avon Skin So Soft that Duncan bought.

"I got that in for you," Henry says, fluttering his eyelashes. "It's back there with the Deep Woods Off."

"I never saw it back there before."

"Well, Duncan came in saying the Off stuff gave him a rash, and Jerry said his wife sells Avon, so there it is. See, thin end of the wedge—you brought in all that Christmassy stuff, and now we've become an Avon distributor." He rolls his eyes to heaven as though the worst possible catastrophe has occurred.

"I'm going to hit the panic button if you don't stop that. Get you hauled to the loony bin." He fakes a super-serious face. "But you know what?" I go on. "You should have three or four of the little bottles sitting here by the register. So guys can just slip it in with the rest of their stuff, all casual."

Henry rolls his eyes again.

"See, that's why. They know you'll give them a hard time.

When I'm here, they'll just slip it in and buy it and put it in their pockets and be gone. Hope you got a good markup going."

We both get busy with customers, and when it calms down again, Henry asks about my new job.

"How did you know I was working?"

"Oh, I heard you on the phone. Thought you'd say something."

"Well, this is my first week. It's part-time, and it's only contract, so it could end any at any moment."

"Any job could end any time," he says rather grimly. "Even when you're the boss man." He looks around.

"You mean the store?" I must sound panicked. I am panicked. I can't stand the thought of the store closing.

"No, no, no. Don't worry. We're fine. Fine enough, anyway. But there were a few years when we weren't. I just meant that any job can disappear."

"Oh thank God," I say, and I mean it. "I'm still employed then? Here, I mean."

"Of course, unless you're ready to give it up. You look like you've had a long week."

"I have, but it's the first week—I'm still trying to remember everyone's name, all the new acronyms. Trying to make a good impression. Next week will be easier and the next week even easier. Unless you don't need me with the boys out of school for the summer?"

"Andrew's starting at Mizzou in the fall, so he'll be gone before we know it, and of course he has his sideline now." Henry looks at the tub and rolls his eyes just a little. The odd little grin comes back and disappears. "Matt is taking more business classes this summer. He's putting grad school on hold for a year while he decides between math and business." He rolls his eyes for real this time, but I can see that he's actually proud. "I'm going to have him do more back-office stuff this summer to get a little feel for it. Ordering, payroll, that sort of thing. And the work schedule. So you can work out your hours with him. If you need to trade days or shifts sometimes, for example."

Walking home, I decide that maybe I will cut back to one morning a week. I'm pretty tired, and I've still got one more conference call this afternoon. Today I walk home on Chestnut instead of my own street, avoiding Flynn even as I tell myself not to be ridiculous. He's probably just being neighborly and that's all.

The day ends with a frantic call from Cassie, in a panic because I didn't submit my hours or my expenses.

"I'm not an actual employee, remember? I can't use the online systems. Just let me know what I need to do, and I'll do it."

I reassure her that it's just startup growing pains, not her fault, things will settle down soon. I hang up, swear a few times, and then send her an email with a list of my hours and my expenses. I bcc Deanna, just in case there is ever a question. Cassie can manager up and figure out what forms she needs to approve.

CHAPTER 42

Andrew shows up right on time Saturday morning and sets about installing the shower. He asks for my phone so he can enter his cell phone number in case I have any problems. He frowns as he's doing that and then hands the phone back. "Needs your passcode for some reason," he mumbles. I enter it and notice that he's got the same suppressed grin going on that his dad did yesterday when we talked about Andrew doing the installation. Those two are up to something.

Cassie texts me with login information to the time-and-expense system, and I close my eyes and stop myself from texting back, "What kind of idiot are you? Don't EVER text usernames and passwords together." Instead, I log in, do what needs to be done, and change my password to CassieisanID10T. I've got to assume that passwords are encrypted and impossible for anyone to see. I think about that for a minute and change my password to AtLeastIHaveAJob. I log out and go to ReStore for shower curtain rods—although I end up buying flanges and pipe to go with the slightly industrial look of the shower hardware. On the way home, I stop at Target for the curtains. No flimsy dollar store curtains—I have a job!

Josie comes over after dinner for ice cream and catching up on neighborhood gossip, which is pretty sparse. She is more interested in my job, specifically how much travel I might have, meaning how often she will get to keep Boris for me. I tell her I'll probably go to Chicago every couple of weeks and that since I'm working and since it's more than just occasional dog sitting, I need to start paying her. She waves that off, and I insist. She stares me down and says that if I pay her, she won't do it, and I cry uncle, and that's the end of that. I'll pay in cookies or ice cream or something, I tell myself. In California, in-kind payment is always in wine. Here, it's tricky. Josie drinks wine if I serve it, but it's not something she would offer to guests, or drink alone, so there's no point in giving it to her. Maybe it's a Baptist thing, although I suspect it's just a Josie thing. I asked her about it once. "Jesus drank wine," she said with a casual toss of her head. "But I don't think he served it. Course, he wouldn't serve it, would he? Women's work, serving." I don't argue that he served it at least once, at the Last Supper. I'm not up for a cross-denominational discussion of transubstantiation. I can bring her Frango mints from Chicago. Everyone loves those.

Dog question settled to Josie's satisfaction, she goes home to watch cop shows, and I decide to call it quits and go to bed. I turn on the shower, feeling like I should christen it with champagne or something. I hear a low rumble of thunder and remember my mother's insistence that we not fill the tub during electrical storms. I can't remember anyone else ever saying that, so I adjust the temperature, note with satisfaction that nothing is leaking, and get in. The thunder is louder, and I hear the crack of lightning, very close by. Where did this come from? I'm now used to Missouri's famously changeable weather, but surely I would have noticed when I was watching Josie walk to her door. One more crack, and I realize that the sound is coming from inside the house. It dawns on me—those father and son grins. I leave the shower on, get out, grab a towel, and pick up my phone. A thunderstorm video is playing. I turn off the shower, and the video goes away. That's why Andrew needed my password. He was installing an app. I send him and his dad a text: "Okay, you got me! But if I find a camera in the showerhead, you will both be hit with something worse than lightning!"

I get back in the tub. Showering with thunderstorm sound effects is pretty cool, I decide.

CHAPTER 43

On Sunday, I stop on the way home from church to buy tomato and pepper plants, which I had intended all along to start from seed but never did. I back far into the driveway and take them in the back door, as if Flynn would somehow see me and know I was lying to him yesterday. I spend the afternoon planting, putting up the rabbit fence, and getting stakes ready, knowing that the plants will sit there and do nothing, and then one day I'll look out and they'll be sprawled all over, too late to tie up.

By four o'clock, I'm ready for an early supper and a relaxing glass of wine. This time when I step into the shower, I'm ready for the thunder. Instead, I get seagulls and crashing waves. Well, that's pretty nice too.

The next week goes by quickly, and on Friday morning, I get a text from Deanna that the acquisition is complete. Five minutes later, I get a call from Cassie saying that I'm on regular payroll with benefits now, although still at thirty hours a week. I drop everything and sign up for health insurance and get back one email confirming my enrollment and a second telling me about the health program I have to complete to qualify for the preferred health plan next year. Will I even be here next year? I like to think it's an omen, even though I know it's just an automated email from the third-party provider. I scroll through the requirements and set a reminder for Friday afternoons to work through one online class a week until I've accrued enough points in the Learn! category. In the Act! category, the easiest seems to be recording steps—I have to average ten thousand a day. Piece of cake, I think. I walk all the time. They'll even send me a Fitbit. I sign up and get a message back that the Fitbit will arrive on Tuesday. I'm psyched—a real job at last. Well, three-quarters of a job.

An hour later, I get a text from Cassie telling me that I need to be in Chicago the following week. We quibble about dates, and she eventually agrees that I can arrive by midafternoon on Tuesday but have to stay through Friday. I call Matt and ask if I can reschedule Friday morning, maybe for the following Tuesday afternoon. He says, "Oh, right, that's on me now. I'll get back to you." I guess this is his first schedule upset.

As I end the call, the doorbell rings, and I look at Boris. He looks back but doesn't get up. So it's someone who doesn't interest him—not a threat, not a friend. It must be Flynn. I think about ignoring the bell, pretending I'm not here. But there's my car in the driveway. I don't want him going around back looking for me. I head for the door. I keep my phone in my hand, though, earbuds attached.

"Hi, Flynn, how's it going? Nice day, huh?" I notice that he's dressed a little better than usual. New jeans, shirt tucked in. Still the same Royals cap, though.

He glances behind him as if to check the weather. Nervous.

"We could get a drink sometime," he says in a rush, like he's practiced. "Or something. I was going to get some chicken—you could come over for dinner. I got ice cream too." Apparently he's running through all the lines he's practiced. I give him a warm smile. It's been obvious that this would happen sooner or later, and I've decided not to duck it. I've practiced my lines too.

STILL NEEDS WORK

"Like a date?" I say, watching his face closely. "Something like that?" He turns red and nods slightly.

"Oh, Flynn, that's nice of you. It really is. But you have to know that I'm not dating." It's lame, but it's true. "You know my husband just died, not that long ago." I state it like a fact, although he may or may not know. "We were married a long time, and I'm . . . well. . . ." I stop there, not sure I ever practiced a good ending. He puts a hand out tentatively, palm down, as if to comfort me.

I tense and then grab the hand awkwardly and shake it.

"We're neighbors, family friends from way back," I say. Unrehearsed. I hope it goes somewhere good. "Just that. We'll always have each other's back, like good neighbors do," I go on, motioning at the nearby houses. "We're all tight here." We're not; he's not part of the little pod just north of Seventieth Street. I hardly even know anyone on his side. But I know we'd all rally if we needed to. "That's the way we need to keep it. No complications. Right?"

I'm nodding, willing him to nod too. If we can get past this moment, I can stop avoiding walking past his house when I'm out with the dog and stop feeling that shred of guilt. "Right? We're pals, that's all. That's better, really. Don't you think?" I shove a question in there to get him to reply.

He's not stupid, and he's a kind man and essentially cheerful. "Yep, that's right," he says, not really cheerful right now. But the nervousness is gone. "Yep, well, gotta get on with. . . ." I don't catch what it is, but he's turning now. "Good to see you."

"You too, Flynn."

I close the door and wish I'd offered him some of the cookies I made last weekend. But no, better not. Who knows what he might give me in return. I'm relieved that this is over, and I think there's at least a chance that he's relieved too. I'm not going to avoid walking past his house anymore.

CHAPTER 44

When I see the first two weeks' pay appear in my bank account, I feel some weight lift. I celebrate with a ten-dollar bottle of wine and a hot fudge sundae, not at the same time. When the next pay appears, I'm in Chicago, and I walk along Michigan Avenue to Hanig's shoe store. I admire the Thierry Rabotin styles that Deanna wears but don't even try them on. I go to Bloomingdale's next and find a Chicago-suitable pair for a quarter of the price of the Thierry Rabotins. They are nicer than the Dansk clogs and the one pair of dress shoes I've been wearing over and over. But that's all I'm willing to spend just yet.

I'm reluctant to give up my hours at Midtown Hardware, and I tell myself that it's because I'm only working thirty hours a week. Or rather, I'm getting paid for thirty hours. I'm working forty or more, and I remind Cassie about this at least once a week. As far as I can tell, everyone else is on a regular forty-hour deal. I use the job at Henry's to insist on not spending full weeks in Chicago, although I don't tell anyone exactly why I can't be there full-time. I do arrange with Matt to work Monday mornings instead of Tuesday, though, which makes it harder for the Chicago team to complain. I try entering forty hours in the timekeeping system, but it rejects anything that adds up to more than thirty. So while I complain at the office, I also want to keep a toe in at Henry's. I'm just not confident that Magetech is forever.

So far, all the work I've done is on the new Magetech system, which we are frantically trying to get ready for our test client. Nothing more has been said about integrating new acquisitions. I seldom see Deanna, and I assume she's working on acquiring more companies. The great big empty space in the office has a few people now, but I haven't met anyone. They keep to themselves and don't seem to be associated with Magetech. Cassie says she doesn't know who they are, and I believe her. She seems put out that she can't answer any questions about them.

Finally, I corner Deanna one evening and tell her that the forty-five-hour weeks at thirty-hour pay have to stop. I'm not quite ready to resign over it, so I try to keep a casual tone. The way I actually say it is: "So, what's up with the thirty-hour thing?"

"What are you talking about?"

"The thirty-hour limit you've got me on. I'm working forty to fifty hours and getting paid for thirty."

She looks at me as though considering how to answer. I wonder if Cassie is the roadblock here or if it's something else. I'm confident that it's not my performance.

"I did give Cassie a budget, and I assume she's doing her best to stay in it," Deanna says carefully.

"Is that why she's always telling me I need to move here? And last week, she asked if I could drive instead of fly." I don't add the sarcastic, *Can't she do the math on that?* that is on the tip of my tongue.

Deanna shakes her head. "I know she's inexperienced." She doesn't elaborate. "But we can't have you working like that." She considers again.

I realize that I've brought her a problem instead of a solution and consider saying that I propose just stopping when I've got thirty hours in, but I don't think she'll be amused. I reconsider and decide that I have given her a solution, or at least that the solution is obvious: switch me to full time. I wait.

"It won't be much longer," she finally says, and my heart drops. Does she mean the job is ending, or that the hours will increase? I decide to wait, not ask. I put on an expectant face and look her in the eye.

"I can give you some shares," she says carefully, and I make sure my face doesn't react. "And some stock options." She looks to see how that goes over. I hold her gaze. "And I think a spot bonus might be in order." She says that with some finality, so I smile and nod once.

"How much are we talking about?" I won't be put off with a hundred shares of no-value stock and a hundred-dollar bonus that will end up much less after the tax is extracted.

"How does this sound? One thousand bonus, paid now, a thousand shares outright, and let's say six thousand in options, exercisable over six years. Or on sale of the company, if that should happen." She says it all so simply that I know this isn't a stretch. She probably has a hundred times that many shares.

"That sounds good," I say. "I'll stop whining and get back to work."

She laughs but stops me. "I don't have to tell you that no part of that is to be repeated."

"No, you do not," I reply, and now I know that she is working on reselling the company. Which is no surprise, since that is what investment bankers do, but it's deflating, a little. Still, I've survived acquisitions in the past. I resolve to put my head down and focus on making the Magetech product sing.

CHAPTER 45

I've been in Chicago so much that I rarely see my neighbors, other than picking up and dropping off Boris at Josie's. Sometimes, for fun, I even skip that: I text Josie, we both open our front doors, and he races into her house in about four bounds. But around Memorial Day, I'm home for five days and the forecast is for no rain, so I invite my nearest neighbors over. Most of them have plans, so we reschedule for Sunday afternoon and then move it to Josie's driveway, which isn't sloped like mine and has a carport for shade. Dave and Carol from across the street wheel their grill down Josie's driveway, and Jennie brings both potato salad and cupcakes, along with Felicity. Bud follows a few minutes later with watermelon and his service dog and Waggo. We put all the dogs in my backyard, since it's fenced but they can still see us. Felicity goes back and forth between the two yards constantly, mostly, I think, because she's entranced with opening and closing the gate and telling the dogs to stay. They all go along with it, although Boris licks her face every chance he gets.

Patrick and Liz come by a little later with their baby, and we all relax and eat hot dogs and hamburgers and potato chips and talk about the weather and how the tomato plants are coming along and what's new in the neighborhood. The house next to Josie is vacant again, and we all think hard about who we might know who would want to rent it. I find out that Jennie's job with the senior-care referral company didn't turn out so well, and I feel guilty until she goes on and tells me that she found a better job as an office manager for a small consulting firm on Troost. Liz has been keeping Felicity, but she's going to start at the Montessori preschool on Prospect in the fall.

"It just costs seventy-five a week, and it's so close. She's just going to love it there. She's already asking how long till she can start school."

I'm excited too, although it means that no one is home during the day looking out for the neighborhood. I am surprised at how much I've come to appreciate that. Jennie is still talking.

"You know, I loved working at home, but now that I'm back in an office, I realize that I really want to be around people." She wiggles her body. "You know, in the same room. It's not like just talking to one person at a time on the phone, even if I talk to a lot of people. You know?"

I tell her yes, I do know, and I do sort of understand. But as much as I'm liking being part of the team in Chicago, it is often wearing, and I can't wait to escape to my hotel room. And I realize that my traveling leaves a hole in Josie's security system, even if it does mean she's got my scary-looking dog right there in her house. She doesn't seem to mind as much as I do, but I wonder.

I get some questions about my job, but no one's really interested in the details, which are pretty obscure. They are more interested in Chicago and what the job means for me in terms of one thing: am I going to move to Chicago? They don't come right out and ask. They just ask if all the travel is getting to be too much, and isn't it pretty cold there in the winter? Too cold, really. I finally get it when Dave says, "You're there so much—I suppose they want you to move?" His tone says, "Although I'm sure you wouldn't," but his eyes say, "Are you going to leave us?"

and I mentally fill in the next bit: *Are we going to have another vacant house on the block?*

I decide to ignore the badgering I've been getting from Cassie, who has her own reasons for wanting me, still the only person reporting to her, to be visible, and truthfully tell them that it hasn't come up. I see faces relax a little and add that Chicago is cold and expensive and that I don't know anything about it beyond downtown. "I've had enough upheaval," I add for good measure. "The last thing I want is to start over again." That seems to satisfy them. Nothing is for certain, especially on this side of Troost, but they can stop worrying about a vacant house, another FOR SALE sign, at least for the moment.

Felicity is sitting on the Christmas swing, which is too big for her to swing by herself. We take turns getting up and pushing her, although not often enough for her.

"Somebody!" she shouts, and her mother tells her to ask nicely. I watch her grab at Boris's collar and huff in frustration. She puckers her mouth and narrows her eyes and slides off the swing. She comes up to me with a huge smile. She's grown past the stage when she led with both hands, grabbing a leg or a waist to get attention. Now she leads with a winning face and a tilt of her head. "Boris needs his leash," she announces, head nodding very seriously.

I think I know where this is going, so I play along.

"Okay, I'll go get it. Maybe you could come help me, and we can get some more ice." I look at her mother, who is talking to Liz about Montessori, and she nods. Felicity tells Boris to stay, and we go up the step into my yard, through the gate, and across the grass. As we round the corner to go in the back door, I stop short. Two young men are huddled at the door.

"Hello?" They turn at the sound, and I hear the tinkle of dog tags. "Sit," I say and hold out a hand to stop Boris if he doesn't sit.

He does, although I can tell he doesn't want to. The men, boys really, are staring at Boris.

"Felicity, go tell your mom we're out of ice." I can't think of any other way to get her away while I figure this out. She goes.

"Now, what can I do for you two?" I've been inching forward, swinging wide around them, forcing them to spin around too. I see they are wearing black suits and ties and carrying books.

"We're. . . ." The speaker looks at the other kid as though he's forgotten who they are.

"Joe-vers Witnessers," the second one finishes.

"Ah. I see. Do you always go to the back door?"

"Um. Ma'am. No one answered, so we were trying the back to. . . ."

"We were going to leave this," the second one finishes again. He holds up a piece of paper. I guess they've practiced a script, although maybe they didn't practice enough.

I should send them away, but I don't. I nod and inch toward the gate. I can hear Felicity talking. "*Two mans*," I hear her say.

"Men," her mother corrects her automatically. "*Mens. Two mens*." Felicity says.

"Well, I'm having a little picnic with my neighbors," I say. "Why don't you come over and talk to all of us?" I wonder how I'm going to pull this off, but at least Felicity has given the rest of them some sort of clue, assuming they believe her. I move closer to the gate, put my hand on it. I see Dave's head appear around the front corner of my house.

"I'll just close this." Now they are kind of stuck going next door. "Come on," I say and shoo them ahead of me. "What were your names again?"

"Uh, I'm . . . uh . . . Joe," the first one mumbles.

Before he gets it out, the second one says, "Joe." They've gone off script.

"Both Joes?"

They look at each other. "Yeah. . . uh . . . ma'am." So "má'am" is in the script somewhere. I wonder if it's their script or someone else's.

We've arrived at Josie's patio.

"Hey, everybody, meet the Joes. They are. . . ." I turn to them. "What did you say you were?" I want to hear it again.

"Joe-vah's Witnessers." They are more confident this time.

Josie snorts. Carol suppresses a snicker. Dave comes back down Josie's driveway toward us. He doesn't sit down, and he doesn't look amused.

"See?" Felicity says, proud of herself.

I tell them to help themselves to food, and they look around, realize they are trapped, and pick up hot dogs. They turn down mustard and ketchup. Josie is looking more amused than ever.

"So what did you want to tell us?" she asks them, all innocence. "Oh, is that *The Watchtower*? I love reading that." She snatches the boy's copy. It seems to be the only one he has, and it's in bad shape. I'm pretty sure it's spent at least one night in the gutter. She starts reading bits and pieces out loud and asking the boys questions. They mumble and make up some answers and say "sir" and "ma'am" a lot. Carol picks up the questioning and starts asking where they live and go to school and if they play baseball.

A black car pulls up and blocks Josie's driveway, and I panic for a moment, thinking it's their handlers. It's clear these aren't Jehovah's Witnesses, and I've been hoping that our little charade will nip their ill-formed burglary plan, if that's what it was, in the bud. Josie and Carol are talking seriously to them now about what classes they are taking and where they are going to apply to college. I pull out my phone to call 911 when I see that it's the Community Relations police car. Officer Carl is walking casually down the driveway. I'm guessing Dave called when he peeked around and saw them talking to me at my back door.

The boys see him and look around for an exit but apparently decide that running is a worse option than brazening it out.

Carl walks up, says hello all around, and gets introduced to the Joes.

"Two Joes, huh? Don't run into that very often. Got any ID? Usually, the JWs let us know when they're in the neighborhood. We want to keep an eye on you, right? Make sure you don't come to any harm." He's very smooth. "Why don't we have a little chat? Maybe I can give you a lift back to your ride. It's getting a little late." He's got them under his spell now, and they move off down the driveway.

We all look at Felicity, who says, "What?" in a loud voice.

"Come here, I'll push you," I say to her. I lift her up and put her in the swing facing away from the patio. I give her a push, and we make loud swinging noises, which gives the others time to talk about what happened. After a few pushes, she turns to me and asks, "Was those mans good mans?"

"Men, Felicity. One man, two men."

"Yeah, but was they good mens? Cuz Boris doesn't think so. See, he's protecking me."

I look at Boris, who is standing midway down the driveway, tail waving slowly. I think he's hoping Carl will come back and pet him.

"I don't know," I tell Felicity. "But I think they could be."

Carl and the "witnessers" leave, and we go back to talking about how much we like the motion-detector lights that Bud installed for me months ago. Liz asks about them, and I let Bud tell her the details, only adding that I do have to knock down the spider webs occasionally to keep them from turning on at random.

The sun gets low, and we start picking up the leftovers before the mosquitoes come. I see Flynn at the end of the driveway and invite him in. He fills a plate and eats standing up. He starts out talking to me, but I move away and leave him to others. They don't know him well but are friendly enough. I hear him mention that we go way back and wonder if I'll need to explain later. We continue picking up and sharing leftovers, and I tell Flynn it was good to see him and gently shoo him off with everyone else. We all pick up our dishes and say goodnight to Josie, and once again I say that we need to put a gate between my yard and Bud and Jennie's, just like the one between my yard and Josie's. Bud offers to do it, and I say I'll take care of it. I make a last trip to Josie's to make sure we haven't forgotten anything, and she asks me to come in and look at her kitchen light for her. I assume that's code for wanting to talk about the boys in black.

"Why did you say that to Bud?" she demands as soon as the door is closed behind me.

"What?"

"He said he would put in a gate, and you shut him down." She's got her hands on her hips and is almost glaring.

"I just thought. . . ." I start, but Josie interrupts.

"No, you didn't *thought*," she says. "He wants to do his share, pull his weight, make things up to you, and you won't let him. Why is that?" She's not only lecturing me—she wants an answer.

"I didn't think about it that way. I didn't want him to have to spend money on something like that. I've let him do other things." I remind her about the motion detectors. She ignores that as not worth mentioning.

"Who says he has to spend money to put in a gate? Didn't you find gates for free? You think he can't do that?"

I guess I did think that, or else I just didn't think. "He probably can . . . yes." Which is true, he and Jennie know a lot more people in the neighborhood than I do. I just got lucky with a Nextdoor post.

"You're right; I'll go tell him I was wrong."

"No, you wait until tomorrow, and then tell him you've been thinking about it and you'd really appreciate it if he'd do that."

"Okay," I say in a small voice. "May I go now?"

"No, I really do want you to change my kitchen light bulb."

So I do that, and she lectures me a little more, but gently now, about how I'm always ready to help someone else, but I don't like to let people do things for me. Like how I keep trying to pay her to keep Boris, even though she's made it clear that she loves having him in her house. "It sets you apart, and that's not what you want, is it?"

"No ma'am," I say, and back out the door, asking her if she could please do me the favor of keeping Boris yet again this next week. She laughs and stops lecturing, and I go home. She's right, and I try not to beat myself up too much, and on Tuesday, I do keep an eye out and manage to be checking my mailbox when Bud arrives home after work. I tell him I couldn't find a gate after all, and if he finds one, that would be great. Before it gets awkward, a black car pulls up, and Officer Carl gets out. Bud gets a panicked look but, to his credit, manages a firm hello. Carl waves him away.

"I just had a question for Marianne," he says to Bud, whose face loses just a little of its concern as he turns and goes inside.

"Everything okay?" I ask. It's been a long time since the shed incident. Boris barks from inside, and I open the door and let him out. He runs over to Carl and levitates his front quarters, just an inch or two to let us know that he could jump up and lick Carl's face but isn't going to. Carl leans over and lets him get in a lick or two and then switches to ear scratching.

"Everything's fine. I just stopped to say hello." He leans over and rubs noses with the dog. "Hello, Boris," he says. "Also, I was going to ask. . . ." But the phone on his belt rings, and he looks at it, and his face darkens. "Okay, got it," he says into the phone. Still talking on the phone, he waves, and the car door slams, and he speeds away.

On Wednesday, I'm back in Chicago, eating dinner in my hotel room, a salad I picked up from the Corner Bakery, where I am now a known entity. I log in to update my step count and realize that I'm falling short of my ten-thousand-a-day goal. Rats. I put on my sneakers and walk down the stairs and out the front door, past the office and on to Navy Pier. I walk to the end and back to Michigan Avenue. I check my step count and go out and back again, then up Michigan to Water Tower Place and back to the Club Quarters. I resolutely ignore the elevator and take the stairs to my room. I fill the tub and soak for thirty minutes before crawling into bed.

In a meeting the next morning, while everyone is getting settled, I ask if anyone else is doing the ten-thousand-a-day step challenge. Several of them are, and I tell them I'm having a hard time keeping up. "I'll have to make a couple of trips out to the end of Navy Pier every day to make it," I tell them.

One guy says he uses a treadmill at home, another tells me that the Fitbit is notorious for undercounting so he uses a regular pedometer, and a third admits to just making it up. "Who cares?" he says. "They don't know me, I don't know them. I'm healthy, I never go to the doctor. I just put in a random number every day between ninety-five hundred and twelve thousand. No one can prove I didn't, right?"

I expect stunned silence, but instead I get agreement. The treadmill guy says he's going to do that too, and the other two people in the room admit to padding their numbers if their Fitbits come up short. They see the whole program as idiotic. I walk out to the end of Navy Pier twice after work, loop south to Millennium Park instead of north to Water Tower Place again, and decide I'm a Goody Two-shoes, but that's who I am, so I'm stuck with it. I log in to the health site to see if there are any other Act! options, but it's too late to start anything else, and counting servings of food by color seems worse than counting steps, anyway.

The following week is a scrum for the coders, so I stay home, just calling in for the daily catch-up meeting. On Tuesday, tornado sirens start shortly before the call, and I grab my phone and laptop and head for the basement. I go back up for charge cords so I've got as much juice as possible if the power goes out. I call in, and while I'm waiting for everyone else to join, I check the health site again and click on the Tips section. In among trite advice like "Walk with a buddy" and "Drink plenty of water," I find one thing of value: each flight of stairs counts as one hundred steps. I can keep track and enter them under the Flights tab, and they will be added to my step total. I decide that I go up and down my basement stairs at least twice a day and that the walk uphill to the hardware store is worth five flights. I make some entries and then walk up and down my basement stairs a few more times, until the meeting starts and I have to concentrate. After the call, I hang a strip of paper and a pencil at the top of my basement stairs and make a tick every time I go up. Sometimes I go back down and up again just for the extra flight. I feel foolish, and I'm glad no one is around to see this, but I can't bring myself to just enter numbers at random. That night, I figure out how far behind I am and start getting up earlier and walking Boris farther, choosing routes with hills.

For the rest of June, I work more and more hours. The bonus appears, but I don't get any notification of stock or options. My weekly report to Cassie includes actual hours, and she never comments. My interactions with her dwindle to almost nothing, but she does approve my time and expenses promptly, which is all that really matters.

By the end of June, I'm exhausted. Several of the engineers and coders are taking off the week of July 4, and I tell Cassie I'd like to take comp time that week. She agrees, which is not surprising since she is taking the week off also.

I talk to my brother about going to the lake, but he says he's going to be working twelve-hour days in his little lakeside general store, since this is his biggest week of the year. And the place will be crazy with cigarette boats and no Coast Guard policing their speeding, noisemaking, and drinking while boating. He's pulling his own boat out of the water so the drunks' boat wakes don't wreck it. I scratch that and think about visiting a couple of cousins, but the weather forecast all over the Midwest is for triple digits, and I give that up. So when I get a rare phone call from Deanna telling me kindly but firmly that I need to spend the week in Chicago, I don't put up a big fight. I don't even ask why, I just book the flights. The day before I go, I get an email from Cassie, who has gone into the travel system and changed my hotel reservation from my usual Club Quarters to the Swissotel. "I know you were looking forward to your vacation, so I thought you should at least have a little treat," her note says.

The truth is that I like the Club Quarters, its compact rooms with a usable desk, a real desk chair, a bookshelf (always three books), and coat hooks on the wall next to the door. I like the casual restaurant attached to it. It's cozy and familiar. But I have to admit that the coziness can feel cramped in the daylight hours, with not much in the way of windows, so that after a three-night stay, my little house feels quite spacious. Still, Swissotel seems like an unnecessary extravagance. I decide to be gracious and thank Cassie profusely. Then I see that she's also rebooked my flight, and I'm arriving Sunday evening and leaving Friday night. So okay, the extra space at Swissotel will be nice. There's not much closet space at Club Quarters.

Not until I arrive at the office on Monday morning do I find out why I've been summoned during a week when most Midwesterners are chilling at one lake or another, or are blowing their fingers off with more or less illegal fireworks. A shoe has dropped. The investment bankers have found a buyer for Magetech—or at least they've found a buyer for the intellectual property. I'm there to explain exactly what it is and how it works.

"Why me, Deanna? I'm not an engineer, and I'm not a coder."

"Because you can actually verbalize what it does, and you can be pleasant about it, and you can keep your mouth shut afterward."

Great, let me put that on my résumé. I don't say that.

"Couldn't you have given me a heads-up? Time to make a PowerPoint?"

"You hate PowerPoint, Marianne. You refuse to use Power-Point. You always say, 'Forget the canned stuff: let the system speak for itself.' Am I right?"

I sigh. "You are right."

"You never prepare for presentations, so I saved you the trouble. The first meeting is at ten."

I don't get the chance to say that while I don't prepare for presentations, I do obsess about them, and now I've got to do all the obsessing in less than an hour. I don't even get a chance to ask about her goals for the meeting. She's gone, leaving the memory of something halfway between a smirk and a nod of confidence. I shove myself back from the table and look at my feet. At least I'm wearing my new Chicago shoes, and at least I've figured out that women aren't wearing pantyhose anymore.

They are wearing makeup, but it's too late for that, even if I had some and knew how to use it. I go to the ladies' room and brush out my hair, twist it up, and shove in a couple of spin pins. Maybe I can pull off "quirky." Maybe I can make them see that they need me, along with the intellectual property.

For the rest of the day, I sit in an overly air-conditioned room with men in their twenties who are dressed in slim-fitting black suits and black shirts and all use the same hair stylist, the one Harry Potter goes to. They are almost indistinguishable. They take themselves very, very seriously. I answer questions and demonstrate how things work. I talk about the platform and security and flexibility and then security again. Uptime is crucial. I suggest we bring in the vendor, since the data are in the cloud, which in reality means on the vendor's servers, which are on the ground somewhere. Or maybe in the ground. I tell them what I know about backing up across servers. I tell them what I know about where the servers are, which is nothing. They may have some outside the United States—it's possible. They can tell you. Let's call them. If something is deleted, it's deleted from all the servers, and it stays on the backup but not forever, and can't we call them? Because I don't know for absolute sure how long it takes for things to disappear from the backup. At a break, I call the vendor and ask the security questions, and he wants to know why the sudden interest, and I lie and say because we're getting close to going live, so people are nervous. He's unwilling to divulge much about the servers, because part of their being secure is that wonks like me don't know where they are.

After the break, I tell them what little I did find out, but they have moved on. Now they only care about uptime. At noon, they ooze away. Nothing is said about lunch, and I sneak out and get a sandwich and eat it in the conference room, pretending to prepare for the next session. They reappear at 12:59 p.m. as though they never left, and the questions resume. At six o'clock, they ooze away again, one at a time, and no one says goodbye or otherwise indicates that the meeting is over or will continue the next day. I realize that they are aliens from another planet and that there is no hope of working with them after the sale. I put my head down on the desk and close my eyes.

"Sounds like everything went well today." I look up and see Deanna. I clear my throat.

"Yeah, great, no problems," I say.

"Good, good. I knew you could do it. Tomorrow we start at eight." And she oozes out too. Is she an alien? I try to ooze, and I trip, scuffing one of my new shoes. At least I'm not an alien. I go back to the Club Quarters, remember that I'm at Swissotel, and reverse course. The Swissotel has just installed a new elevator-control system, where you swipe your room key card on a reader in the elevator lobby and then wait for one of the elevators to announce your floor. It's supposed to group people going to the same floor together so each lift can make fewer and faster trips. What happens is that people just get on any elevator that opens and then panic when there are no buttons inside. I explain that to everyone on my elevator, which goes to my floor, seventh, and stops. I get out. Half the people get out and hit the button to go back down, and the other half stay on and expect me to make it go on up to their floors. I realize that if I can't explain the elevator, I have no business explaining Magetech. I go to my room, change into jeans and sneakers, and walk down the stairs to the lobby, where staff are trying to get people onto elevators.

"Take the stairs," I say to no one in particular as I pass through the lobby. I walk through DuSable Park and out onto Navy Pier and stand in line with all the tourists and eventually get on the Ferris wheel, which swoops me up and over. I look for the alien spaceship but don't see it, so I admire the city, which

I love, even if I don't want to live here. I get off and walk out to the end of the pier and then make two more loops, until I tire of bumping into tourists. I go back to the Club Quarters for a quiet dinner and then brave the lobby of the Swissotel and walk upstairs and lock myself in my room.

Tuesday is much like Monday except I don't try to make jokes. At noon, I go outside and eat street food for lunch. Okay, I eat ice cream and call it lunch. I get a large iced coffee and take it back to the conference room, which has no coffee setup, another clear indication that these are aliens. Today they don't ooze away until almost seven, but one of them does sort of smile at me as he turns to ooze and disappears. Or maybe that lift of the lip is what initiates the disappearing act.

Deanna materializes shortly after and asks me if I want to get a drink. We go to the Palm Restaurant at the Swissotel and sit on stools at the end of the bar. Deanna orders a single malt, and I order a Ridge zinfandel because it's the only thing I see on the wine menu that I'm sure will be delicious. Deanna tells them to bring us something to eat, any small plates they like. We talk about the weather (nice) and the Cubs (I nod at whatever she says) and how many people are in Chicago with their kids for the holiday. I contribute the thought that the Ferris wheel is fun.

We get refills, and I know it's not a good idea, because I'm thirsty and drank the first one too quickly. I ask for a sparkling water and let the wine sit. "It'll be better after it breathes for a while," I say by way of explanation and ask the waiter for another small plate, something not fried this time. Maybe a vegetable of some sort. I know Wisconsin is only a few hours away, but fried cheese? Come on. He brings us lightly cooked asparagus. Doesn't go with wine, but it's delicious otherwise. I eat a couple and drain my glass of water.

"So tell me, Deanna, are those guys aliens from outer space, or are they from some sort of finishing school for MBAs?"

Scotch comes out her nose, which makes me laugh so much I don't even apologize, I just hand her my napkin and ask the waiter for another. I feel a lot better after that and finish off the asparagus and ask for more fried cheese. It was actually pretty tasty.

"Okay, I'll admit they're a peculiar bunch, but they're happy with what you're telling them. Happy with you *and* with what you're telling them."

I file that away to think about later. Maybe they will want me to stay on. God, how could I work with them? Later—think about it later.

Deanna asks for the check and says she'll see me Thursday.

"What time do we start tomorrow?"

"Tomorrow's the Fourth. Go have some fun. See you Thursday."

She leaves, and I finish the cheese and my second glass of wine, which really is much better for having taken a breather on the bar. More people come in, and I realize that the nudging is for real—people want my barstool. I go upstairs, walking up all seven flights, and make a note to record that just in case it still matters. I admire the view and breathe in the idea that I have tomorrow off, free of aliens. I check my Fitbit, sigh, and change clothes. I can't face Navy Pier after dark, swarming with drunks, though. I go down to Millennium Park and walk under the giant silvery bean, trying to remember its official name. I finally come up with Cloud Gate and wonder if I can work that into tomorrow's session. No, not tomorrow. Thursday. Tomorrow is a free day.

CHAPTER 46

I put the Do Not Disturb sign out and sleep late. I skip the $17 breakfast at the hotel and go in search of coffee and pastries and a free sidewalk table on the sunny side of Michigan Avenue. Then I find a spot on one of the many architecture boat tours that cruise the Chicago River. The one that happens to have a seat available motors through the Loop and then out through the lock into Lake Michigan, where it gets up enough speed to make the kids and some of the parents on the boat start squealing. We wave at the Ferris wheel, and no one barfs, and afterward I eat hot dogs for lunch and then walk until I hit my ten-thousand-step goal. I walk an extra two thousand just to get ahead and then walk up the seven flights to my room and fling myself on the bed. It's not much of a holiday, but it's also a fantastic holiday. I order room service, which arrives just as it's getting dark. I have the perfect room for watching the fireworks.

Thursday is much like Monday and Tuesday except that I don't really care anymore, so I am not as exhausted at the end of the day. I go back to the hotel at noon, get a sandwich from the lobby kiosk, and eat sitting in the window seat in my seventh-floor room, watching a storm move in and change the view from cityscape to rain streaming down the large panes. I didn't bring an umbrella or a raincoat, and I ask the concierge if he has any.

"Long gone," he says but points me to underground passageways, which I find will get me back to my office without going outside. I pass a subterranean Dunkin' Donuts and get a large iced coffee to get me through the afternoon.

It's still raining in the evening, so I put on my sneakers and go to the hotel fitness center. I open the door and recoil at the extremely loud music, the damp warmth, and the smell of sweat and a dozen different body sprays. Everyone else is rigged out in full workout gear, no gym shorts or cotton socks in sight, as long as I don't look down at my own outfit. I push my way into the fug and look for an available bike or treadmill or even stepper. I edge up to a rowing machine, whose current occupant seems to be getting up. A shiny, hot-pink form steps in front of me, towels the seat, and hops on. "My turn," she says over the music noise with a smug smile. "You need to check in." She nods vaguely toward the far corner. I tear my eyes from her lime-green shoes, which look nothing like my running-style sneakers, and her eye makeup, which is not running in spite of the sheen of sweat on her face, and her hair, which matches her shoes in color, and the aliens in my office in style. I head for the far corner.

The guy at the kiosk in the corner is talking to the twin of the woman I just left. Same outfit, different color palette. When he finally turns to me, he looks me up and down and hands me a release form. I read it over and look up to ask him a question. He's talking to another customer, and I take in his silvery, skintight shirt, his piercings, and the constellation tattooed on his neck. I look around the room and feel my head throbbing from the music and the body-spray cocktail swirling in the air. I realize this is another sort of alien meetup. Kiosk Alien turns to me, and I hand the form back. "I just remembered I have some earthling things to do," I say with a smile.

"Kerfling?" he yells over the music. "We don't have that."

"I didn't think so," I say to no one as I find my way back to the exit. The lights have been turned down, and strobe lights are now flashing. I can't get out fast enough. I go out onto the street, walk to the end of Navy Pier in the diminishing rain. Not all the tourists have been driven inside by the weather, although I'm the only one out with no rain gear at all. I order a few 99-cent taquitos from a food stand that has a counter under cover and then realize I don't have anything with me other than my room key. I hold it up sheepishly and tell him I'll be right back with some cash.

He waves me away. "Two bucks, no worries today." A dad buying tacos for his kids tries to pay for mine too and argues cheerfully with the vendor. I thank them all around and leave them to it. *I love Chicago,* I say to myself, and thank God there are still a few earthlings on the streets. I keep walking, but now I'm aware that I shouldn't be out here alone after dark with no cell phone and no wallet and soaked to the skin. I get a glimpse of myself in a store window and realize that I look more alien than any of the visiting aliens.

CHAPTER 47

I don't see Deanna at all on Friday, but I run into Cassie at noon in the ladies' room. She looks rather forlorn, and I spontaneously invite her out for lunch before remembering that she is the boss and if anyone's going to do the inviting, it would be her. But she seems grateful, and we choose a pizza place that has an outside table open. I love Chicago-style pizza, until I've finished a slice, and then I lapse into food coma and swear I'll never eat it again. The waitress comes, and I see with a shock that she has spikey pink hair and tats and a lot of metal in her ears. But at the same time, she exudes earthling vibes, so I smile at her and order a pizza salad instead of a coma-inducing pizza. Pizza salad is a large green salad with one-inch squares of thin pizza scattered over the top.

Cassie is quiet, which is unusual for her. I wonder if it's because she knows something, or because she doesn't know any- thing when it's obvious that there are things to be known. Or is she mad at me about something?

"How's it going?" I ask to give her the chance to say anything she wants.

"Great," Cassie says. "This is a great opportunity for me."

I nod my head—nothing to say to that. I don't know if she means the lunch, or her job, or something I've not picked up on. Then she huffs, and I raise my eyebrows.

"It's just that I don't know what's going on." She stops talking, probably realizing that she shouldn't say that to a direct report. I decide to sympathize. Maybe I'll find out something while I'm at it. She is my boss, right? Supposed to keep me informed?

"Yeah, things seem pretty fuzzy to me too."

"But at least you're there in the meetings," she says, shrill now. "I'm just, just, well . . . making arrangements." I think she was going to say she's just making travel arrangements and ordering the lunches that I see go into the boardroom. I suddenly wonder if my aliens have been eating lunch in the boardroom while I escape to the streets. I never see them in the lobby or the elevator or outside. Maybe they bring in their own alien food. Maybe they don't actually eat.

"Well, Deanna does depend on you," I say. "And I appreciate your. . . ." I almost say "support" but change it to, "I appreciate how you have my back." It's a stretch, but I want her to calm down.

"I'm supposed to be chief of staff," she says through gritted teeth, "but where is the staff I'm chief of?"

I put on a goofy face and point at myself with both forefingers, hoping she'll laugh and ease the tension. Instead she sighs and pokes at her food with her fork. Neither of us says anything for a few minutes. She finally takes a drink of her iced tea and says, "Well, it looks good on my résumé."

"There is that," I say with confidence, and in a desperate attempt to improve the mood, I add, "And I'll give you a good reference." And then I quickly add, "If you ever need it, and they want to hear from your staff." *Could I have said anything more awkward?*

I realize I'm not going to learn anything from Cassie, which is just as well, so I shift the conversation to the weather and then make a show of noticing the time. I pay the check, which is dicey because she's the senior, if lower-paid, employee, but I don't remember that until it's too late. Chances are no auditor will catch it, and if they do, I don't mind a few mea culpas.

We go back to the office, and I let myself into the conference room for what I hope is a short last meeting. The aliens are more intense than ever, although they don't cover new ground. I assume they are new at this and are just making sure they don't forget anything, and I keep my answers short and to the point and try to keep moving along toward the minute I can leave for the airport.

On the tick of five o'clock, they get up and gather their papers and laptops and start disappearing. I get a rather formal, "Thank you for your help" from the alien I've picked out as their leader, and he oozes away after the others.

"Don't be strangers," I say, but they have dematerialized. I collect my luggage, look around the office, find no one, and go out onto Wacker to hail a cab to the airport.

I'm almost to Midway when I get a call from Deanna, who opens in typical sorry-less Deanna style: "I missed you at the office—we need you to stay over the weekend." When I don't say anything, she goes on: "There will be an announcement on Monday, and we have to wrap up a few things."

I sigh, and she finally adds, "Please, Marianne. I know it's an imposition. Can we meet for dinner?"

"Okay," I say, dragging out the word and laying on the resignation. "I'm in a cab, just pulling into Midway. Let me see if he can take me back without violating any cabbie protocol. And I'll have to check with my dog sitter and also see if I can get my hotel room back. Oh, and change my flight." I look at the time. "Which boards in forty minutes."

"Cassie will do that," she says. "See you in an hour." I tell the befuddled cabbie to take me back to the office, text Josie about keeping Boris, lean back, and close my eyes while we struggle through Friday evening traffic. By the time the cab stops in front of the office building, Cassie has sent my new reservations. I check the flight—next Friday, an entire week away. She has put me back at the Swissotel, and I'm pleased. The Club Quarters would feel a little cramped after a week in the big room with the spacious view.

My new room is on a higher floor, but the view is different. More lake, less city, and smaller overall. It feels odd, shut off from the river and the Trib building. I keep turning to face the city and seeing my closet instead. I unpack and realize I have a laundry problem. I check the prices on the laundry ticket in the closet; buying new would be cheaper. I wash out my underwear and then wash out my silk and knit tops too, unwilling to trust them to commercial washers. That leaves a skirt and two pairs of pants, plus my gym shorts and casual T-shirts. I bag one pair of pants and my casual clothes to drop off downstairs, hoping for the best, and find it's time to meet Deanna. But all my clothes are now bagged or wet. I put on the best pair of jeans and nicest T-shirt and tell myself we'll have to go casual for once, although it's hard to picture Deanna in a casual eatery. I run down all eight flights.

I don't see Deanna in the lobby, so I wander around, keeping an eye out. I finally spot her in the gift shop, looking at earrings. She has a weakness for expensive, artsy earrings. "Feel free to expense a few things if you need to," she says. "I know you didn't pack for a two-week stint." She looks at my jeans and T-shirt. "Not to criticize, but there are some nice summer tops over there."

It seems like this should be embarrassing, but I remind myself that we've known each other a long time, and she's trying to make up for the change of plans as casually as possible. She's also telling me to buy a sweater, not just suggesting it. A clerk in resort wear suggests a dressy, lightweight cotton sweater with a jewel neckline and three-quarter sleeves that I think is suitable for both jeans and the office. I take all three sizes to the dressing room, trying them on without checking the price, and come out wearing the medium.

Deanna is chatting with the clerk, who discreetly removes the tag and rings up the sale. I have my credit card out, but she shakes her head and nods toward Deanna, who has moved away and is trying on a scarf. I feel like a teenager taken shopping by an aunt. "Come back in the morning," she says, handing me her business card. "Your boss explained about the crisis at the office." She gently takes my old T-shirt, puts it in a palm-logoed shopping bag, and tucks it under the counter. "I'll be here from ten until five tomorrow." She smiles, and I catch up with Deanna.

"I guess I sent my laundry out a little too quickly," I say as we walk out. Deanna ignores me and gets in a cab, and I hurry around and get in the other side.

"Greek tonight," she says, and I am instantly hungry. I can't remember the last time I was in a Greek restaurant.

She orders for both of us, which is fine with me. She is known here, I find to my amusement, and speaks if not Greek, at least a Greek-flavored restaurant patois that ingratiates her with the waiter.

Tonight, she doesn't bother with small talk, which is a relief because it's either rainy or sunny, and all I know about the Cubs is that they play baseball and the stadium is called Wrigley Field. And that it has been called that for eons; it's not one of those naming-rights things that results in names that change along with corporate takeovers and the rise and fall of bottom lines. I'm too tired for small talk anyway. For that matter, I'm too tired for any talk. Deanna, however, is energized by her week's work.

She opens with: "Tomorrow morning we'll work on the final documents, press releases, and so on." I raise my eyebrows. That's not really my forte. "Tomorrow afternoon we have a final one-hour presentation to the buyer's team. Meet at eight, rehearse at ten, and they come in at one."

"Who's 'they'?"

"You'll find out."

"Who's included in 'we'?"

"Me, you, our attorney, and Jason the tech genius. Cassie on drums."

"Bongo?"

"PowerPoint."

"Got it." Deanna needs someone to flip slides. At least it isn't me. "What's my job?"

"Sell yourself." She smirks but in a friendly way.

"Translate that. They aren't buying people."

"Doesn't mean they don't need people. They need you and the tech genie to get this thing to market. They know they need Jason; they don't know they need you."

"How do I sell me?"

"That's always your weak point." She sighs like I'm her below-the-curve student. "You can sell anything but Marianne."

I put a stuffed grape leaf in my mouth by way of reply and pour more wine in my glass.

"You have eight minutes and six PowerPoint slides," she says.

"I hate PowerPoint," I say, and she mouths it along with me. "Oops, knee-jerk reaction. Six slides it is."

She starts telling me a story about a meal she ate in Greece once, and it's clear she's finished talking about the presentation. I half listen and wonder what I'll say tomorrow. For once, I'm forced to prepare, since I need slides. I'll be up all night obsessing.

"Ouzo?" the waiter is asking. Deanna has one finger up, meaning she's having one, and they are looking at me.

"No, no thank you. No ouzo, please. *Limoncello,* if you must." A night of PowerPoint is bad enough; tasting ouzo all night will make me want to puke. "Actually, no *limoncello* either. I'll have a *metrios.*" He smiles at my attempt at Greek and goes off to get the ouzo and the coffee. I cross my fingers under the table, hoping he brings Deanna a glass of ouzo, and not a glass and a bottle. Worse, two glasses and a bottle, and he'll pull up a chair.

But no, he brings just the glass, and Deanna doesn't dawdle. We walk back toward the hotel. The stores are closing, but she stops at the window of the Eddie Bauer store and says, "You're an Eddie Bauer type. Expense whatever you need. Don't worry about Cassie—you can change the approver to me for this. No need to upset her."

At the hotel, she heads for the bar, and I take my overfed self up eight flights of stairs. Deanna's been fiddling with her phone all the way back, so I assume she's meeting someone for some other last-minute prep. A half-hour later, I go down to the lobby for toothpaste and see Deanna outside talking to a bellhop. She's turned away from me, but I'm sure it's her. A cab pulls up, and she gets in. I walk back upstairs, musing about where she's going now. I don't know if she lives in Chicago or not. For all I know about her workplace idiosyncrasies, I know nothing about her personal life. No one does. But there have been great rumors over the years: She was once a NASCAR racer, an air force pilot, a sniper in the Israeli army. She spent her teenage years in juvenile hall. She lived on an ashram. She was kicked out of the Peace Corps for teaching girls to kickbox, although I think that last story was originally assigned to Deanna's head of communications, who actually looked like a kickboxer. I can't remember her name.

— — —

I have no idea how to sell myself to unspecified buyers who don't know they need me. I stare at the blank PowerPoint screen and slowly make my slides: one for job history and education, two more for projects, and another for accomplishments. *So boring.* That's four slides down, two to go. Goals: Make Magetech the Go-to Infrastructure Software. *One more.* My phone buzzes, and I pick it up. Enrollment is open for the conference I attended last fall in San Francisco, the day I was laid off from my last job. I get out my corporate credit card and sign up. I email my contact there, saying I want to be a presenter; I want to tell them how we've used their platform to build Magetech. I click Send, go back to PowerPoint, and create my last slide: Put Magetech on the Map.

CHAPTER 48

Deanna puts on an amused face when I go through my slides. Six slides, eight minutes exactly, because I'm watching the clock. She has me do it again, and then she tells me to lead with the last slide and go to the others if I have time. Whatever. I reorder them and send them to Cassie to insert in the group presentation. She's struggling a little, and I sit with her for the rest of the morning, keeping her calm and helping her when she runs into trouble. Lunch is brought in, and I spend the time on my feet, talking to the lawyer, or rather, letting him talk. Deanna tells us to turn off our phones now, all the way off, and put them out of sight. Laptops go back to our desks except for the one Cassie is using to project the slides. I go to the ladies' room just before one o'clock and get back just after. Maybe it's not leaning in, but I have to separate myself from Cassie or I'll be the assistant slide flipper and an impossible sell.

The prospective buyer team comes in looking like a different sort of alien. New York? London? Moscow? I've lost my touch. I introduce myself, shake every hand, say a few words. Their accents are hard to place. Coffee is brought in, and Deanna begins: "Let's get seated." I see with relief that name cards have been set out, and I look for mine. I'm at one end of the table, near the door and next to Jason, the tech whiz. Deanna is at the other end with Cassie, trying to look like a chief of staff, beside her. I give Cassie full marks for her dark business suit, even though the skirt is barely long enough to sit on, and she's wearing bright red stilettos. The buyers won't forget her.

"I'm going to change up the agenda a little," Deanna says, and I recognize this as a tactic she uses to make it clear that she's in charge. I grin into the folder in front of me.

"We're going to hear from Marianne first," Deanna goes on. I'm surprised but not worried. "She'll stay for the technical discussion, and then both she and Jason have to leave. They've each got a lot to do before Monday morning." I nod knowingly, face serious, although I have no idea what it is I have to do before Monday. I can text her later. Jason makes a noise beside me, and I ignore him. I stand up, and Cassie flips through the title slide and the welcome slide and other useless crap that all PowerPoint presentations start with, and stops when she gets to Put Magetech on the Map. It looks awesome in the format Cassie has dropped it into, dark plum background and gold letters. She's put a globe behind the words, barely visible, and a suggestion of fireworks in the background. I smile at her and give her a tiny nod, and she beams for a second and then puts her chief-of-staff face back on.

I look up at my slide and then at the audience, using my Toastmaster training to let a short pause create a little expectation. "I like it," says the head dude, and the rest of my eight minutes is spent by me answering questions and ignoring the slides: my favorite kind of presentation. At exactly ten past, Deanna winds up my section and firmly moves on. When Jason gets up to talk, she makes sure everyone is paying attention to him and then gives me an I-told-you-so look. Her eyes then narrow and go to the folder in front of me. I open it and see that it has a copy of the PowerPoint presentation and behind that, a brown envelope. I pull the presentation out as though I want to follow along and see that the envelope has my name on it, along with "personal and confidential." I look up, nod once at Deanna, and focus on Jason.

A few questions come my way during Jason's presentation, and I answer them quickly and turn them back to Jason. I want to stay on his good side in case we end up working together. He finishes, and Deanna turns to the next item on the agenda, giving me a barely perceptible "get out" signal with her eyes. I pick up my folder, nudge Jason, and leave.

"What was that about?" Jason asks as soon as the door closes behind us. I walk away quickly, motioning for him to follow. I don't say anything until we are back in the cubicle area. Alien ears might be keener than human ones.

"Either she's sparing us the tedium or, more likely, she's making sure we don't know anything we aren't supposed to know. Also, she likes to be center stage, right?"

"I don't mean that; I mean what do we have to get done by Monday? She promised me I could leave by two. I've got kids I never see anymore."

"Oh. Well, maybe she made that up to get rid of us." I fish out my phone and turn it back on. It buzzes, of course—thirty minutes of email queued up. "Oh, look at this. She texted both of us: 'Just kidding, you're finished until Monday. Thanks for a great effort.'"

Jason frowns at his phone and shoulders his backpack. He stalks to the door, muttering. I think he says "Crazy lesbo," but I'm not sure, and I've called him on this sort of comment too many times to count, and besides, he's gone. Right this minute, all I care about is that I'm free until Monday morning. I could almost fly home. Not worth the hassle, though, and I can't expense it. Also, now that I think about it, Deanna could text at any moment expecting me to be here, in Chicago. Then I remember the brown envelope. I wonder if Jason had one too. I look around. His folder is gone, so if he had one, it's gone home with him. I take mine out. It's sealed, and I'm sure the handwriting is Deanna's, not Cassie's. Cassie would have typed a nice label anyway and found a stamp to mark it "private and confidential." No one is around, but I go back to my cubicle anyway before I open it. Inside are the certificates for shares of stock and stock options and a note thanking me for the extra time I put in. I feel a little uncertainty drop away, even though I know these are not publicly traded stocks, so the value is anywhere from zero to wow.

I decide that hanging around won't look good, and if there is any drama, I don't want to be a witness. I hurry back to the hotel, stow the envelope in my room, and change into jeans and sneakers, noticing that the sneakers are a little smelly from their soaking a few days ago. I switch to flip-flops and head for the lobby shop, where the clerk has two more tops and a pair of pants waiting in a dressing room for me. The pants are a little narrower and a little shorter than my old ones, more au courant. My wardrobe is stuck in three-years-ago Silicon Valley dweeb, not much improved by two years of telecommuting and working in a hardscrabble hardware store. All my clothes are black, white, or blue, the black extending to dark charcoal gray, and the white to pale cream. The blue spans the spectrum from ice blue to sky blue, meaning it's all pretty much the same. The clerk has brought out a dark-green top.

"Almost blue," she says. "Give it a shot." Then she suggests a silky, dressy version of a black hoodie: "Just a suggestion of tech," she says. I thank her, she sends it all up to my room with a bellhop, and I escape to Michigan Avenue. I go back to Eddie

Bauer, because Deanna seemed to expect it, and get another pair of jeans, also snugger and shorter than the old ones, and another T-shirt. That seems like more than enough, but when I get to Bloomingdales, my feet are sore from the flip-flops. So I buy a new pair of sneakers, flashy ones like everyone else is wearing in Chicago, along with disappearing socks. I put them on and head on up Michigan. I make it all the way up to Holy Name Cathedral in time for five o'clock Mass, which calms me down from my long week. The singing alone would have been worth the walk. Other than the shower, where else can you sing, with people who are uncritical of your talent, if you're not good enough to join a chorus?

I walk back down and across the river on State Street. I'm not up to eating alone in downtown Chicago on a Saturday night, so I stop at a ramen shop and take a bowl up to my room and eat it gazing at Lake Michigan. I turn my phone to silent, put out my Do Not Disturb sign, and sleep for hours.

On Sunday, I'm suddenly at a loose end. I'm mentally tired but physically too antsy to stay in my room. For once, I don't really have anything that has to be done. I wonder what is going on at home. I miss my dog, my house, my shower, my mornings at the hardware store. Whoops—I didn't let Matt know that I won't be in tomorrow. I send him a text and worry until I get a text back saying I owe him one. I catch up with personal email, am grateful for autopay, and check in with Josie. At eleven, I put on my new jeans and T-shirt and sneakers and go outside, thinking the Art Institute is a good idea. But when I get there, I keep going, glad to be outside and walking. I walk all the way to the south end of Grant Park, cross Lake Shore Drive, and walk back north along the lake, up to Randolph, where I cross back over and walk south again through all the little parks that make up Grant Park:

Peanut Park, Maggie Daley, and Buckingham Fountain, which almost makes me feel like I'm back in Kansas City. Almost. It's getting chilly here by the lake, and chilly is not something that happens in Kansas City in July. I buy a Chicago hoodie, dark pink—way out of my color palette. I blame the clerk, with that blue-green top, but I like the pink. I finally get back to my room, mentally refreshed and physically exhausted. I take the elevator upstairs.

CHAPTER 49

The announcement to staff is made on Monday afternoon at two, which surprises me because bad news is usually delivered on Fridays. But the unnamed buyer presents this as good news, meaning with smiles and congratulations and thanks. Business as usual, we are told. He doesn't ask if there are any questions, and raised hands are ignored as the suits shake hands and leave the room. Deanna goes with them.

After the announcement, I walk into the daily scrum meeting, where no one gives a report and everyone talks about the sale. Each person seems to remember some different phrase, and we dissect them all in the worried tones of people who may have just lost their jobs.

Tuesday morning's meeting starts late. After a cursory round of reports, everyone talks about job hunting. I remind them to update their LinkedIn profiles, which are mostly crap. At Wednesday's meeting, I do a LinkedIn tutorial. At first, I worry that they'll ask me if LinkedIn ever got me a job, and I'll have to admit that it hasn't done squat for me, ever. Unless you count getting my hopes up, which is worth something on some days, even if the hopes have always been dashed later. I needn't worry. In this situation, 90 percent of people's attention is on themselves, and the 10 percent that's on other people is narrowly focused on what those people can do for them.

So I critique their About sections and remind them to be scrupulously honest about education and past jobs. That goes over their heads, so I tell my story of Phil's bad behavior and subsequent disappearance from his new job. Some of them look sheepish, and some of them look at me critically, wondering if I'll rat them out.

"It's just a cautionary tale," I tell them. "I'd report you if you tried to impersonate me. You would too, I'm thinking." Oddly, that reassures them. They are coders and engineers, and they see me as someone with only girly soft skills. I wonder why I bother helping them and decide it's because it gives me something useful to do. I think about that. It's not useful. I stop thinking about them and focus on my own situation.

Thursday night, I make Deanna swear that I can leave for sure on Friday. On my last run up to the eighth floor, I realize that I'm not getting winded until the fifth floor and my legs feel great. Maybe there is something to this stair-climbing thing.

When the cab drops me at home, after midnight, and I've tipped the cabbie extra because I can see that he's terrified to be so far east of Troost, I peer at Josie's to see if any lights are on. I don't want to go in my house without Boris, but I'm not going to wake her up.

I see her door open a few inches, and Boris bounds out. "Talk to you tomorrow," Josie says, and the door closes. I go into my own house, which is hot and stuffy and smelly. I've left bananas on the counter, and several generations of fruit flies seem to have colonized them. I seal them in plastic and banish the entire colony to the freezer to await trash day. I turn on the window fan while I shower, then turn on the air conditioner and go to bed.

I'm exhausted, but I can't sleep. I get up and unpack, hanging my new clothes on wire hangers instead of the wooden Swissotel hangers they are accustomed to. The clerk removed the price tags before she even showed me the clothes, but I saw what other things there cost. What are these clothes doing in this house, in this neighborhood?

I'm home for one week, and then Deanna tells me that the buyer wants to keep me on, and I'll be commuting to Chicago Tuesday mornings and leaving Thursday nights for the time being. I know I won't get an answer, so I don't ask how long "the time being" will last. Probably until the buyers put some lipstick on Magetech and resell it. I mostly work on test cases and preliminary system testing, wondering who we will get to do the real testing, the user-acceptance testing. I can only verify that it meets written requirements, not that it meets real-life needs and expectations in the hands of actual users. It's no use if the users don't log in. What would happen then? Attendance at daily meetings dwindles, as the engineers and coders get other jobs and the ones left stop caring. Jason is one of the first to resign. Temps are brought in to replace the ones who leave, and I start flying to Chicago on Monday afternoon and leaving on Friday, trying to keep the coders focused on getting through testing instead of complaining about the previous coders' work. Things break, and they blame the older code. I can't write code, but once in a while I can spot errors, and that annoys them to no end. I'm only a tester in their eyes.

A temp who goes by Marh, although that's not his full name, is especially annoyed by my error sleuthing. One Friday morning, I'm testing a particularly tricky function and run into several obvious and basic errors. I know it's Marh's code and quietly ask him about the most obvious error, which is only a missing comma. He corrects it, and I wait a while before I ask about the next problem. This time I tell him what's not working, so he can find the error himself. He tells me it works the way the requirement says it should, so I say maybe it wasn't all that clear and just ask him to change the code so I can keep going. He sees that it was his error, and I watch his face tighten and hear the anger in his voice when he tells me he changed it, but I should have logged it as an error in the requirements, not the code.

"Right," I say as though I plan to log it that way, which I'm not going to do.

I think about how to tell him about the last issue, which is a bigger code error. I don't have edit access to the code and wouldn't trust myself with it if I did, never mind that it would be a gross violation of protocol. But I want so badly to fix the code and not deal with Marh. Maybe my squirming tips him off that I'm about to prod him again, because when I finally open my mouth, he jumps up from his seat.

"What the fuck, why are you even here?" he shouts. "You don't know shit. God, you can't even dress yourself. You wore that same thing yesterday. You look like someone's Aunt Gladys."

A few of the other coders look up, glance at me, and look back at their keyboards. I should have calmly said, "The code is still wrong," or maybe laughed and said, "You really can't tell this black top from the white one I wore yesterday?" But I've let him get to me, so I don't stay calm, and I don't say either of those things. I glance down are what I'm wearing—I'm pretty sure it's not the same—and lash out at him.

"You've worn the same gray T-shirt with the same sweat stains all week," I say instead. "I'll bet your mom tried to throw that thing out when you were fifteen."

"So what?" he sneers. "I'm a coder. I'm a guy. I make five times what you do. It doesn't matter what I wear." He grabs his backpack and stalks out of the room. I log the error and set the test case for retesting after the error is corrected. And I don't let myself think the obvious: he's right on all four counts. I don't think about that; I think about what I'm wearing, until I remember that yesterday's ice-blue silk sweater got mixed up with an iced coffee incident and is hanging in the closet drying, after a night soaking in hotel shampoo in the bathroom sink. I sigh out loud. Maybe he doesn't make five times my salary, but I'm sure he makes at least double, and he doesn't have to spend any of it on looking professional.

I get called into meetings periodically with people who are introduced to me by first name only—I don't know who they work for or what their roles are. Deanna is around but stays in the executive area. I don't run into her, even in the ladies' room. Chances are she has a private one and only uses the general one when she wants to seem like part of the gang—although the female part of the gang is negligible. Cassie is pouty and finally complains to me that she's been told that she has six more weeks and will get a bonus if she stays until the end. That information turns a screw in my chest, and I stop imagining a future with the aliens and start looking for a job.

Unlike last year, I don't slink away, grateful to avoid the coming train wreck. I don't waste time telling people that it will all be fine. I don't know if it will be fine, and I don't care. And I'm not leaving any friends behind to deal with the fallout. In all probability, we're all on waivers.

I call the vendor rep, who owes me for initiating the contract that's now going to open the door to a new client—the purchaser of Magetech, whoever that is. I meet him for lunch. I tell him I'm looking for a new job, something more challenging. I leave no room for sympathy, because I suspect he lacks the gene for that. I ask him which clients in his portfolio are struggling to understand all the great things their software can do, meaning which ones aren't buying more modules as fast as he would like. I remind him of all the things I've done to smooth the extra licensing he's sold to Magetech. I'm not collecting on a debt; I'm trying to make him see that I can increase his commissions if I am working for one of his underperforming accounts. I point out that I don't live in Chicago, I'm not tied to Lake Michigan, farther afield is fine. By the time we've finished our espressos, I'm exhausted, but I think he's starting to see me as a potential asset.

I subscribe to the *Kansas City Star* digital version, since I'm rarely home to read the paper version delivered to my front step every morning. I'm not looking at the job ads; I'm reading the business section and the local news stories, looking for something that indicates a need for what I do or what I might be able to do. I make cold calls. I have to pump myself up to do it for a while, but after the first five or six, I tell myself that however much I hate cold calls, I hate unemployment even more.

During the first week of August, the project is declared complete. I concur, with the caveat that there is no way to do real-world testing. I fly home, wondering if it's for the last time. By now I know everyone at the Club Quarters, everyone at the Southwest Airlines counter at KCI and Midway, and every flight attendant. I even get the same cabbies sometimes. I'm relieved to be staying home, but I don't quite know what I'll be doing now.

CHAPTER 50

It's hotter in Kansas City than Chicago, and I'm already sweating when I get to the hardware store early Monday morning. Working here feels different today; I'm not thinking about getting home and changing clothes and hoping the cab shows up to take me to the airport. The store seems both shabbier and friendlier. I take more care sweeping today and ask Henry if we should think about doing a little painting, maybe the vertical face of the counter, which is scuffed from a thousand work boots, and maybe the trim on the outside.

"Well, good to have the old Marianne back," is Henry's response. "You haven't told me how to run my business all summer. I thought you didn't care anymore." He's grinning as he says it.

I give him a guilty look and tell him yeah, I'm back, and then tell him I'm still employed but not at all sure where things are going. But I'm happy to take on some painting between customers.

He points out that painting the west-facing trim on the front of the building is hopeless in August, and pretty much every other month unless we get some cool dry weather in October. But he doesn't object when I start sanding the face of the counter and open a can of forest green high-gloss paint.

"The guys don't care about that," he says, because he has to rib me about it.

"The painters will; they spend all day making things look spiffy."

"They'll want to see your union card."

We go on to talk about my next home projects, which are kitchen counter and kitchen floor, both currently dating to my parents' era, 1960 to be precise. The Formica counter seems to have taken some heavy blows and more than one hot skillet, and the linoleum floor is down to the jute backing in the doorways and is peeling up along the front of the sink. I might hire Jimmy Cooper to do both jobs. He did a lot of repairs when I first moved in, and I like his careful way of working. But if I'm unemployed, I'll do it myself, even though it seems intimidating right now.

"If I'm getting sacked, I almost hope they do it soon," I tell Henry. "The worry is killing me." We both know I don't mean it, not entirely. A paycheck is a paycheck.

I spend the afternoon making cold calls, to no avail, but late in the day, I get a call from the vendor I had taken to lunch in Chicago. He's been thinking about what we talked about that day, he says, and he has a lead for me.

CHAPTER 51

He's not very specific, but he gives me a name, Marjorie Fletcher, at the Kansas City public school district. He tells me only that the school district is one of their pro bono clients, which means they get free use of the software platform and a modicum of free support from the company. But what they do with it is up to them. Marjorie is struggling, he says, and I should call her.

I try to press him for more information, but it's clear that he doesn't know much. I conclude that he wants her to stop calling him and possibly wants to keep me from calling him too, since I'm as good as gone from Magetech and therefore of little further use. I do some googling and call Marjorie Fletcher. It's a little after five, but I figure that's good. I can leave a message, and she can get back to me when she has time to talk, if she even wants to talk.

She answers, a warm voice not intended to intimidate the caller.

"Oh, hi," I say and introduce myself. I tell her where I got her name and number.

"Oh, that guy," she says.

She leaves it at that and tells me a little about her problem, which is that she's got a system, and she's got a lot of data and a lot of questions that the data might be able to answer, but no way to fit the two together. I get the impression that she thinks I'm with the software company, part of the pro bono deal. I tell her I can probably help her, but that she needs to understand that I'm looking for a job—someone to pay me to do that. I cringe, expecting either a little swearing or a sad silence.

"Yeah, okay . . . that makes some sense," she says slowly. "We're not getting anywhere the way we're going. Seems like we do need to pay for what we get."

I put my palms together, take a breath, and lift my eyes to the ceiling, which needs paint. I close my eyes and breathe a prayer that I can help this woman—and get paid. Oh, and full-time with benefits, please.

We set up an interview for Thursday, and I peruse the KC Public Schools website trying to figure out what they do and how they dress. On the day, I wear my new pants and one of the tops and the new shoes, all low-key in black and white. Marjorie is not wearing the school administrator clothing I pictured, a downscale version of Deanna. She's wearing a flowing tunic and cropped pants and a black hat, a sort of oversized pillbox, with gold stars.

"You look fantastic in that outfit!" I say before I even introduce myself.

She opens her eyes wide and shoots right back with, "Don't you even try it, girl. You too pasty white and too skinny."

We both laugh, and puts on a professional face. "Let's get to it," she says, and takes me to her office. She doesn't waste time. She logs into their nascent system and shows it to me, starts asking questions. If nothing else, she's going to get a little help session out of this interview.

"So your man, Jeremy, sets this up and then hits the road. Look at it. He says, 'Oh, you can add any field you want,' and he adds Race, like he's all wise to what we do here and says, 'See, you can pick Black, White, Hispanic.' Like that's all there is."

"What would you actually like?" I say softly. "Or maybe the question is, what do you need to report? And do you need some hierarchy? Maybe a place to enter something not on the list?"

I let her think about that before I go on. "A couple of other things to think about: Who is going to be choosing—are you going to have a self-serve portal where parents can view a few things and update just some of them? Or is an employee here going to do it?"

We talk about options for a few minutes, and I make a few changes, and she gets excited and wants to go on to other fields. I hold her back and ask if she's got data somewhere else, maybe a spreadsheet. "We can load that up and then modify it from there. It's a pretty cool feature, but everyone has to be onboard with ditching the spreadsheet once it's in here. Sometimes that's the hardest step."

We go on to talk about who has an interest in the system and how interested they really are and how much controversy she expects to run into. "People can get pretty crazy about what you call something," I warn her. "Even First Name and Last Name can get thorny."

We go over my credentials, for the record. She asks how much I know about schools, and I tell her, "Nothing."

She frowns, pen poised over her notes. "You went to school, though, right?"

"Yes, I went to Blenheim and later to Hogan," pronouncing it "Blen-hime" and leaving the "Bishop" off Hogan.

"I guess you did go there, or you'd pronounce 'Blenheim' like they do in England," she says, looking at me closely.

"Most of the kids on my block said 'Blem-hine,'" I tell her, "but my mother was a stickler for proper pronunciation and

grammar. Of course, she wouldn't have known about Blenheim Castle—she grew up on a farm in the Ozarks during the
Depression. She didn't get to finish high school, which bothered
her all her life. Grammar was important to her."

She looks at my application form, sees my address. "You still
live over there?" Disbelief is clear in her voice.

"Yeah, I know. East of Troost." I give her the short version
of the rise and fall of Marianne and my move here from California, and then add, "Full disclosure: I only went to kindergarten
at Blenheim, and I went to Hogan when it was still a Catholic
school. I went to St. Louis school for grades one through eight.
So back to your question—the full extent of my public school
experience is Miss Rose's afternoon kindergarten class."

She stares at me for a full minute and then says, "Well, we've
got a lot of people who know about public school. What we don't
have is someone who knows what questions to ask."

After that, I ask her a lot of questions about her vision, about
what she wants to do with the data she is hoping to collect and
store and analyze. Quite a lot of her vision is related to grants
and jobs. I get excited at her plans for keeping kids in school,
getting them jobs, even very small jobs, so they can earn money
of their own while doing something positive. "Even if it's just an
hour after school," she says, "it interrupts the problem of teens
hanging out unsupervised, and it gives the kid an easy way to say,
'Sorry, can't do that—I gotta go to work.' It makes them proud of
themselves, in a good way."

She takes me around to meet other people in her area. She
tells them I went to Blenheim and Hogan without elaborating.
She tells them I live east of Troost, and they nod like that's a
normal place for adult humans to live. I notice that all of them
call her Arjo. I ask her about that.

"Oh that—it's something my brothers and I did when we

were kids. It's the middle of your name. Stephan was Tepha and Jonathan was Onat—it kind of spread around the neighborhood, and now it's taken hold here."

"So I'd be . . . Aria?" We both squint, picturing my name. "Arian wouldn't be so great."

"Ouch. Aria is fine—you just make this thing sing for us."

After ninety minutes, she looks at the clock and apologizes for taking so much time. "Can I get you to fill out some forms?" She goes on to warn me that things can take time, especially in August, but then tells me that she's got an ace up her sleeve, a technology grant she applied for and was just awarded. "It's for a technical person," she tells me, and I don't argue that I'm not really that technical. "Plus a part-time after-school student helper. That's the catnip I put in grant applications. Don't tell anyone my secret."

The next day, I go for drug testing, and then Marjorie calls me back for a second interview, this time with more administrators and, at the end of the day, a few teachers. I learn about their mentor program, which does everything from repairing bikes to make sure kids can get to school, to organizing intramural sports to keep them there after school. "No kid wants to be in after-school care, but if they can sign up to be in a musical or to play dodgeball or something, that's a completely different thing." They need statistics to convince the school board and grant-givers and even taxpayers that it's worth the cost.

"Return on investment," I murmur, and the administrator looks at me intently.

"Yes, ROI," she says. "Can you give us that?"

"If we can define it and collect the data, then yes, we can get that." I notice that I've switched from "you" to "we."

Marjorie walks me out the door at the end of the second interview and thanks me for my time. She muses about her long-term dreams. "I want to keep the kids in school, sure, but I also want to keep them in the same school, keep the families together and in the same home or at least the same street, where they know each other. People say 'strong communities,' and I don't think they have a clue. Mostly they're just mouthing words. Staying put, that's the key, and the rest follows. And then," she goes on with a dreamy look, "we need to do that for the teachers too. They don't stay, for all kinds of reasons: money, fear, burnout. . . ."

"Long commutes?" I add. "That's easy to document."

She shifts her gaze to me. "Are you concerned about the commute?"

"Me? No. That expressway that doomed my neighborhood in the seventies gets me here in ten minutes, twelve tops."

She looks off into the distance again and sighs. "We're east of Troost here too," she says. And she's right; we are standing on the sidewalk on the east side of Troost. She promises to call soon, and I leave with my head full of ideas.

Marjorie doesn't call Friday, but I don't expect her to. She doesn't call Monday, and I tell myself not to worry, it's still early, and it is summer, and people are away, and this isn't another crazy situation like with Deanna and her startup. She does call on Tuesday, and she tells me my background check came back clear, and she has permission to make me an offer. The salary will be revealed in the contract, which will arrive in the mail in a few days. I can hear her roll her eyes when she tells me this. "It's just how we do things. Maybe they think it looks like more when it's written down."

I'm so excited, I start chipping up the kitchen floor and calling around looking for linoleum dealers. Small as my kitchen is, I know I'll never find enough linoleum at ReStore, although I will make the circuit, just in case. My big worry is moving the stove. I worry about that to avoid worrying about the job offer.

When I've got all the easy sections of linoleum up, I take a break before moving the refrigerator. I look out and see that Bud's truck is in his driveway. Why not ask for help? I run out and ask, and he seems thrilled that he can help me do something. It takes quite a while because Felicity and the two dogs come along to assist. Bud looks at the stove and offers to help me disconnect it when I'm ready. He says he'll get Pat or Dave to give him a hand. I'm grateful, because I'm pretty sure I'm not going to be able to shift my share of the weight. He gathers up kid and dogs and herds them out the door.

My phone rings while I'm surveying the disgusting mess in the corner where the refrigerator was. It's Jason, the Magetech genius, who had resigned but has now been hired by the buyer to do a major overhaul and roll out the new software. He has a VP title. I kick myself for not thinking of doing that.

He can't or won't tell me the name of the buyer, but he is calling to tell me that they are offering me a job, the same job I was doing a few weeks ago. Technically, I'm still doing it; I'm still on the payroll, and I still call in to meetings that last maybe ten minutes, because nothing is actually happening. Technically, this is a transfer as part of the sale to the investment bankers and now to this new unnamed buyer. Technically, he's just letting me know. I assume he keeps saying "technically" because he's nervous. He tells me that there has been a shift in focus, that the product will be pitched to the tech industry, companies like Google, for storing data about—and there he stops. "We can go into the details later," he says abruptly. "I'm in a rush right now."

I ask about salary and benefits and potential for stock and bonus. He says that HR will explain all that, but since it's an acquisition, there won't be any changes from what I had at

Magetech. He will send me the particulars and a new nondisclosure agreement, and he'll need confirmation in two weeks.

The call ends, and I realize that I don't need the school district job; I still have my job. I won't have to sign up for insurance or jump through hoops or learn the jargon. I'll get the same pay I get now, or maybe more, and have a chance at a bonus. My phone buzzes, and it's a text from Jason, saying that he forgot to tell me that it's a regular, full-time position, not thirty hours. A second text says: "The job is in Chicago, you'll have to move here." I text back: "Move package?" And get: "Probably."

I text back, "Thanks, good information" and turn my phone to silent. I now have an ironclad excuse for leaving my still-shabby house in its dodgy neighborhood. I sit down on the floor and wonder why I'm not elated.

When the packet arrives from the school district on Friday, I look at the envelope for a long time before I open it. The salary they offer is at the top of the range for teachers, but only half what I will make working for Jason. On the other hand, the school district job is for a thirty-two-hour week, and has all the teacher holidays: winter break, spring break, and a month in the summer. I can get involved in other things, do some volunteer work. Or maybe I could do a little consulting on the side for more money. I get excited again, and I think about Marjorie and how much I liked her and what she is trying to do. I even have a nickname. I'm Aria! And there were no aliens.

Marjorie calls to make sure I got the package and tells me she's going on vacation for two weeks, so there is no need to make a decision until she's back.

CHAPTER 52

I call Jimmy about the kitchen floor, and he comes over and admires the bathroom and the other work I've done.

"You could almost sell this place now," he says, and I must look shocked, because he says, "I just mean it's looking really good. When you moved in here. . . . Whoa, what a mess! I couldn't believe you really bought it—especially to live in it yourself. I gotta say, at first I wasn't sure if you were crazy or lying to me. But now, it's really nice in here. Or will be when we get this kitchen floor done."

He's right. I could sell it and move to Chicago and live someplace safe, maybe a smallish house in a close-in suburb, or a cool high-rise apartment with a view and no worries about leaking roofs and showers. We agree that he'll start in a few weeks. Whether I stay or go, it needs to be done. I order the linoleum and ponder kitchen counters. It's easy enough to buy Formica and have Jimmy switch out the old for the new. If I'm leaving, why bother with the tedious counter-tiling job I've been contemplating? We agree on a price and a start date and also agree that it would be nice if the weather cooled off a little by then.

Instead, it gets hotter and more humid, every day in the high nineties, and barely getting down to the seventies at night. I miss the breeze off Lake Michigan. I take Boris out at daybreak, but we are both miserable and don't stay out very long. I work and sleep in the room with the air conditioner, grumbling to myself about the noise of it but grateful for the cool. I wish my shade trees would grow faster. I miss the backyard tree of my youth and dream up ways to shade the east windows temporarily, but they all involve working outside, so I don't do anything.

Early one morning, I pass a house that has newspaper taped over the outside windows on the unshaded west side. I sigh at the tackiness and hope they take it down when the heat wave breaks. The next morning, a woman is replacing the newspaper with what looks like an old white sheet. She sees me and smiles sheepishly.

"Looks awful, doesn't it?" she says. "But it does seem to help."

I go home and tape newspaper on the outside of my east windows. "We're now the worst-looking house on the street, Boris," I tell him. I dampen a tea towel, drape it over my shoulders, and settle down at my computer.

Jason calls and asks if I can spend two days in Chicago working on next year's plan and budget. I quickly check the temperature in Chicago and tell him yes. It's fifteen degrees cooler there and will be even cooler near the lake. I'll be able to go outside and breathe—and save a few bucks at home by not running the air conditioner. Boris will enjoy a few days with Josie. I take the newspaper off the windows before I leave, picturing it coming loose and ending up in Josie's yard.

Jason has rehired a couple of the coders who quit early on, and at the end of the first day, we all go out for pizza, the deep-dish kind. A few former coworkers join us, including Mary Mola, a program manager I worked with years ago. Over drinks, we get caught up, and after the fried calamari and cheese stick appetizers, along with a glass of Chianti, I'm done. Then, four pizzas show up for the eight of us, and I eat the smallest slice I can find, savoring each bite, knowing I'll regret any more than that. Talk has gotten louder as pitchers of beer are consumed, and the only topic now is recounting past drinking binges. The guys move on to a bar, and I say goodnight, not that they notice and not that it matters in the least.

Mary takes the opportunity to escape too. She gets the waiter to box up the leftover pizza, and we head off toward Millennium Park. There is no hope of walking off deep-dish, but a little movement has got to help, and it's a lovely evening. The pizza boxes in their plastic carry bags are heavy, even though we're down to leftovers. We speculate about how many pounds of cheese must be consumed in Chicago every day.

"What are you going to do with all this pizza?" I ask Mary, thinking she'll take it to her office for lunch tomorrow.

"We're giving it to hungry people," she says instead. We get to the park, and I let her hand out the boxes. We discover that it's not so easy to decide who is homeless or hungry, but Mary doesn't let it worry her. She just walks up and asks if they want pizza. Most people she approaches do want pizza. When it's gone, we say goodbye, and I walk back to the hotel wondering why it's so easy for Mary to walk up to strangers and give them pizza and why I would find it so hard to do such a simple thing. Then I wonder how hungry you have to be to accept used pizza from a total stranger on the street. Not starving, I decide. Just hungry. And then I worry about how many hungry people we found so quickly. And then I mentally slap myself, and go to my room, and wish I hadn't had the fried calamari and the cheese sticks and the pizza. Surely there was something green on that menu?

When I get back to Kansas City on Friday night, it's no cooler than when I left home. On Saturday, Matt comes by earlier than usual to mow. When he's finished, he asks if there is anything else, anything I want trimmed or spaded up. But he is backing away as he says it, willing me to say no, so I do. I also tip him a little extra, and he leaves smiling.

The Sunday forecast warns of highs in the triple digits, and after Mass, the priest announces that the church basement will be open all day for the next week for people to come in and cool off, as long as enough people sign up to act as hosts. Almost everyone volunteers. He also asks for a little extra to cover the August electric bill.

On Monday, there is a tornado watch, which is all anyone talks about at Henry's. By the time I head home, the watch has turned to warnings, and the air is still and sticky. As the afternoon wears on, the sky turns greenish, the wind picks up, and then a ferocious storm breaks. Thunder and lightning replace all other sensory perception as the storm rolls over. Boris howls during the worst of the thunder but doesn't seem upset. I wonder how Waggo next door is doing. I picture Felicity petting her and telling her it's okay, it's just a "sto-erm." I turn off the air conditioner and unplug it and my computer.

Just before sunset, the clouds move out, and the air is cool and fresh. I open all the windows for a few minutes, then lock them all up again and get the leash.

I test the concrete sidewalk to make sure the rain has cooled it enough for Boris's paws, then start off to the south, for no reason other than that the sun is slanting enchantingly through the wet trees in that direction. I breathe like I've been deprived of oxygen for days, and Boris sniffs like he's never walked up this street before. We walk south as far as possible and then east, reveling in the cool air. People are out walking and talking to their neighbors. I chat with several of them, mostly because they want to pet the dog. It starts to get dark, and I realize that we've gone farther than usual, but I feel safe on residential streets with my big German shepherd. There are still a few people out, but not many.

I consider how to get home. I've got to cross Gregory and Cleveland, and I can stick to residential streets otherwise. But I miscalculate and end up where the two intersect. There are businesses here, but all have closed for the day except the gas station. I hurry across and head up the hill on Gregory one block, where I can turn right and get off the busy street and into my neighborhood. It's quite dark now.

Just before I turn off Gregory, Boris stops to sniff the shrubbery. I've been hurrying him along, so I give him a minute to check out the smells. He rustles in the leaves, pushing through the bushes.

One or two soft footsteps—that's all I hear before my baseball cap is slammed down over my eyes. The brim smacking my nose brings tears to my eyes, but the hands reaching into my pockets cause fear to wash over me in a suffocating wave.

The cap is being held down, so I can only see the ground, and it registers with me that there are two attackers. I stomp the toes behind my right heel as hard as I can, and at the same time I feel fur slide past my right arm. Boris makes contact, and my cap disappears. Some of my hair goes with it, and the sharp pain of hair leaving scalp lifts the fear and replaces it with anger. I remember one line from my single one-hour self-defense class: Get angry, and use the anger to save yourself. I scream, "You little jerk!" although I might have used some other noun and adjective. I call him several other things after that, all at full volume.

Without the cap, I can see that it's the person in front of me who is scrabbling in my pockets. His head is down, and I knee him in the groin. He jumps back, bending over, but I am angrier than ever now, and I kick him again. He grabs at my foot, and I start to lose balance. My right hand comes around with an empty leash in it. I don't even register that Boris has pulled out of his collar; I just swing the leash wildly at the person in front of me, and the big metal clasp whips around his neck like a bola, and I yank it instinctively to stop my fall. He claws at the leash, and I kick him and kick him and kick him. Groin, knees—I don't care. I hear screaming, but it doesn't seem to be coming from him.

And then he's on the ground, face down, hands under his body. He's not moving. I realize that I'm the one screaming, and I stop. I look at the leash in my hand and realize that Boris is not attached to it. I look around for him and hear barking in the distance. I think I see movement farther up the hill, but I'm not sure. My vision seems blurry. I can't think, I can barely breathe. I try to call Boris, but nothing comes out.

The guy in front of me moans, and I refocus. I put my foot on his back and shout at him to stay still. My voice is raspy from screaming, but he obeys or maybe passes out. I feel for my cell phone, which is in a zippered pocket low on my thigh. They didn't get to that pocket. I pull it out and stare at it for a moment. What's my passcode? I see the word "Emergency" and press that.

When the dispatcher answers, I have trouble forming words, but she calms me down, and I tell her where I am and what happened. I remember Boris, and panic again. She is patient as I tell her that he's disappeared with the second attacker. I can't describe the attacker other than that he may be being chased by a large German shepherd. I panic again.

"Don't shoot the dog. It's my dog. His name is Boris. Call Officer Benning—he knows Boris. Don't shoot him. Please don't shoot him." I realize that I'm bouncing on the back of the person on the ground as I'm pleading with the dispatcher. I stop bouncing, but I don't even think to see if he is alive, if he is breathing.

The dispatcher assures me that they don't shoot dogs that are chasing attackers, but I'm skeptical. I don't know where he is, and I have his collar in my hand. It will look like he's just a stray attacking a random person.

All this takes enough time for the first cruiser to arrive. The dispatcher is asking if the officers have arrived and are out of the car. I tell her they are and end the call. They approach me warily, until the woman who seems to be in charge gets off the radio.

"Are you Marianne?" she asks, and I tell her that I am.

"Could you move away from this gentleman?" She is speaking very calmly, very slowly, and pointing, which is good because I am not understanding what she means by "gentleman."

I look down and see that I still have one foot on the attacker.

"Oh." I back up.

"But stay here."

"My dog," I say and then cough. My voice is still raspy from screaming. My throat hurts.

They seem to know about the dog. "We'll get him."

I wish she had said "find" instead of "get," but I can't form a sentence about that.

The first officer is checking the guy on the ground, and he rolls onto his side but doesn't get up. She calls for EMTs. I want him in handcuffs, but I don't say that, either.

The first officer stays with him, talking to him, asking for his name, asking if he can breathe okay, and telling him he needs to stay on the ground until the EMTs arrive.

The second officer is male and very young. He has me move away a little and starts asking me questions, starting with my name, my address, why I am in this place at this time. I realize that I'm maybe more than a little hysterical and try to calm down. It occurs to me that the man on the ground may be seriously injured and that if he is, I am the one who injured him. I need to be rational. The officer tells me to take a deep breath. I think he said that earlier, but it didn't register.

The first officer is talking on her radio again. She turns to me. "What does your dog look like?"

"He's a German shepherd, about ninety pounds, black and brown."

"What kind of collar?"

"Black," I say. "Oh." I hold up the leash with the collar still attached. "No collar." She goes back to the radio.

"Why isn't your dog on leash?" my cop asks, and the absurdity of the question stuns me. I realize that I'm about to laugh hysterically, and if I start, I won't be able to stop. So I take another deep breath and tell him that the dog *was* on a leash until I was attacked, at which point he pulled his head out of the collar and jumped on the attacker, the one who pulled the cap down over my eyes and who has now run away.

This has the effect of focusing my attention and giving me my voice back. I can feel anger rising though, and that scares me a little. I take another deep breath. I'm afraid that he's going to tell me that the collar should have been tighter, so I say, "If he hadn't pulled his head out, he would have yanked it out of my hand anyway. I had two guys on me—I couldn't fight them off and hold onto a ninety-pound dog at the same time."

He seems to be a little abashed by that but maintains his professional face, which keeps me from really lighting into him and reminds me to stay calm.

The EMTs tell the first officer that their patient may have broken ribs and they are taking him to the hospital. I can't hear what the cop tells them. The EMTs head north on Cleveland.

As the siren fades, I hear howling faintly, from the west, in the direction I last saw Boris moving. I look at the officers.

"I think that's my dog howling. Is it okay if I call him?"

The younger one looks at the older cop, and I add, "He howls when he hears sirens."

The older one talks into her radio for a while. The siren and the howling have stopped. I practice deep breathing until I realize that I might hyperventilate. I focus on the middle distance and try not to think about anything. And then I find myself on the ground, the officers patting my face and telling me to wake up. I realize I've fainted.

I've fainted before, so I'm familiar with the feeling and try to reassure them, but the words come slowly. Finally, I'm able to tell them that I'm okay, it's probably just shock, and could I just sit for a minute? One of them goes to the car and returns with a bottle of water. I remember the howling.

"What about the dog?"

"If you're feeling better, we can take you to him."

"Where is he?" I ask and wonder why they said they can take me to him instead of saying something like, "They've found him, and he's okay." Surely he's okay if he was howling. Maybe it was another dog howling. Maybe Boris is dead.

They don't answer, but they open the back door of the squad car and walk me to it, and I feel like everyone in town is watching me do a perp walk. At least they don't put a hand on my head as I get in, but maybe that only works with sedans. I'm now in a large SUV.

We drive up Gregory and stop at the curb where another squad car is parked, lights flashing. I try to open my door, but of course the back doors can only be opened from outside. I feel like a perp again. They ask for the leash and leave me alone in the SUV. The windows are tinted, the red and blue lights are flashing, and it's dark outside, so I can't tell what's going on. They seem to be very interested in the collar and leash.

Finally, I hear a firm, "Sit" followed by, "Stay," and then a different officer with Canine Unit on his shirt opens the door. Boris is sitting next to him, wearing a muzzle. He whines but holds his position.

"Is this your dog?" the cop asks with a deep voice and formal tone.

"Yes, it's Boris." At the sound of his name, Boris whines, wags furiously, and starts to rise but doesn't quite. He sort of bounces.

"Okay," the canine officer says to Boris, who bounces up and licks my face through the muzzle, which I've tried to discourage for years but now don't mind at all.

I slide off the seat onto the sidewalk and ask if we can go home now. "It's only two more blocks."

"Not quite yet," he says, not unkindly but not very encouragingly, either. "We need to go to the station."

I give him a questioning look and he adds, "We need to get a statement from you. Let's drop your dog at home, and then we can go."

"Can't he stay with me?" I struggle to think of a convincing reason. Boris licks my face. The officer pauses.

"I guess so."

Things are very formal at the station. If I had thought about it, I would have expected a bit of sympathy, but that didn't even register at first. I tell them everything I remember, and then I have to tell it again, starting with leaving the house after the storm, and then they ask question after question, going over it a third time and maybe a fourth. I was losing track. I ask for more water and a bathroom break. I wash my face and see that the bridge of my nose is bruised where the brim of my cap hit my glasses. I'm probably going to have black eyes.

When I return, there is only one officer in the room. I get a little courage back and say, "What's going on here? These two mugged me. Why so many questions?"

She left and was gone for a minute or two and then came back with another officer. I hoped for the one cop I know, Carl Benning, but it wasn't him.

"Your dog bit one of the young men. There is some bruising, but he didn't break the skin, so we don't have to quarantine him. But you will have to have him evaluated before you can take him off your property. He'll have to wear a muzzle when he's outside, even in your yard."

"He probably saved my life."

"Maybe, but that doesn't mean he isn't dangerous." I look at Boris, who is lying on the floor with his head on the officer's shoe. I roll my eyes. I roll my whole head.

"I know." He almost smiles. "Rules." He hands me a form with an address and phone number. "Make an appointment, and get it done. You have seven days."

I'm stuck with this, but I can live with it, so I go into get-me-out-of-here mode.

"No problem at all," I say. "Can we leave now?" But then I remember the attackers. "Will those guys be held?"

"Overnight, yes. We still have to get a formal statement from the one you kicked. I've just talked to the juvenile officer who is at the hospital with him. He claims your dog attacked him."

I sputter. "My dog attacked the one who ran!"

"And then he says you attacked him."

"Well, yeah, I did. He had me in a clench with his hands in my pockets. Wouldn't you try to get him off you?"

"Did he take anything?"

"I didn't have anything except my cell phone and my house key, and they were zipped into the side pockets." I show him. "He was in the other pockets." I point those out.

"So he didn't injure you, and he didn't steal anything?"

I can see where this is going—juveniles and no injury or theft. Maybe they are first offenders to boot. They may be home before I am. I feel tears and sniff them down. Boris gets up and puts his chin on my knee. I run the back of my hand across my face and wince.

"He jammed my cap down over my eyes so I wouldn't be able to see," I said. I take off my glasses and show him the bruise and hope it looks worse than it did five minutes ago in the bathroom. "Where's my cap?" I add as though it might have found its way to the police station.

Apparently the cap did find its way. "The officers recovered it; we didn't know whose it was. We'll keep it for evidence." He makes a note and asks for a description.

I give him the name of the software company emblazoned across the front. No way could it belong to a juvenile delinquent.

"We didn't find anything on him or at the scene that either of them could have taken," he says again. I don't have any anger left at this point. The adrenaline is gone, and I'm exhausted. My head is throbbing. I reach in my pocket for a tissue and don't find one. I check the other pocket, the one that usually has a couple of plastic bags for the inevitable. It's empty. I stand up and jam my hands in my front pockets.

"Poop bags," I say. "And Kleenex." I look up at the officer. "I can't swear to the Kleenex, but I know I had poop bags—I was walking the dog."

"You want to charge him with theft of poop bags?"

"No, I'm saying that they're gone because he had his hands in my pockets!"

He doesn't display chagrin, but he writes a short note and leaves the room. The female officer stays but doesn't say anything, doesn't make eye contact. I think she is trying not to smile. She is very busy writing in her notebook.

The officer returns with a roll of green plastic bags. They are in an evidence bag. "These yours?" he asks.

It takes another hour to finish up and sign my statement. They tell me I can leave. I blink a few times. It's five long blocks home, not very far, but do they really expect me to walk? I guess they think I'll call someone. They know I have my cell phone; the days are gone when they would have asked if I needed to call someone to pick me up.

"Um, can I borrow that muzzle?" I'm not even being sarcastic.

No one answers; no one is paying attention. They are on to other things. I get up and walk out. If Boris poops on the way home, I'll just have to leave it.

But when I get to the curb, I pause, afraid to cross from the well-lit parking lot to the darkness beyond.

"Marianne!" I hear a voice behind me. "Wait up, we'll take you home."

The female officer who was first on the scene pulls up. Boris and I get in the back, and she drives the five blocks to my house. The darkness and the pain in my head and the screen between us discourage conversation. But when she lets me out, she tells me that someone will be in touch the next day. I ask her if she'll wait until I get some lights on before she leaves. She parks and goes to the door with me. I let Boris in first. He goes to his bowl and drinks for a long time. I open the basement door, and he goes downstairs, sniffs around, comes back up. I thank her, and she leaves. I haven't turned any lights on.

I sit on the sofa and cry for a long time. I wish I had someone to hug me. I'm fine on my own; I really am. Until a moment like this, when I want someone to sit and hold me until I can sleep and gather the courage to face another day. Boris leans on my knee, and I slither off the sofa onto the floor, taking a sofa pillow with me. I wrap my arms around him and bury my face in his ruff. I huddle there, with my back against the sofa and my dog between me and the rest of the world. I don't sleep until I see the gray light of morning.

CHAPTER 53

When I open my eyes, the room is bright with late-morning sun. Boris is nosing at my face and whining. I claw my way onto the sofa, check the time: ten thirty. I stumble to the kitchen, the bathroom, the back door to let Boris out. I wake up my computer—emails, texts, hours of missed messages. I answer the texts that seem most important, start the coffee, answer some emails. I don't apologize in any of them.

I block out noon to one o'clock on my Outlook calendar and take a shower. I drink more coffee and make toast. I let Boris out again and remember about the muzzle. It doesn't register with me as important, although I do make sure the gate is securely latched, and I do make the call to schedule his evaluation. They are very businesslike when they hear that it is a police-required evaluation. I give the clerk my credit card number and am grateful again that I have a job.

In midafternoon, I realize that I am on edge, jaw clenched, waiting for the promised call from the police. I imagine the conversation, shoo it away, imagine a worse one. I give myself a shake and focus on the screen in front of me.

I'm almost caught up with email when Boris leaves my side and bounds toward the front door, arriving just as the doorbell rings. It's Officer Carl.

I'm glad it's Carl but still worried about what he's got to say. I've imagined being charged with assault, imagined losing Boris. I've had a whole range of exchanges in my head in which I am told that the two juveniles were not charged. I have already imagined them coming after me, breaking down my door, kicking me unconscious, killing my dog. In my head, I am selling my house and moving to Chicago before the weekend.

"Hi, Marianne."

"Hi, Carl."

I see that he's in a Community Relations car, not a black and imposing SUV. I hope that's a sign that the kid didn't die and I won't be doing the perp walk. I invite him in, and we sit at the kitchen table.

"You okay? Boris okay?" He is rubbing Boris's ears. Then he's looking at my bruised eyes, although he doesn't mention them.

"I'll be okay if you tell me the perps have been moved to the part of Alaska accessible only by bush plane. Boris will be okay if he passes his evaluation."

Carl smiles and seems relieved that I'm not hysterical—or at least not hysterical in a way that requires him to take action.

"So. Those kids." I don't take it as a good sign, his calling them "kids" instead of the foul attackers that they are. But I keep quiet.

"They're first offenders, although we suspect them in another attempted mugging. They're trying to get into a gang—or maybe I should say, the gang is recruiting them. Anyway, that's what this was about. We were lucky that you and Mr. B here managed to split them up and that we got to them separately. Made it hard for them to keep their stories straight. We got some shreds of gang info from them too." He pauses and clears his throat.

"Mostly, we scared them, you and Boris and then us, reminding them that the gang doesn't like it when they screw up and get caught and then squeal. So as of an hour ago, they each separately agreed to plead guilty to simple assault and spend six weeks at the Ranch down near Warrensburg. To them, Warrensburg is half the world away from here and the gang. After six weeks, they'll be back, but they'll have a strong motivation to behave. By the way, they aren't from this neighborhood. The gang handler drove them over here from the Kansas side."

Great. I have another punk gunning for me, an experienced one. "Is the handler going to come here and take it out on me?"

"Nah, they'll stay in their own space. Besides, you must have looked like some sort of ninja to them. Weird, but they sort of respect that. Ninjas and cool dogs." He leans down and lets Boris lick his face.

"Lovely, maybe they'll recruit me." It's weak but Carl seems glad to hear a little sarcasm in my voice. "So I'm not being charged with assault on a juvenile?"

"Nope."

"Or with owning a dangerous animal?"

"Not unless he fails his eval, and really not even then."

"But I might have to relinquish him?"

"I don't know. Depends, I guess."

I think he's being evasive about that, but I let it go.

"Look, this dog is not dangerous," he says, "so don't worry about it. I've seen dangerous dogs and this is not one of them. He's a protector, not a killer."

I am going to worry about it, but I am a little reassured.

"Okay now?"

"As okay as I can be."

"Okay enough for me to lecture you about walking alone on busy streets after dark?" He's grinning when he says it, though.

"No, not that okay. But I'm not walking anywhere at any time of the day right now."

He nods, looks away, looks back. I think he's going to say something, but he just nods and resumes his cop posture and strides away to his car.

I go back to my desk and open a file to work on for Jason, but the words blur, and I put my head down on the keyboard. Boris scrambles to his feet, and the doorbell rings again. This time, it's Josie, and she's carrying a large casserole dish with two pot holders.

"This is heavy," she announces, pushing past me into the kitchen. She puts the dish on the table and faces me.

"I know something bad happened," she says. "You don't have to tell me about it just yet, but you do have to eat. Sit down."

She gets plates and silverware as if it were her own kitchen, which it practically is, since hers is almost identical, with the same limited storage: only one obvious silverware drawer and one obvious dish cupboard.

She serves my plate and then hers, wisely giving me small portions.

"You can have all you want. Did you eat anything today?"

I think about it. "Toast?" I'm not even sure.

Steam rises from my plate, bearing the irresistible aroma of sausages, mashed potatoes, carrots. My mouth waters. I take a bite and then another. When I've cleaned my plate, Josie leans across the table and scoops on a little more. I'm still looking at my plate. I realize that tears are running down my face, and there is nothing I can do about it.

Josie gets up, finds a box of tissues, and puts it on the table. She leaves me alone with the tissues for a minute while she rummages in my refrigerator for a bottle of wine, then pours an inch into a tumbler.

"Talk."

CHAPTER 54

I talk. I start with, "These two guys," and go from there, skipping backward and forward and sideways. She doesn't ask any questions, just pats my arm and murmurs now and then, things like "Oh, honey, no," and "Attaboy, Boris."

Eventually, I run out of words and go to the bathroom to wash my face. I sit back down, and neither of us says anything.

"Tell me again."

My head pops up.

"Again? I told the police over and over, and I just told you everything."

"And you told it all to yourself all last night and all day today, didn't you?"

"Well, yeah, sort of."

"So just get it all out, so you can use that space in your brain for something else."

This time through, I don't try to get it exactly right, and I tell her how nervous the young cop seemed to be and how I heard Boris howl from far away. And for the first time, I say out loud how scared I am about how angry I got.

"When I was kicking him, I was out of control. After the first kick, the one that dropped him, maybe I should have stopped. Or after the second kick, anyway. But I didn't, or I couldn't. I feel like I could have killed him and then stomped the other guy too. Is this how murderers and wife beaters get that way?"

"Whoa, there—that's a huge leap. What you did, that's human nature. It's how we survived in the wilderness. The important thing is that you did stop. He didn't die. It sounds like he wasn't even hurt that bad. I mean, he was hurting!" She chuckles. "Probably still is hurting. But not damaged. And you won't do that again unless it's life or death." She thinks for a minute. "Actually, you should be happy to know that you can do that, if you have to. Not just curl up and get yourself stomped."

I stick close to home for the next few days. I tell myself it's because I'm not allowed to take Boris out without a muzzle, and once people see the muzzle they will forever assume he is dangerous. But really, I'm just scared—scared of the cops and scared of the robbers. We stay in the house, mostly, with forays only into the backyard. I tell myself I need to catch up on work. I call a real estate agent about selling my house. I ask her to just drive by, and I send her pictures of the inside rooms. I tell her I'm just thinking about it, not ready to sign a contract. I don't want her parking her real estate–agent car out front and walking up to my door in her real estate–agent clothes. Everyone will see her and know. Why do I care? They'll know soon enough. But not yet, not today. She knocks on my door anyway, and I like her in spite of myself. She's around my age, a Black woman with a realistic attitude and no fear of east of Troost.

I tell her about the new kitchen floor and counter, coming in a few weeks. She tells me my house is charming, which we both know is just adspeak, and later she calls it "cozy," which we both know means really small. I ask her if she wants to see the basement, and her face says she doesn't, but we go downstairs anyway. She perks up a little when I flip the light switch, which lights both the steps and the area at the bottom. I hear her sniff.

"Nice and dry down here," she says, and I'm glad I've put the time in to get it clean and aired. She looks at the washer and dryer, the pallet table I made for folding laundry, the shelves. She runs her hand along the top of the table and makes an approving noise.

"Birdcage?" she asks, nodding at the cage-like box hanging from the joists that catches the laundry sent down the chute in the bathroom above. I laugh for the first time since she knocked on my door.

"It does look like that, doesn't it?" I unhook the door and show her. "My dad made it, I suppose. It was always here."

"Your dad?"

I have to explain my history with the house then, a story I've grown tired of. I want to just be the person who lives here, not the person who grew up here and then came back when the world beat her down. We go back upstairs as I finish, and at the top I end with, "And he built all this part," waving my arms around. She seems to look at everything more carefully now.

We go back to the kitchen, and she asks if the siding is asbestos, knowing it is, and I shrug. I know it is too. Then she surprises me by saying that it's not a liability as long as it's in good shape, not crumbling. She points out that it never needs painting and tells me where to buy replacement shingles that are identical but asbestos free, if I need to replace any. She knows I do. But I didn't know about the cement replacements, which would make it possible to do something wild, like moving the bathroom window.

She suggests an asking price. It's almost exactly what I paid two years ago, even though I've paved the driveway and built the garden shed and refinished some floors and gotten rid of the smell of neglect. I blink a few times, and she puts on her concerned real estate–agent face.

"There's no garage," she says softly, and I wish with all my heart that I'd figured out how to build a garage instead of a shed, which I know was impossible without losing most of the backyard, and which would then mean she'd be telling me there's no yard.

"And no dishwasher," she goes on, and I think, *Where would you even put a dishwasher?* but I don't say it, because of course that's what she's really saying.

"And things just aren't moving very well right now, not right here. We can ask for more and maybe get it, but if you want to sell before winter, this is the price that will make it happen. We could get someone in here pretty quickly at this price."

I wonder how quickly. I picture myself throwing my things in boxes and loading a U-Haul, then backing out the front door with one last look at my empty house. My eyes tear up. I see other people moving in, putting their dishes in the cupboard, and I feel a weird sort of panic. She misreads whatever she sees in my face.

"Were you hoping the neighborhood would gentrify?" she says, empathy mixed with disbelief in her voice.

"No," I tell her. "No. I just wanted a place to live. A really cheap place."

She looks at me steadily. It gets too late for either of us to make the obvious joke about getting what I wished for, so neither of us says anything for a while.

"We could try for more if you've got time to let it sit. You could replace the broken shingles, amp up the curb appeal a little. Eventually one of the corporate buyers will make a lowball offer, probably lower than this, and we can try to bargain back up. But they don't really care. They'll rent it as long as it's rentable and then hold onto it, because it won't cost anything to sit and wait and see what happens to the neighborhood." She lets that sink in, and I think about asking if that's what is going on with all the vacant lots, but I don't have the heart to ask. Better not to know, at least not today.

The agent puts her card on my kitchen table and gets up to leave. I mumble a thank-you and fake a smile. I hate her now, for the simple reason that she's pointed out the obvious: that my house is worth more to me than to anyone else on the planet.

I hope none of the neighbors saw her shiny red heels and giant briefcase. I go outside and look at the asbestos siding, which is chipped on the front corner where someone did a bad parking job. More than once, from the look of it. It's the first thing you see when you walk up to the front steps. I call Jimmy and ask if he can find the siding and fix the corner, instead of the kitchen floor. He says he can and that it's easier on the knees anyway. I tell him he may still get the chance to crab around on my kitchen floor, but I don't elaborate. I can lay the linoleum tile if I decide not to move, and I'll call him back if I need it done quickly.

Online, I look at houses for sale in Chicago near the train lines that go downtown. My house, if it sells at all, will bring enough for a smallish down payment. I look farther out, and then even farther out. Condos don't allow ninety-pound dogs. Rentals don't, either. To buy a house with a mortgage that will leave me a bit to sock away each month, I won't be living in Chicago at all. I'll spend hours on the train. I picture myself walking the train from end to end, trying to keep my step count up. People will call me the Crazy Train Walker, and one day the Metro police will take me to the psych unit for a seventy-two-hour hold. Meanwhile, I won't spend enough time at my remote home to meet the neighbors, and they won't call me to change light bulbs and get things off the top shelf. They'll wonder if I'm in witness protection. I'll have to board the dog when I travel. I look at the cost of that. I make a spreadsheet and try to figure out if I can come out even at the end of the year. I call Deanna and make sure that my shares will pay out if I decline the job. "Of course," she says. "Of course. There was a sale, that's all that matters. I made sure. You aren't chained to the new owners, whoever they are. That job is just an option that you earned." So whichever job I take, I'll be able to repair some of the damage to my retirement account brought about by my late husband's sickness and the recession—if the shares turn out to have any value. That's for the future. For now, I don't have to figure it into the equation.

One day, when Boris and I are outside, a police helicopter circles several times. I worry that they are checking on us, knowing that is absurd, and then worry more that they are searching for a mugger loose in the area. I take out my phone to call Officer Carl and ask, and then put it away. No patrol cars appear, and I go back to worrying about dangerous-dog evaluations, about which I know nothing at all. I wonder if they simulate the "incident" to see if he will bite. I wonder if he will. I worry about what happens after that.

On Sunday, I am too crabby to go to Mass, but at the last minute I go anyway, not bothering to change clothes because . . . because I'm crabby, and that will just show . . . who? What? I go back in and change. In the car, it occurs to me that the people I see at church have probably had worse things than my almost-mugging happen to them, and I have no business being crabby around them.

In the first reading, Jeremiah is captured and dropped in a well, and although there is no water in it, there is plenty of mud, enough to sink into. Okay, that mugging might have been worse than mine. He had to sit there and hope someone found him—no cell phone, no 911. The second reading is from Paul to the Hebrews, and I'm no big fan of Paul, who I think of as the Whining Apostle Wannabe. But I will admit that *sometimes* the reading we get is not one of his all-about-me letters or one of his clueless exhortations, like the one about covering your head in church. Today we get, "Think of the way he stood such opposition from sinners, and then you will not give up for want of courage." I'm okay with that; I could use some courage. Finally, in the gospel: "I come to bring fire to the earth." I'm over my crabbiness now, so I don't say to myself, *Move over, Prometheus.* The priest gives us the homework assignment of being encouraging to someone, somehow. I think about how to do that.

I stick around after Mass and ask the priest if I can go to confession. I want a little extra help coping with the feeling in my gut that I could actually kill someone. He does not dismiss my concern, and he also doesn't act like I'm a danger to society. He nods thoughtfully, tells me I've learned something important about being human, gives me absolution, and sends me off with a reminder about being encouraging to others. I get in the car and think about being encouraging to . . . whom? Henry and his team? Sure, no big deal, part of the fun, and I get paid, so it doesn't count. Marjorie, if I take the schools job? Absolutely, that's the whole point, but I'll get paid for that too. Jason and his crew of aliens? Hard to even picture. They have money to encourage them, and what will I be encouraging them to do but make more money? Magetech's original mission of creating software to support urban infrastructure seems to have vanished.

I pass Josie's house and turn into my driveway. Dave and Carol, Liz and Pat, Bud and Jennie and Felicity. And Josie. Do I encourage them? Only by being here. Just being here. Here. I put my head down on the steering wheel. Can I stay in this place?

CHAPTER 55

The canine evaluation day arrives, and I log out a little early to give myself extra time to make our five-thirty appointment. I put the police department muzzle on Boris, and we drive off to meet our fate. The evaluator's office is in a light industrial area, and it takes me a while to find the right roll-up door, but at last, we are inside.

The evaluator starts out all business, checking my paperwork and the file emailed to her directly from the police department. She has me put Boris in a cage and remove the muzzle and then tells me to leave the room. I'm not happy about that, but she says I can watch through a one-way window.

She starts by talking to Boris through the cage, offers him a toy, takes it away. He is wagging and trying to lick her through the bars. She slips on a leash and takes him out, touches him with a towel, a rubber hand, another toy. She gives him a chew toy and takes it away. She has him sit, lie down, stay. He is focused on her face and utterly willing to please her. She lifts his lips, picks up his paws, grabs his tail. He worries about his tail but only whimpers and looks at her with a questioning face.

In five minutes, she's finished and filling out forms. I'm optimistic, but assume the next phase will be attempting to stimulate aggressive behavior by yelling or lunging or something. She waves me into the room, and I expect her to test him for being overly protective of his owner. Instead, she gives me a broad smile and reaches out to shake my hand. Boris crowds in for petting.

"I'm Sally, by the way," she says. "Sorry I have to start out all gruff. Can't risk any friendliness tainting the evaluation."

"You mean that's it? Did he pass?"

"Of course; he's a great dog! Come into the office, and we'll finish up the paperwork."

I sit down across from her desk, and she talks while she writes.

"I shouldn't even take your money; they should never have required an evaluation. They aren't filing charges, and it's pretty clear that the so-called attack was defensive. I don't think he even used his teeth."

"They told me the kid had bruises."

"Look at the photo." She spins her monitor around to show me. "Those aren't fresh bruises—see the yellow and purple? They're like the ones on your face are now—about five days old, right?"

"Yeah."

She peers closely at her monitor again. "I think those are finger marks, not teeth marks. Someone grabbed at him. But hey, I'm just here to check out the pooch." She takes both hands and rubs Boris's face. "And you are one perfect dog, aren't you just?"

"I thought there would be more to it. You didn't do anything to see if he would bite someone to protect me."

She narrows her eyes and looks me full in the face. "That. Is. His. Job. We don't diss dogs for that."

"Ah. I've been worried for nothing."

"Right. As I said, they shouldn't have required this at all. This is just CYA. The bozo said your dog attacked him." She points at the screen again but doesn't show me. "So even though he later admitted that he was trying to mug you, they aren't taking chances. Especially with a juvenile." She looks up at me again. "Did he get anything?"

I start laughing at that and then laugh even more from sheer relief. "Poop bags," I finally manage to say.

CHAPTER 56

Driving home, I feel intoxicated. I want to sing and wave my arms around. I leave the car at home, and we start off on foot toward the police station, muzzle in my hand instead of on my dog. I feel like skipping. I say hello to everyone I see. I do tense up a little when we get to Gregory, then pretend I'm a runner and sprint across, maintaining the pace for another hundred feet or so, until I remember I'm not a runner and slow down to catch my breath. We arrive at the police station in high spirits. I plunk down the muzzle on the narrow rim of counter, then push it through the slot in the bulletproof glass along with a copy of the form Sally gave me, stamped "CLEARED" in three places. The officer at the desk looks it over and nods. I guess I was expecting an attagirl or something, but all I get is a distracted thank-you. Well, maybe her evening is not going as well as mine. I think about asking for a receipt for the muzzle but decide to leave before anything can spoil my mood.

The trip home is mostly downhill, so I jog, wondering if a runner is less attractive to muggers than a middle-aged woman ambling along with her dog nosing the bushes beside her. Unused to the fast pace, Boris bounces beside me, dancing and leaping up toward my face. Maybe he's trying to figure out what's going on in my head. Half a block from home, I realize that I don't have any poop bags and arrive at my front door still laughing.

Inside, I drop the leash and grab a quart of ice cream from the freezer. A minute later, I'm ringing Josie's doorbell.

"We passed! Let's celebrate."

Josie turns off whatever cop show she is watching and listens while I describe the entire evaluation. It takes longer to tell than it did to experience, since I provide a lot of commentary and include selected bits from my imagined scenarios. We eat almost all the ice cream. She doesn't speak until I finish talking, and we both put down our spoons.

"Sounds like you've got a new friend, this Sally," she says. "You need that. And I hope you remember what she told you: it's Boris's job to protect you, and it's not a crime if he does."

We think about that for a few minutes, and then Josie changes subjects again.

"And what about Carl?"

"Carl? He never really thought Boris was a threat, either. He was pretty clear about that."

"I don't mean that."

I look at the floor and then at the ceiling. Josie's kitchen ceiling has a hairline crack in the same place mine does, near the chimney.

"What do you mean then?" I say evenly. I am pretty sure I know what she means, but, just in case, she's going to have to say it. And if she does, I'm not sure what I'll say back. I reach out and scratch Boris behind the ears.

She picks up her spoon and smacks me lightly on my hand. "Don't act like you don't know what I'm saying. Do you like him or not?"

"Like him?" I'm just stalling, and she knows it. She smacks my hand a little harder, and Boris the great protector licks her hand.

"Are you going to go out with him when he finally asks you for a date?"

"Probably," I say. And then, because I can feel my face get red, I add, "Not that it's any of your business."

She nods and gives me a self-satisfied smile. "All right then, now you know."

"You mean, now *you* know," I say right back, but we both know that she meant exactly what she said.

And then, because we're being forthright and gutsy as all get-out, and because I really want to change the subject, I decide to ask Josie something that is none of my business but that I've been wondering about for months.

"Josie, can I ask you a question? Why do you still live here? I know this neighborhood isn't the worst one in town, and it's the best some people can afford. But I get the idea that you don't have to live here. What happened last month makes me want to run for the hills. Seriously, I was ready to sell up and move to Chicago. But you, you're still here. Why is that?"

"Oh, Marianne, I'm here for the same reason you are, and the same reason Bud is, and that guy Flynn, and the same reason a lot of folks are here. This is home." She sighs and looks out the window. "Maybe it won't always be home for you, or for me, either. But that's why we're here right now. And it's why you're going to stay, at least a few more years."

Lying in bed that night, wide awake, I think through the whole of the past week. I really and truly had decided to move, to find a safer place in a new city. I feel differently now. I have a place here, a job and a home and friends, and possibly someone who might become more than just a friend. None of these are like what I had before. I shift gears and wonder which high school those "bozos" attend. I wonder if they have something to do after school that doesn't involve shaking down people like me for their poop bags.

I wonder for the hundredth time if Josie is right, if I really belong here. For Josie, I can see, my being here makes a little bit of difference, or maybe quite a lot of difference, much better than the vacant and derelict house that mine was before I bought it. And that probably makes a difference for the other closest neighbors too. My leaving would let them down. Leaving would let me down, too, selling out after all I've been through. And Josie was certainly right when she told me that I can protect myself. Not from everything, but from the thing that I have feared most ever since the day I moved here. I'm not going to let the bad guys decide for me. I'm not going to let them. I'm not going. I'm not. I get up and send Jason a "thanks but no thanks" text and then I text Marjorie, accepting her job offer. I think about Carl and smile and tell myself that Josie was right when she said that now I know. I get back in bed and fall asleep in seconds.

ACKNOWLEDGMENTS

Inspiration for Marianne's experience in this book came from the many corporate jobs I've had, the stories told by my friends and colleagues (including colleagues who are friends), and all the things I lay awake at night thinking *might* happen on any given day at the office. Not the least of these friends and colleagues are the people at She Writes Press, who got this book to press, and my cohort of SWP authors, who support each other so well during the Herculean labors that burden writers in the dark period after the joy of writing and before the thrill of publication day.

I am eternally grateful for my high school classmates, who so thoroughly feel for Marianne's struggles in her Kansas City neighborhood.

Thanks also to all those who knowingly and unknowingly inspire me:

The Washington University community in St. Louis, which supported me financially in my youth and continue to celebrate my success.

My Los Altos and St. Louis book clubs, my art club buddies, and all the other friends and relatives who read my first book and demanded a second.

My husband Tom, my alpha reader and omega proofreader, maker of the wine and bread that sustain the writer in me.

Boris the real-life dog, who has not suffered the indignities he endures in this novel, and who still proudly refuses to do stairs and still sings the song of his people.

All the strangers who wrote notes and reviews of my first novel, *East of Troost*, reminding me that fiction teaches and touches people in unknowable ways.

Librarians around America who graciously accepted my suggestion to carry my novels.

Finally, the people who work and live in the fictional Marianne's real neighborhood in Kansas City, especially Nick Gadino, owner of the Midland True Value at Gregory and Prospect and the inspiration for Marianne's boss Henry at Midtown Hardware in *Still Needs Work*.

ABOUT THE AUTHOR

Ellen Barker grew up in Kansas City during a period of demographic upheaval and returns there in her novels. She has a bachelor's degree in urban studies from Washington University in Saint Louis, where she developed a passion for how cities work, and don't. She began her career as an urban planner and then spent many years working for large consulting firms, first as a writer-editor and later managing large data systems, jobs rich in corporate drama large and small. She is the author of *East of Troost*, which introduced readers to the neighborhood where *Still Needs Work* takes place. She now lives in Los Altos, California, with her husband and their German shepherd, Boris, who is the inspiration for the dog in this novel.

Learn more about Ellen and her books on her website: http://www.ellenbarkerauthor.com

SELECTED TITLES FROM SHE WRITES PRESS

She Writes Press is an independent publishing company founded to serve women writers everywhere.
Visit us at www.shewritespress.com.

East of Troost by Ellen Barker. $17.95, 978-1-64742-229-5. Troost is a real street. East of it is where you can buy a house if you're Black. It's also where our middle-aged white narrator grew up—and where she has just returned to reboot her life. How will she fare in this vastly changed world? This fictional story, punctuated by factual memoir, is by turns soul-searching, entertaining, and heartbreaking.

Andrea Hoffman Goes All In by Diane Cohen Schneider. $17.95, 978-1-64742-099-4. Written for everyone who's had a love/hate relationship with their job, this smart, funny novel by a former Wall Street sales pro reveals what it was like for a woman to build a successful career and a satisfying personal life in the macho world of 1980s stock trading.

The Best Part of Us by Sally Cole-Misch. $16.95, 978-1-63152-741-8. Beth cherished her childhood summers on her family's beautiful northern Canadian island—until their ownership was questioned and a horrible storm forced them to leave. Fourteen years later, after she's created a new life in urban Chicago, far from the natural world, her grandfather asks her to return to the island to see if what was lost still remains.

A Better Next by Maren Cooper. $16.95, 978-1-63152-493-6. At the top of her career, twenty plus years married, and with one child left to launch, Jess Lawson is blindsided by her husband's decision to move across the country without her—news that shakes her personal and professional life and forces her to make surprising new choices moving forward.

What's Not True by Valerie Taylor. $16.95, 978-1-64742-157-1. Just as a soon-to-be divorced woman commits to reviving both her career and love life, a conniving woman from her husband's past forces her to protect and defend what is legally and rightfully hers.

All the Right Mistakes by Laura Jamison. $16.95, 978-1-63152-709-8. When the most successful of five women who have been friends since college publishes an advice book detailing the key life "mistakes" of the others—opting out, ramping off, giving half effort, and forgetting your fertility—they spend their fortieth year considering their lives against the backdrop of their outspoken friend's cruel words.